CHILLERS

Tales Inspired by Classic Horror Films

Bela Lugosi as Murder Legendre in *White Zombie* (1932)

CHILLERS

TALES INSPIRED BY CLASSIC HORROR FILMS

COMPILED AND COORDINATED
BY BRAD BRADDOCK

EDITED BY DWIGHT KEMPER
AND CHRISTINE SOLTIS

MIDNIGHT MARQUEE PRESS, INC.
BALTIMORE, MD, USA

**This book is dedicated to
our heroes of classic horror that are gone,
but they will never be forgotten**

Table of Contents

"*White Zombie* (1932) is one of the most fascinating of all horror movies. As played by Bela Lugosi, its villain Murder Legendre has remained a mystery, an enigma. That is, until now. Brad Braddock's wonderful novel removes the veil and unleashes the classic character in an all-new narrative."
  –Gary D. Rhodes, author of *White Zombie: Anatomy of a Horror Film*

Foreword
by Brad A. Braddock

When the idea for this anthology first hit my brain like a bolt of lightning in Dr. Frankenstein's laboratory, I was at Creepy Classics Monster Bash Octoberfest in Canton, Ohio. It was the fall season, Halloween and cool air on the rise. Pumpkins and, more importantly, pumpkin beer. No better time for Ron Adams' follow-up to his June Monster Bash extravaganza than a two-day weekend at the Palace Theatre, where one could watch every Universal studio Frankenstein film from the 1930s and '40s! A real treat for fans of classic horror and for Monster Kids!

In addition to watching these classic films in an old-time theater, equipped with a pipe organ, that between movies filled the theater with its delicious macabre sound, were the wonderful artists and guests who make appearances at various Monster Bash venues in Mars (how fitting), Pennsylvania. Artists like Terri Mount, with her Terri-IFIC monster-themed clothes and gifts. Artist Christopher Fry, with his amazing masks, from Frankenstein's Monster to the Creature from the Black Lagoon. I couldn't help but buy one. Martin Stephens, who starred as a child actor in *Village of the Damned* and *The Innocents*, was there and was he ever a nice guy! But the fellow I wanted to meet the most was Lugosi and film historian, Frank Dello Stritto … and I just so happened to bump into him and his lovely wife Linda while heading into the event.

Over the weekend, we talked about various book projects, from his groundbreaking novel (no pun intended) *A Werewolf Remembers*, to his Lugosi study, *Vampire Over London: Bela Lugosi in Britain*, about Lugosi's latter days on tour in the stage play *Dracula*. It is truly one of my favorite books.

I had written a prequel to the 1932 classic *White Zombie*, starring Bela Lugosi, titled *Memoirs of Murder*, and had so much fun embellishing on that horror classic that I couldn't wait to do it again! And I thought, with great writers like Frank Dello Stritto and what I had seen him do with his, "A Werewolf Remembers," I thought, why don't some writers and historians who are so passionate about classic horror get together and write an anthology of bloody horror!

And it began … with writers like Gregory William Mank, author and historian of so many wonderful classic horror-themed studies joining the team. The one and only Dwight Kemper, of *Who Framed Boris Karloff?* fame. Kurt McCoy, who writes for various classic horror-themed monster magazines.

So many other wonderful talents, like Danielle DeVor, Bob and Stefanie Kokai, Todd Shiba with his wonderful dark wit, Luca Winer, Brian Carney, and my dear friend, Christopher Gauthier, with his poetic talent, started to pour their soul into this little idea that became an anthology of classic horror-themed fiction. Special thanks to Christine M. Soltis for her guidance and knowledge of editing and writing as well! To all involved, I am (beyond the grave) grateful!

When I thought of a publisher, the first thought that came to mind was Midnight Marquee Press. Gary and his wife Susan have produced and published so many wonderful and informative titles over the years. When they showed interest in our project, I was thrilled, to say the least. I wish to thank them for their long-time dedication to the classic horror world and all they have contributed to it, from scholarly works, to classic horror-themed fiction. They truly are one of the keystones for the world of classic horror today.

I'd also like to thank Frank Dello Stritto and Greg Mank for their contributions to the world of classic horror. These gentlemen provided the energy and the lightning in the lab that helped bring this monster to life. For their kindness and help, I am truly grateful.

To those who read this anthology inspired by classic horror, I truly hope you enjoy … and remember, *there are such things!*

A WEREWOLF REMEMBERS

The Testament of Lawrence Stewart Talbot

FRANK J. DELLO STRITTO

Colin Clive and Mae Clarke as Henry Frankenstein and Elizabeth from Universal's 1931 classic, *Frankenstein*

Elizabeth

by Gregory William Mank

{Author's Note: In *Frankenstein* and *Bride of Frankenstein*, the character of Elizabeth, Henry Frankenstein's fiancée and later wife, was clearly of keen interest to director James Whale. He went for two different characterizations from two very different actresses: The lovely, rather straightforward 21-year-old Mae Clarke in *Frankenstein*; and the angelic, wildly stylized 17-year-old Valerie Hobson in *Bride of Frankenstein*. Since my earliest viewings of both films, I've wondered: How did Elizabeth cope with the notoriety and nightmares of having been the wife of the "Maker of Monsters"—and having been in the clutches of the Monster himself? Read on for my musings. Incidentally, while writing the story, I imagined Valerie Hobson as the aged Elizabeth; my wife Barbara pictured Mae Clarke. You're invited to conjure up either lady as you read this story. Enjoy.}

The moon in the December sky had a ring around it, almost a halo—often a prophecy of snow. The wind off the sea was sharp and bitter, but as she walked along the cliffs, carrying a candle-lit lantern for light, she stood tall, despite her age and the weight of her memories.

She was 70 years old, willowy, as she'd always been. She imagined that, in her long coat and shawl, she suggested the aging heroine of a Gothic novel.

That's precisely what I am, she thought, with humor and sadness.

The sea was roiling, as if joining in her mourning. Yes, 25 years ago, on this night, her Henry had died.

She hadn't been with him when Death came. Nor had his body ever come home to his ancestral England for burial. The villagers had taken his corpse to the ruins of the old laboratory. When she'd written to the village, pleading for his body's return, a crude letter had come back, refusing her request, spitefully noting the epitaph that marked his forsaken grave:

MAKER OF MONSTERS

They'd even exhumed Henry's father from the cemetery, she'd learned, burying him in the ruins as well. The Frankenstein family was judged not fit to rest in holy ground. The villagers had vindictively decreed they belonged in *un*holy ground.

She felt a chill, perhaps from the night wind, perhaps from her memories ... maybe both.

Yes, she and Henry had been young and happy, once upon a time. Fifty years ago, they'd loved walking along these cliffs. She grinned slightly as she remembered the vanity and sensuality of her youth: how she wore her hair, as she put it, "in long, sad tresses"; how she often wore her favorite dresses without any lingerie beneath them.

I thought myself so terribly wicked, she mused.

Especially joyful were the early years of their marriage, after they'd come home from Germany, back to the family's English estate by the cliffs and above the sea. These were the nights of romance and rekindled passion, and the days of realizing Henry's plan of devoting his life to research, living down the raging infamy of his disastrous experiment. These were the years of the births of Wolf and Ludwig.

But then, Henry had to go back.

The obsession with his tragedy had insidiously returned like a recurrent illness. He'd leave her and the children, traveling back to the castle in Germany. He'd go there despite the danger from the villagers, who'd bless themselves at the very sight of him, and who'd regularly express their desire to kill him. He'd arrive in the middle of the night to try to avoid them, but inevitably they'd see the lights in the castle above the village. They'd know he was there.

He'd become a ghost, haunting the sites of his personal tragedy. After midnight, he'd walk the village square where he'd once led a torch-lit parade of men to destroy the Creature. He'd climb to the site of the windmill, burned and never rebuilt, where the Creature had thrown him from the balcony and nearly killed him. He'd even go to the mountain lake, where the Creature had drowned that poor little girl.

When Henry came home to England, he'd tell her these things. When he spoke to her about the drowned child, he'd wept bitterly.

Henry, she'd realized, had become an addict—an addict of his own tragedy—and it had eventually killed him.

She stood very still, and then instinctively faced the moonlit ocean, allowing the full force of the wind to hit her. She was always strong ... defiant. Even at her age, and with all the memories, she was *still* defiant, still tall ... still strong. Henry had failed, but she'd vowed to stay strong, even after more than half a century of nightmares.

The worst ones, of course, were about the Creature.

She'd first seen him on the day she was to have been married, when she'd turned in her boudoir, and his gaunt, horrific face was only inches from her own. She'd screamed, fainting on the bed. The story had spread that the Creature had attacked her, violated her, but he had not. And strangely, her most vivid memory of the episode was not his height, nor his stitches, nor the horribly obvious evidence that Henry had sewn him together, a livid patchwork from various corpses. Her clearest memory was the Creature's eyes.

 CHILLERS

They were, by some wicked irony, actually beautiful.

Later, after she and Henry had married, the presumed-dead Creature had returned, having lived through the windmill fire. He'd come for her, kidnapping her, pulling her from her vanity table before she and Henry could depart on their honeymoon. She'd screamed again, and he'd taken her to a mountain cave, binding her to a stake like a captured beast. He'd stare at her from across the cave, through the flames of the fire he'd built to warm her. He'd growl at her, as if to menace her, but she could tell that what he truly felt for her was pity.

Finally, there'd been the night of her escape. She ran from the cave, her honeymoon dress fetid and soiled, up the stairs to the tower laboratory. The door to the laboratory was locked, but there was a barred window, and she looked through it, as if peering into a demonic zoo. There was Henry, the Creature, and that awful Dr. Pretorius, looking like Satan himself. And there was the female creature. Tall, proud, the red hair, the silver streaks ... the stitches in her neck. There was an aura of spite and defiance in her, and she remembered a strange jealousy spiking her hysteria as she realized Henry had intimately pieced this woman *together* ...

The Creature, rejected by his Bride, had seized a lever that, as Pretorius had warned, would "blow us all to atoms." She'd begged Henry to flee with her, and he'd actually refused—hellbent on staying with his creatures. It was the Creature who'd looked at them both with a tear running down his cheek and had commanded in a broken voice:

"Yes ... Go! You live ..."

And then, to Pretorius and the female creature ... "You stay. WE BELONG dead!"

She and Henry had fled, the old tower exploding magnificently, almost Biblically, an Armageddon. Henry had comforted her, but she realized that terrible night, as she would for the rest of her life, that it wasn't Henry who'd saved her.

It was the Creature.

So, it was back to this dreadful scenario that Henry had made pilgrimage, time and again. He was away from her, away from their sons, longer each time, and eventually he never returned. Finally, one December night, 25 years ago in Castle Frankenstein, he'd died alone in his bed, a Bible on his night stand. The villagers claimed he'd died during a hellish storm, in lightning and freezing rain, "fire and ice," as one of them said. He'd never made peace with the sorrow he'd spawned and had remained especially agonized by the Creature, having saved them both.

One night, Henry had feverishly rambled to her that he'd defied God by creating his own man. Yet God had enjoyed the last laugh, giving the Creature what Henry could never have given him—a soul.

"That day in the laboratory," Henry had said. "Just after his creation. He'd reached for the light ... he'd begged for a soul ... God had given him one. The Monster proved it that night ... saving us ..."

Henry had always referred to him as the Monster. Yet she always thought of him as the Creature.

It was growing colder, windier, and the candle had burned low in the lantern. She knew she best return home. She'd soon have to address Christmas plans. She wished she'd see her sons, but it wasn't possible now. Henry had deeded that, if 25 years passed after his death with no evidence of the Creature returning to life, Wolf, as first born, could claim the estate and inheritance in Germany. Wolf had written her that he was planning to do this next year, leaving his physician practice and college professorship in America. He would take along his wife Elsa and son Peter and she hoped all of them would be safe there. Her second son, Ludwig, was based in Europe, not far from the Frankenstein ancestral village, acclaimed for curing diseases of the mind. He was a widower with a beautiful daughter. She was very proud of both her sons, and they revered their father, although they'd never really known him.

Later tonight, she'd sit by the fire, remembering Henry. His fallen-angel handsomeness, his poetic talk of looking beyond the clouds and the stars ... and learning what changes darkness into light. Still fervent, even after the decay had set in, trying to believe he'd perhaps come close to discovering "the Divine plan." She'd recall his brilliance and passion, before it became anguish and torment. Maybe he'd visit her tonight in a dream, as he often did. Sometimes, the Creature was with him. The two of them came peacefully, with no enmity between them. And what she'd notice first about the Creature in the dream, as in life, were his eyes.

Henry had never understood why all this tragedy had happened, why God—if there is a God—had coldly and capriciously allowed all this to be. Maybe now, he knew and understood. And if the Creature had truly possessed a soul, as Henry had come to believe, maybe he understood too.

Perhaps both were now at peace.

Elizabeth pulled the shawl tightly around her hair, standing tall and strong. She wiped a tear that ran down her cheek, and under the moon with its halo, walked briskly toward home.

About the Author:

Gregory William Mank is the author of such books as *It's Alive! The Classic Cinema Saga of Frankenstein*; *Bela Lugosi and Boris Karloff: The Expanded Story of a Haunting Collaboration*; *The Very Witching Time of Night: Dark Alleys of Classic Horror Cinema*; *Laird Cregar: A Hollywood Tragedy*; and most recently, *"One Man Crazy!" The Life and Death of Colin Clive*. He's written many magazine articles, written and narrated a dozen DVD audio commentaries, and appeared on numerous film history documentaries. He and his wife Barbara live in Delta, PA. In regard to "Elizabeth," his short story in this anthology, Greg is proud to have interviewed Mae Clarke (in 1983) and Valerie Hobson (in 1989), the respective Elizabeths of *Frankenstein* (1931) and *Bride of Frankenstein* (1935).

Poster art created for the 1945 production of *The Picture of Dorian Gray*, starring Hurd Hatfield as Dorian Gray

CHILLERS

The Profile Picture
of Dora Gray
by Miranda Morrow

{Author's Note: Oscar Wilde's *The Picture of Dorian Gray* has always haunted me, and I love consuming adaptations of this great classic. I have watched semi-serious attempts at bringing to life its dark psychology, such as *The Picture of Dorian Gray* (1945), and silly, swashbuckling versions which were light on philosophy and heavy on one-liners (I'm looking at you, *The League of Extraordinary Gentlemen*). In reviewing these adaptations, it struck me that though this story has its origins in Gothic horror, it also lends itself beautifully to be a lens with which to explore our modern-day emphasis on social media. Social media increasingly shapes how people perceive their social worth, even though a person's public social media persona often differs wildly from their real, private self. Being inundated with social media pictures of other people's "highlights reel" (while being acutely aware of one's own ups and downs) sets up people to feel inadequate, and the prevalence of filters indirectly sends the message that a person's real body, unvarnished and unedited, is simply not good enough.

When you add teenagers into the mix, teenagers with wobbly self-esteem, and give one of them the possibility of a social media presence of Dorian Gray-like perfection, the outcome you get can be, well, horrifying.}

Dora pulled herself up the stairs and her dry breathing rattled her emaciated chest. Her heart felt like a feral thing, clawing against her ribs, trying to escape. She held her cell phone over her heart with one hand, and with the other clutched the banister. Her milky nails were long and created small crescents in the soft wood as she propelled herself upwards. She stumbled past the first door, the second, until she reached the one at the end of the hall. Dora sobbed as she pushed open the door, leaving a smear of red on the white paint. She stumbled into the room and locked the door. There was no sound now, except her own blood pumping.

Dora sank down to the carpet, collapsing within herself, creating a small pile of person, as she normally might with clothes. Her bones creaked in protest, and her nose throbbed.

Her hand vibrated. "Leave me alone!" she sobbed. The phone vibrated again, insistent. Dora knew what she would find. She still couldn't stop herself from looking.

A new Instagram post. A young woman looking coyly up at her, her long limbs perfectly arrayed, her eyelashes flirtatious and her smile wide and white. Behind her, there was another woman slightly out of focus, her face a pale blur, her hands outstretched reaching for the first woman's neck. A third woman, a blonde, was leaning against a tree, a small smile on her face, one finger tracing a line down her bare throat.

"No," Dora whispered. "No!" Her phone continued to vibrate, notifying her that people liked the photo.

"I know what I have to do," Dora whispered. And she held up the phone and snapped a picture of herself. And posted it. Without a filter.

Earlier that summer …

Dora stood in front of the bathroom mirror, holding a curling iron in one hand, and a fistful of limp brown hair in the other. The soap dish precariously propped up her phone, in its ladybug case. The voice emanating from the phone was cheerful and competent.

"Smoothly move the iron down your hair until it reaches the end of the strands!" Dora jerked the iron down her hair.

"Then begin to curl the hair upwards against the shaft of the iron, rotating upwards!" How come when Dora did it, her hair got caught in the iron?

"Hold for three seconds and tease the iron open!" Was hair supposed to steam like that? Dora sniffed the air in alarm.

"Ah!" Dora yelped as the iron kissed her neck. She dropped the device and it crashed into the sink, knocking her phone to the floor.

"Voila! A perfect curl!" came the muffled voice. Dora hastily unplugged the curler and looked at herself in the mirror again. She eyed the shiny red burn emerging on her neck, before glumly noticing her crisped hair, her puffy face, the acne scars, and the pimple volcano on her nose. Dora picked the phone up from the floor, sighed, propped it against the soap dish, and plugged the hair curler back in.

A few hours later, Dora unveiled the results. "What do you think? They okay?" she asked her best friends. Sibyl lay on the bed, her legs against the wall, doing yoga stretches. Baz sat on the floor by the bed, Dora's laptop on the legs of her overalls. She chewed a little on her hair as she scrolled through the pictures. Dora sat on the floor as well, applying "Vant to Bite My Neck?" to her toes and trying not to breathe in the ethyl acetate.

Dora heard Sibyl make an evaluative sniff. Unsure whether it was because of the fumes from the polish or commentary on her photos, Dora stuck her foot in Sibyl's face in retaliation. Sibyl laughed.

Baz, in her usual Baz fashion, was taking photography quite seriously. "I still don't think you need to Photoshop your photos at all. You always look good."

Sibyl sighed at Baz's naiveté. "We could all use a little help, you know, to present our best selves. Remember I had you edit my headshots? And look at me now! I got into *Beauty and the Beast!*"

"Yeah, in a teenager-only community theater production as, like, *Candlestick number 7*," Baz muttered.

Sibyl picked up Dora's hairbrush from the nightstand and held it in front of her mouth. "This coming live from Los Angeles, Sibyl Vane in her breakout role!"

"Uhuh, like you're the next Angela Lansbury."

Dora played peacemaker. "Focus, Baz. Fix me, make me pretty. You know you are the best at this."

Baz still looked skeptical.

Dora decided to sweeten the pot. "You are such an artist." Always one for that particular compliment, Baz moved the laptop to the desk and began to work her magic.

Sibyl decided her abs were taut enough for now and moved onto her arms. She eyed the leftover pizza on the floor. "I take it your mom is still out of town?"

Dora grinned. "Busy. She was in, like, Egypt or someplace last week, came home just for a day." Dora rolled over on her stomach. "She definitely feels bad leaving me alone so much though. She gave me her spare credit card. She's not gonna be back until school starts up again."

Sibyl's eyes gleamed. "That's, like, almost two whole months! We are going to have the best senior summer ever. Party!"

"I guess." But Dora's face fell. "It's not like anyone else will come over. Except you two, of course." Dora poked at her stomach fat absentmindedly before shaking her head with disgust.

Sibyl was still in full-on daydream mode. "We could always throw a big party and invite Henry. He'd see me across a crowded room and our eyes would meet ..." Dora threw a pillow at Sibyl.

"Like a guy like that would ever ..."

"Hush!" Baz loved to be imperious. "I've edited the photos a little—put you in front a purple wall, v. fab bee-tee-dubs, colorful walls are in for some reason—edited down your arms, added some highlights ... what do you think?"

Dora leaned over Baz's shoulder. Sibyl crowded next to her.

"I still look like me," Dora said, in a small voice.

Baz frowned. "Me is good."

Dora looked at Baz and Sibyl, Baz looking childish in her oversized overalls and an overabundance of piercings from Claire's, Sibyl, looking the same, with her leggings and dramatic eye makeup. One was trying too hard to be an original artiste; the other trying too hard to be cool. Both utterly failing and hanging out with Dora on Saturday night. Just like always.

Sibyl gave a fake little laugh. "Let's take a photo together. For the insta!" Before Dora could respond, Sibyl held her phone up and clicked.

"So, we can always remember this moment," said Dora quietly.

"So, we can know that we always have each other," Baz countered, defiantly.

After Baz and Sibyl left that night, Dora looked at that photo of the three of them, Sibyl smiling, her hair a messy blond nimbus, Baz looking concerned, her straight dark hair falling into her face, and Dora … looking like Dora. Dora then looked at the photographs Baz doctored for her. Hours of makeup and battling with hair torture devices, even Photoshop touch-ups, and she was still her. Plump in all the wrong places with a crooked smile. No one would *heart* the girl looking back at her from in front of her stupid purple wall, except Baz and Sibyl. And they didn't count.

"I just want people to like me," she whispered. "Cool people. People like Henry." As she drifted off to sleep, Dora muttered, "I wish my insta made me look like the person I know I could be, not the loser I am now."

The next day, Dora decided that any social media presence was still better than none at all. She had created a new username for herself recently in yet another attempt to reinvent herself, and she might as well populate it with more than pictures of Technicolor food artfully arranged on plates. She uploaded the photo Baz had edited and clicked through the filters. Clarendon, Juno, Walde … Dora reached the last filter. Dora's finger hovered over it, a filter she had never seen before. *Bast.* She clicked it.

"Dora is being such a brat." Baz fumed, punching a pillow on the couch. It was hot outside, and she was cranky.

Sibyl sighed but didn't speak. Apparently, Sibyl needed to "rest her voice." The musical was only a few days away from curtain, and from the way Sibyl told it, her "unique sound" was not given its proper respect by the director.

Baz couldn't let it go. "Is she, like, too good to hang with us now? 'Cause of the popularity of her stupid photos?"

It started with just a few changes. Like with the photo that Baz had edited for Dora with the purple wall. Dora must have tweaked it further, because she looked great. Dora was always pretty (as Baz was constantly telling her, despite Dora's insecurity about her weight) but now she looked … radiant. Her smile, slightly apologetic before, now looked confident and sly. It was like she was inviting the viewer to join her in knowing a secret, and it was a good one.

Later that same week, Baz invited Dora and Sibyl to meet her at work and check out the darkroom. Dora did show up, but late, and kept her sunglasses on the entire time. She said her eyes were being weirdly sensitive to light. Baz was concerned, but before she could inquire further, Sibyl said she wanted to get a haircut, and the subject was dropped.

 CHILLERS

"Darn it, they can't see us today, it's too packed," Sibyl reported back to Dora and Baz, who waited outside the salon.

"We can try again next weekend," Dora said.

But a few days later, Dora must have gone to the hairstylist without them, because her latest insta photo showed her with an asymmetrical bob of carefully messy red waves. Did she get green-eyed contacts too? Dora's eyes had never looked so large and luminous. Maybe it was the new makeup she was using. Baz sent the Hearts for Eyes emoji but felt a little weird about the whole thing.

"Why'd you go without me?," Sibyl asked Dora the next time they met up after one of her rehearsals. Much to Dora's displeasure, they were at Ben and Jerry's downtown. Despite the heat, Dora was wearing a hoodie, with the hood pulled up tight over a baseball cap, and she was wearing the same damned sunglasses. You couldn't even see her new haircut or contacts. Baz sat in between them, focusing intently on her Phish food in order to get the perfect ratio of marshmallow fluff to chocolate swirl in her mouth, without courting disaster.

Dora's tone was oddly haughty. "I know you just love going to Silvio's, but I wanted to try that new salon on Main. And you know, that place is kinda pricey … I just didn't want you to feel like you had to go there too. I know that money is tight for you and your family."

Sibyl gasped and dropped her plastic spoon. Dora quickly began to chatter on about this new fitness routine she was starting and how it, and the juice cleanse diet, was absolutely, like totally, changing her life.

After that, it didn't surprise Baz all that much that she and Sibyl and Dora somehow didn't see each other for a week or so. Sibyl's rehearsals for *Beauty and the Beast* were intensifying, and Sibyl was also putting in more hours bagging at the grocery store, to pick up enough cash to buy a red dress she had been eyeing. Baz herself hardly had a moment to breathe due to being promoted at the studio, but still, this was hardly the way Baz had imagined the summer before her senior year would go.

Baz knew Dora was still doing well though, by watching her Instagram feed. Dora must have stuck with that workout routine she found in that magazine, because every day she looked fitter and fitter—it was like the pounds were melting away. Dora's Instagram was getting tons of likes. Cute boys, boys with names like Kaden or Liam, were hearting her posts. Dora texted Baz and Sibyl to tell them that people were suddenly following her for fashion and makeup advice. She had over three thousand followers now on Twitter. She was busy coming up with new content to feed the insatiable appetites of her digital acolytes.

Baz stopped at Dora's house one evening, just to see if she was there. Dora had posted a photo from her bedroom less than an hour earlier. But when Baz rang the doorbell, no one answered. The light on in the bedroom must have been on a timer.

Dora also wasn't answering her phone very often anymore. Finally, Baz started a group text. *It's been weeks, Dora. What gives?*

Dora was slow to reply. *Just been so busy, drop it.*

Sibyl tried next. *But you are still coming to my show, right?*

The three dots quivered and hesitated, but the answer came. *Yes.*

The more that Dora cut them out of her actual life, the more obsessed Baz and Sibyl found themselves with Dora's digital one. Thumbing through the photos, Baz and Sibyl were treated to a side of Dora they had never seen. Dora, the hiker, standing on top of some mountain, looking cute and fit in a crop top which revealed a belly button stud. Dora, the sun goddess, in a strappy black bikini, her legs looking long, lean, and tan as she smiled provocatively at the camera, her knees slightly apart, an ocean behind her. Dora, the cultured sophisticate at the opera, looking fancy in a red dress that hugged her in all the right places.

"Isn't that the dress you were looking at?" Baz asked.

Sibyl got very quiet. "Not anymore."

And now here Baz was, sweaty and irritable in the heat, lying on the couch in Sibyl's living room as Sibyl "rested" her voice.

"Dora is being such a brat." Baz's phone vibrated, and she reached for it instinctively. Dora had just posted. This time it was Dora, the fun girl next door: Dora was standing on a boardwalk, a Ferris wheel behind her. Next to her was a guy, with his arm slung over her shoulder. Baz's eyes widened as she recognized him.

"Dora?" Sibyl asked. Baz held the phone, uncertain.

Sibyl raised an eyebrow, noting Baz's reaction. "Pass it."

"I don't think I should," Baz said, but she handed the phone to Sibyl anyway. Sibyl looked at the photo and closed her eyes.

"And now Henry."

Baz had no response to this.

Sibyl rallied. "She'll still come. The show opens this Thursday. She promised she'd come. And hey, maybe she'll bring him." Baz made herself smile and promised Sibyl that regardless of what happened, Baz would be there, cheering her on.

It wasn't quite as bad as Sibyl thought it was, but if Baz were being truthful, it was still pretty mortifying. After what happened opening night, Baz sent Sibyl text after text, getting no response. Baz even reluctantly texted Dora, telling her what happened, asking her to reach out to Sibyl. No response from her either.

Two days after it happened, Baz went to Sibyl's house, but Sibyl refused to see her. "Go away," she cried from behind her bedroom door. Baz tried to comfort Sibyl through the door, telling her that even though Sibyl's gaff had indeed gone viral, and had been seen by everyone in the school and then some, that eventually people would forget all about it. Baz would always be there for her, too. Sibyl just kept crying from behind the door, so after about an hour, Baz gave up and went home. After all, as Baz reminded Sibyl before she left, though it felt bad now, no one actually dies of embarrassment.

The next day Baz's father picked her up from work. "Leave the bike, it's okay," he said in a hollow voice. His eyes looked hooded. Baz felt a swooping sensation in her stomach, as she got in the car. Her father turned off the engine and turned towards her.

"Dad?"

"Basil, I am so sorry."

She had never seen him cry before.

Sibyl's funeral was a muted affair. Baz felt like she was somehow far away from it all, like she was fumbling through cotton batting. She kept expecting to see Sibyl come through the crowd, explaining it was a sick joke, that she was fine. But she wasn't fine, and she wasn't there. Except in the coffin being lowered into the ground.

"I feel so bad for the mother. Imagine finding your daughter just hanging there," a woman whispered to her neighbor. Baz's mother compressed her lips and strode over to her, as Baz's father tugged Baz away. Baz let herself be led, scanning the crowd.

She couldn't believe it. Dora wasn't there. Dora still wasn't there.

So late it was early, Baz heard her phone vibrate on her bedside table. "Dora?" she croaked. She had fallen asleep with her glasses on. Baz rubbed her eyes and she picked up the phone. It had to be Dora texting her, Dora explaining where she was, why she missed the funeral, Dora telling her that it was okay to be angry with Sibyl.

Indeed, it was Dora.

Baz looked at the photo and felt a white-hot fury. In that photo of Dora, looking mischievous, her fork was about to descend into a decedent looking slice of chocolate cake. And there was Sibyl, sitting next to her, looking luminous, laughing, and stroking her throat.

"You sick ... sick ..." Baz stuttered.

As Baz watched, another photo was uploaded—this one of Dora in a swing, her skirt floating up her knees. Sibyl was in this one, jumping off a swing next to Dora. The photo caught the moment where Sibyl's body was totally in midair. Sibyl's neck stretched upwards at an odd angle, the smile on her face vacant.

It was surprisingly easy to sneak out of the house. The night was still heavy as she biked over, the darkness swallowing the small beam of light from the headlight on her handlebars. She swerved into Dora's driveway and deposited the bike on the lawn.

"Dora!" she howled, her voice breaking as she pounded on the front door. Then Baz remembered, and she raced around to the back. Baz reached down, and her fingers found the hole in the bottom of the stupid ceramic cat sitting outside of the kitchen door. The key wasn't coming out, so Baz smashed the cat against the ground and picked the key out of the rubble. Baz entered the kitchen.

Baz was about to turn on the light, when she heard a rustling noise. Yes, the noise was coming from Dora's basement. Baz threw open the door and began to descend the concrete steps. Baz was so incensed that she took the stairs two at a time and did not bother to turn on the light.

"How dare you, Dora! How dare you Photoshop Sibyl into your photographs—what kind of sick, perverted person are you!"

"Don't come down!" screeched a voice from the darkness of the unfinished basement beyond. But Baz didn't listen, didn't care. At the bottom of the stairs, Baz marched over to the wall, and began to fumble for the light switch. Her fingers had just found the plastic cover when a bony hand closed over hers. Baz yipped.

"No light!" came the voice.

Too late. Baz's disobedient finger flipped the switch.

Before her was a monster.

It was a pale, emaciated creature of spine and rib. The creature was stooped, the wings of her shoulder blades prominent even underneath the faded tee-shirt. Almost bald, she had only a few stringy brown hairs still clinging to a scalp of blue veins. Her small black beetle eyes glittered at half-mast in the sudden light, her bloodless thin lips opened in a wordless cry to show sharp, yellowed teeth. Worst of all, the monster was wearing pajama bottoms with dinosaurs on it. In the monster's hand was a phone with a ladybug cover.

"D-Dora?" Baz whispered, horrified.

The creature shrank back from Baz, but then bared its teeth in a grotesque grin. "Don't you recognize me? Aren't I … beautiful?" Baz watched as the creature deliberately raised her cellphone. The creature made her mouth into a performative pout. Baz heard the click.

"And now I apply the filter …" The creature looked at Baz expectantly. Baz's phone buzzed. Moving slowly, Baz took the phone from her pocket and looked. There was a photo of Dora, stunningly beautiful and perfect, pouting at the camera. And in the photo, Sibyl stood behind her, her hand on Dora's shoulder. Baz looked at the photo and then to the emptiness that lay beyond the creature.

"But … how …" Baz couldn't stop staring at the photo, at Sibyl alive in the frame.

"Everything comes with a price," the Dora monster hissed. "Since Sibyl … she is in my photos now. Every time."

"So as your photos became more … you turned into …" Baz searched for a word to describe what Dora had become and failed. "This?"

The Dora creature nodded. "It was like the filter read my mind, how I wanted to look, who I wanted to be seen with …"

Baz noticed then that Dora's cheeks were wet.

"You see why I couldn't come," Dora said, pleading, holding her phone limply in her hand. "To the show. To the funeral." Baz and Dora stood for a moment, silent.

Baz took in a deep breath. "You know what you have to do, right? To fix this?"

Dora drew back. "Do what?" Her voice was hard and held warning. Baz didn't notice.

"You have to post a photo of yourself as you really are. No filter. Just you. Maybe, just maybe, if you do that, the changes will reverse."

"But then everyone will know. I can't do that, I won't do that!" Dora's voice came out in a hiss.

Baz looked at her with pity and love. "I know," she said softly, and with astonishing speed, plucked the phone from Dora's hand, and started to race up the cement steps.

Dora charged after her. Baz was nearly at the top of the stairs. Dora screamed in fury and frustration. Baz paused for just a second. It was enough. Dora slammed into Baz, grabbing her waist. "Give me that!"

The cell phone went flying.

And with a small gasp, so did Baz. She hit the wall, and then, with shocking speed, fell towards Dora. Dora saw stars as Baz's head hit Dora's nose with a sickening crunch. Baz continued to fall, and her head hit the wall and then a concrete step. Baz's body only stopped rotating when it landed at the foot of the stairs. Her limbs were splayed in a morbid approximation of a starfish. Her skin looked ghostly white in the fluorescent basement light, except the bruising that was already rising under her skin.

Dora slowly sat up in a daze and noticed that her nose was bleeding. Pinching the bridge of her nose, Dora looked down the stairs at Baz. There was blood coming from Baz's head too, and her neck was twisted at an impossible angle.

"Baz?" Dora whispered. Dora crept down the stairs. She stared at Baz, and then at her cellphone, halfway down the stair. Tilting her head back, Dora closed her eyes.

And then she heard slight movement.

"Baz!" Dora cried out. But it was just Dora's phone vibrating, rattling against the step. In a daze, Dora picked up the phone with shaky fingers, streaking blood across its surface. There was a new photo on Dora's Instagram, a photo of Dora at the top of her basement stairs. Dora's face was a mask of cruelty. And there was Baz, about to fall, her hand outstretched in supplication. Sibyl stood behind Dora at the top of the stairs, and she appeared to be laughing.

"No!" Dora screamed and doubled over, her organs shifting inside her. As she fell, Dora thought she heard Sibyl laughing and Baz crying out, and their voices slithered and mingled in senseless cacophony in her mind. A searing pain lashed through Dora's body as all her muscles seized and released, repeatedly, in sickening waves. It seemed to last forever, the voices and the seizures contorting her body.

With a sudden gasp, Dora awakened to herself, and found that she was curled on top of Baz's rapidly cooling body. Horrified, Dora flinched backwards. Dora reflexively tried to wipe the blood from her face, smearing it further. She shakily stood up, using the wall for support. Dora took one last look at Baz's body broken at the bottom of her basement. And then, deliberately, Dora turned away.

Slowly, so slowly, Dora walked up the basement steps. Softly, almost gently, she closed the basement door. Dora stumbled blindly out of the kitchen, into the living room. Dora pulled herself up the stairs, clutching her phone in one hand, and the banister tight in the other. She felt so tired.

Baz was right. She couldn't take this anymore; she couldn't have this happen to her anymore. Dora finally knew what she had to do.

Dora pushed open her bedroom door. She locked the door behind her and sank down to the carpet in weary defeat. She held her phone, feeling it vibrate with yet another damned photo of her, of Sibyl, and of Baz. Even as she cried out "no," her phone continued to vibrate, notifying her that people liked the newest batch of photos. But Dora calmed herself. At least now, she knew what she had to do.

So, she held up the phone, and aimed the camera at her face. And she looked at herself as she was reflected there, really looked at herself: at her bloody face, the red streaks of blood merely exacerbating the whiteness of her skeletal features and of her nearly bald scalp. Dora looked at her own haunted eyes. And then Dora took the photo—of herself as she truly was—and posted it.

Of course, Jillian Gray had rushed to come home once she heard the news about Sibyl from Baz's mother. She couldn't believe that Dora hadn't told her. Her daughter must be suffering beyond belief, without her mother there to comfort her! But how could Jillian have accounted for the monsoons that knocked out the Wi-Fi and grounded planes for three days in Goa? And once she finally made it to Paris, it certainly wasn't her fault that the unions were striking again, and she had to take the Chunnel to London to get on the redeye from Heathrow.

CHILLERS

When Jillian finally made it home, she went to the back door to enter the house through the kitchen, just like she always did. Her eyes widened as she saw that the spare-key statue was broken, and the door to the kitchen was unlocked. Jillian held her keys tight in her right fist, and softly dropped her bag just inside the door.

"Dora?" she called tremulously. She listened. No sound. There was something though. A smell? Steeling herself, Jillian walked further into the kitchen and then into the living room. Not seeing her daughter, Jillian went to the second floor. There, she found Dora's bedroom door shut and marked with a brownish-red stain.

"Dora, are you in there?" Jillian rattled the doorknob. The smell was stronger now. "Dora!" Jillian shrieked, and with strength she didn't know she possessed, Jillian kicked down the door.

After she broke into her daughter's bedroom, Jillian Gray found Dora lying on the floor, her body curled around her phone. Dora's brown eyes were open and glassy, and her nose was a mottled bruise. Dora's bushy brown hair was tangled and matted with dried blood. Jillian was too busy screaming to notice Dora's phone vibrate with one last update.

Had Dora's mother not been occupied with cradling her daughter's plump, limp body, she would have seen there was a new photo of Dora with her arms around her two best friends. And maybe Dora's teeth were a little crooked, maybe her cheeks were acne-pitted and her hair mousy brown, but didn't she look happy?

About the Author:
Miranda Morrow lives in Washington D.C.; she lawyers by day and writes by night.

Boris Karloff plays Imhotep in the 1932 Universal classic, *The Mummy*.

 CHILLERS

Cryptic
by Robert J. Kokai, Jr.

{Author's Note: As a writer I have written for print, radio, and television. But the most fun I've had as a wordsmith took place over a period of nearly 10 years when I wrote, produced, and acted in weekend murder mystery theatrical performances. Over that decade I wrote more than 20,000 pages of story and dialogue. It was during this period that I came to love the detective and film noir genres. At the root of each of these stories is a crime. *Cryptic* blends a story inspired by the classic horror films we all love, in this case *The Mummy*, with a first-person noir style narration that takes you inside the mind of a criminal as he plots a big heist.

Who among us hasn't suffered betrayals, treachery, and theft? What is the most precious possession that could be stolen from you? Consider that and guard it carefully.}

The old man was going to be an easy mark.

It was an autumn Friday afternoon at The Cleveland Museum of Art and I was looking for a big score. I needed a mark. That's where I spotted him milling around in the Egyptian section. He was an octogenarian wisp of a man, frail and delicate, who looked like he could keel over at any second. But he was dressed like a million bucks. He wore a classic blue blazer and gray flannel slacks with an ascot that made him look like he had stepped out of a men's shop on Savile Row. He also carried a walking stick, and the way he carried it, mostly by leaning on it, suggested it was more for show than necessity.

On anybody else the ascot and walking stick would have seemed like foppish affectations, but on the old man they seemed to fit. The way he was dressed, elegantly, and the way he carried himself, aristocratically, gave him the air of money. Even better, it gave him the air of very old money and lots of it. So that was the first thought that naturally crossed my mind.

The old man was going to be an easy mark.

That simple thought crossed my mind because it was my occupation to think that way. I'm a confidence man. Or at least, I was. I was well versed in the tactics of Machiavelli and could recite Sun Tzu's *The Art of War* chapter and verse. These strategies were all about manipulation. Their writings were guides about how to control people and their desires to get what you want, and I was charming enough to use that knowledge to open just about any door I wanted to. The moment I spotted the old codger I knew his door was going to be worth opening.

After deciding he was my target I kept an eye on him with my peripheral vision. He loitered around the room moving aimlessly from artifact to artifact, as if he was actually interested in seeing them. But once he settled in front of a specific piece, he really didn't seem to take any interest in it at all. It was like he was milling around just waiting to be noticed. At one point he must have sensed that he had been noticed when I made the mistake of looking directly at him. That's when he turned and made eye contact with me and gave me a gentle smile. He had weak eyes and yellow teeth, but his smile was still pleasant and friendly. I smiled back and then immediately diverted my attention to something that I had no interest in at all.

This was going to be easy.

In the few seconds that our eyes met I got the impression that the old man was lonely and just looking for somebody to talk to. That was my invitation. So, I casually made my way to a position in the room where I could make co-incidental contact with him. On the way I checked my reflection in the glass of one of the showcases I passed by. I was the fair-haired blue-eyed boy that every mark trusted. Fair haired with a tenor voice that neared a falsetto verging on feminine. Who wouldn't trust me? I was harmless. My diminutive appearance had opened the door of every sucker I'd ever taken to the cleaners.

I continued to where our incidental contact occurred. It was in the middle of the room in front of the Egyptian section's centerpiece, which was an ancient, ornate sarcophagus. The sarcophagus was covered from top to bottom and inside and out with hieroglyphics. Unlike the other artifacts the old man had pretended to study, he looked at this piece as if he were truly interested in it. His eyes moved over the hieroglyphics following a distinct pattern. I observed his study for several seconds before intruding.

"Excuse me, are you actually reading that?" I asked.

The old man turned his head slightly to look up into my eyes and smiled that friendly yellow-toothed smile. "I can read some of it. Not all of it. It's from a later period, the 21st Dynasty, and I'm not as familiar with that as I am earlier Dynasties."

"Really?" I asked, doing my best to sound sincere and interested.

"Yes." The old man nodded, "This is the coffin of Nesykhonsu. It's nearly three thousand years old."

"Wow!" I exclaimed and then asked, "Is it really that old?"

The old man shrugged matter-of-factly. "Yes, it is that old." Then he added, "But mine is older."

I did a stunned double take. "You have one of these? One that's older than this one?" I wasn't acting interested at that point. My curiosity had truly been piqued.

"Yes," the old man nodded again, "many of the pieces in this Egyptian collection were purchased or donated to the museum before ground was broken on this building. And many came from one of Howard Carter's early archaeological expeditions. But mine came from …" he hesitated for a moment before saying, "… a private collection. It's substantially older than this casket."

"Are you a collector?" I asked.

The old man chuckled. "I suppose you could say that. Collecting just sort of happened. So I suppose I am and have been collecting for more years than I'd care to admit."

"And?" I asked, "you have things in your collection that are even older than these?"

The old man replied, again matter-of-factly, "Oh yes, substantially older."

"That's incredible." I remarked. "I'd love to see them."

The old man's face became serious as he turned to face me. "Do you have an interest in Egyptology, young man?"

He had taken the bait and my hook had been set. It had been that easy. I nodded my head affirmatively and in a solemn voice replied, "I'm fascinated by it."

The old man's eyes narrowed and he looked at me as if he was judging me. It was an uncomfortable moment until he smiled, extended his hand, and said, "My name is Akil El Sayed."

I bowed slightly at the waist as I took his hand and introduced myself. "I'm Chris Allen. It's a pleasure to meet you, Mr. El Sayed."

He hesitated for a moment as he thought and then asked, "Would you really have an interest in seeing my collection?"

I answered, "I would love to see it!"

"There may be other things that would interest you in my collection as well. I have historic pieces from many eras that I've collected over the years. But the majority of them, the best pieces, are Egyptian. Those pieces and the artwork are the prizes of my collection." He volunteered.

I hoped my eyes didn't betray my thoughts as I asked, "You collect art as well?"

"Oh, yes. I have an extensive collection of art. I have so much of it that I can't even display it all properly. My house doesn't have enough wall space so most of it is stored in empty rooms and closets and in the attic. It was all purchased when it was cheap, before people saw the real worth of it." Then he added, rather cryptically, "Always see the value in something and buy it cheap, young man."

I responded with feigned awe, "I would love to see your collection."

The old guy was getting better by the second. Not only did he appear to have money, but it was becoming apparent that he had a collection of relics and artwork that could be worth millions. My mind was reeling; if I played my cards right, I could fleece the old goat and be gone before he ever knew what had happened. It sounded like he had so many treasures that it could be years before he even realized that something was gone. Or, he may never miss it at all.

While I was pondering this, El Sayed had taken a pen and pad out of his breast pocket and began scribbling something down. He finished writing and tore the paper from the pad. "I'm always happy to share my collection with somebody who will appreciate it. Are you free tomorrow afternoon?"

I nodded. "Yes, I am."

He handed me the paper and smiled. "Then here is my address. I'll expect you for tea tomorrow at one o'clock."

I thanked El Sayed and told him I'd be there and he shook my hand. Even the touch of his hand had the feel of old, cold, money to it. Then he excused himself saying that he had to go home and feed his cats. I nearly laughed when he said that. It was another thing that a rich, lonely, old man would collect—cats.

The next afternoon I pulled through a wrought iron gate into El Sayed's driveway at five minutes after one. I'd arrived fashionably late. Not late enough to be rude, but late enough to build some anticipation for my arrival. When I saw his house my head reeled. It was easily the biggest house, or mansion, I'd seen in my entire life. It was nearly as big as the museum where we had met and it stunned me that El Sayed had said his house didn't have enough wall space to display all of his art collection.

How much artwork did the old coot actually have? How many artifacts did he have?

I got out of my car and approached the door, and as I did, it opened. A tall powerful-looking black man greeted me. I assumed he was El Sayed's servant. He looked at me with dead eyed disinterest, and in a deep, flat, accented voice asked, "Mr. Allen?"

"Yes." I answered. The servant stood aside for me to enter.

"Mr. El Sayed is expecting you. He is in the study." I stepped into the foyer and the servant held out his hand to point the way as he crossed to the room on my left. He stopped at the doorway and held up his hand again as an invitation for me to enter. I thanked him and went into the room.

The study was dark considering that it was early afternoon, and when El Sayed's manservant closed the door behind me, it became even darker. Before the door completely closed a black cat ran through and shot past my feet. The cat startled me and I stopped short. That gave me an excuse to stand still for a moment and allow my eyes to adjust to the darkness. Thick velvet drapes covered the windows on the outside wall and were pulled together tight to keep the sunlight out. Two wingback chairs were in front of a fireplace opposite the door with a coffee table between them. The only light in the room came from a small fire in the fireplace and a lamp on a table next to one of the chairs. The effect of the two tiny pools of light in the cavernous room was somber.

El Sayed sat in one of the chairs reading a book, and the black cat that had raced past me jumped up onto his lap. The cat looked at me with bright green eyes, as if I was an unwelcome intruder, and then curled up on the old man's lap to take a nap. In the near darkness of the room El Sayed looked even frailer than he had at the museum the previous afternoon. In the shadows he practically looked like a corpse. As the cat put down its head, the old man raised his and noticed me and smiled. The act of smiling seemed to be an effort for him, and in the near darkness the strain made his smile seem wicked, not friendly, like it had been at the museum.

"Good afternoon …" He began and halted. He coughed a dry cough to clear his throat and continued in a croaking voice. "Good afternoon, young man. Thank you for coming."

"Good afternoon, Mr. El Sayed." I replied. "Thank you for the kind invitation."

El Sayed urged me to have a seat in the chair opposite his. I did and took in my surroundings again. The interior walls of the room were lined from floor to ceiling with shelves that held thousands of volumes of antique books. There were even shelves flanking the fireplace, and in the space between them, above the mantle, hung an oil painting. It was a portrait of a man and it was easy even for me to see that it was hundreds of years old. I studied it for a moment and then commented on it.

"Something about the man in that painting looks familiar to me." I said.

El Sayed looked up at the painting and nodded. "I thought so, too." He offered. "That's why I bought it. You'd never know it looking at me now, but the man in that painting resembles me when I was a young man."

I looked back up at the painting and observed, "It's the eyes. His eyes look like yours." I turned back to El Sayed, who smiled and winked impishly. Then I added, "The style of the artist looks familiar. I think I've seen that painting somewhere before."

El Sayed shook his head slowly. "The style should look familiar. It's a Rembrandt. But I doubt you've seen it before. I purchased it a long time ago and it's never been on public display." Then he changed the subject. "Would you care for a cup of tea or coffee?"

"Coffee would be good. Black, please." I answered.

"Very good." El Sayed put aside the book he had been reading and gently removed the black cat from his lap. Placing his hands on the arms of his chair, he painfully pushed himself up to a standing position. He then collected his walking stick and began slowly making his way to the door. I noticed that in the privacy of his own home he didn't appear to be as well tailored as he had been in public. The robe he wore looked like a relic from a bygone era and draped around him like it was several sizes too big for his frame.

"Excuse me." He said, "I'll have Kek prepare drinks. I'll be back shortly."

The very act of walking appeared to be a painful chore for him as he shuffled to the door. The moment he was gone I began taking stock of the room again. As I cased it my eyes were drawn to the coffee table between El Sayed's chair and the one I was sitting in. It was cluttered with books and papers and from beneath them was a glint of a sparkle that caught my eye. The flame from the fireplace was reflecting off something metallic underneath the clutter, and I reached forward and fished out the shiny object. It was a gold figure of a scarab beetle that was about three inches long. As soon as I picked it up I could tell by its weight that it wasn't made of pot metal or lead. It was heavy. I was certain it was made out of real gold. It was like winning The Irish Sweepstakes!

I shot a glance at the doorway to make sure that the old man wasn't coming back into the room yet. Once I was satisfied that I was still alone and wouldn't be seen I slipped the gold scarab into my jacket pocket. I was pleased with myself; I had picked the right mark. I hadn't been in the house for more than 10 minutes and had already scored a piece of art that could be worth hundreds of dollars or more. It could be worth a lot more if it were one of the actual relics the old man had hinted he had.

As I basked in my achievement I got the unsettling feeling that I was being watched. I looked up and saw that the old man's black cat was sitting across from me, atop the back of his chair, staring at me. The creature had a look of disdain in its eyes, as if it was telling me it knew I had just done something wrong. It didn't move. It just sat there and glared at me with contempt.

I told myself that I was being ridiculous, that the cat was just a cat. It couldn't possibly have any idea what I had just done. But nevertheless, it gave me the creeps as it sat motionless with its green eyes locked upon me. I wouldn't have thought it was possible to be able to hear a cat breathe, but the two of us remained so still that I was sure I could. Then, finally, thankfully, El Sayed returned and sat down in his chair again. Once he did the sentry cat stretched and jumped down from his perch and ran from the room.

After the old man situated himself back into his chair he engaged me in small talk. He asked questions about my background and I lied. I told him I had recently gotten out of the service and was preparing to apply to several colleges to continue my studies. I told him I couldn't decide whether to concentrate on ancient history or art since both of them interested me. He bought my lies and attempted to make some helpful suggestions. After a few minutes the man servant, Kek, arrived with our drinks and we nursed them for the next 15 minutes. Then El Sayed put his cup on the table and exhaled heavily and smiled.

"Would you like to see my sarcophagus now?" El Sayed had a gleam in his eye as he asked the question. He was happy. He had no idea how truly eager I was to see the sarcophagus and the rest of his collection. I told him I would love to see his sarcophagus and he laboriously raised himself from his chair again and cackled, "Then, let's go down into my crypt!" I laughed at his joke and followed behind him as he made his way out into the foyer and down the first floor's main hall to the cellar stairs.

There was artwork everywhere on the walls, and as we walked down the hallway, one particular piece caught my eye. I paused to admire it. It was a sketch on parchment paper that appeared to be of the same man in the Rembrandt painting, above the fireplace. El Sayed stopped and leaned on his walking stick as I studied the sketch.

"Do you like it?" he asked.

"I do." I replied, "Very nice."

"Of course it is. It's the work of a Master." El Sayed explained, "It's a Leonardo da Vinci sketch. It's another piece that I managed to get cheap."

"And," I observed, "this sketch appears to be of the same man in the Rembrandt painting. They both have the same eyes."

"It does appear that way, doesn't it?" El Sayed agreed, "Perhaps both artists knew the man. That would be an amazing coincidence, wouldn't it?"

"It certainly would be." I nodded and looked at the wall on the other side of the hall. Another painting was hanging there and I recognized the artist immediately. It was a Pablo Picasso painting of a man done in his cubist style. I knew that because I had read an article about Picasso in *Time* magazine. "A Picasso!" I exclaimed.

"Yes. Do you like it?" the old man asked.

I tilted my head and looked at the painting from top to bottom. I squinted in the dim light to take in the painting's details, of which there were few. But the one detail that I did notice was that even in the cubist style the man's eyes bore an eerie resemblance to the man in the Rembrandt and da Vinci pieces. I didn't mention the similarity and simply nodded that I liked the painting.

"I paid a bit more for that painting than I liked. But I bought it directly from the artist." El Sayed said matter-of-factly.

"You've met Picasso?" I asked.

The old man shrugged off my question, "Yes, in Paris."

He called for Kek, who immediately appeared, as if he had been waiting to be called. El Sayed told his manservant that we were going down to the cellar. Kek opened the cellar door and turned on a light and then picked up El Sayed, effortlessly, like he was a rag doll, and carried him down the stairs. The old man explained that at his age and in his condition he didn't dare try to navigate up and down stairs anymore out of fear of falling and breaking a hip. At the foot of the stairs there were doors on each side and one in front of us. Kek gingerly put El Sayed down and opened the door that was facing us.

Kek stepped back and El Sayed moved aside and motioned for me to enter the room in the dark. "I'll turn on the lights once you're inside. That way you can get the full effect of the room all at once." He said it with a tauntingly wry look on his face, so it was with a bit of trepidation that I stepped into the pitch-black void. I got the feeling that I was about to see something pretty spectacular. I knew I was right with the first step I took. There was something gritty under my feet and I realized that I was actually walking on sand. The floor of the entire room was covered in sand.

Once I had taken about a half dozen steps into the room, El Sayed turned on the lights and what I saw surrounding me was amazing. There, in the cellar of his suburban home, was an authentic-looking Egyptian tomb. No detail, from the hieroglyphics painted on the walls. to the statuary and furnishings had been overlooked. In the middle of the far wall was the sarcophagus he had told me about. It was standing upright and its lid was propped up against the wall next to it. Inside the sarcophagus was a well-preserved mummy. In the middle of the room was the funeral bier that the sarcophagus would have rested on. Around the walls were braziers, canopic jars, and statues of the Egyptian gods.

El Sayed looked over his shoulder at Kek. "Light the braziers so Christopher can get the feeling of what this room would have actually looked like over four thousand years ago," he said.

The manservant immediately began lighting the dozen braziers around the walls. As he did, I turned to El Sayed and exclaimed, "This is incredible! It's better than anything we saw at the museum!"

The old man beamed with pride, "It should be. Everything here is authentic and it all came from the same tomb and stands here exactly as it did forty-five hundred years ago."

The moment Kek had lit the last brazier, El Sayed turned off all the electric lights in the room. I stood in awe and looked around me at the tomb lit only by the flames from the braziers, just as it would have been in ancient Egypt. I stared at the paintings of the gods on the wall: Ra, Amon Ra, Thoth, Anubis, and Isis. Painted eyes of Horus flanked me on opposite walls and seemed to be looking right at me. And the shadows cast by the statuary danced in the light of the brazier flames across all of them. Once I had taken in the spectacle around me, my eyes settled on the mummy in his sarcophagus. I felt a bit sad for him. I thought about how long that poor devil had been in that coffin and wondered what he would have thought about ending up as a curiosity in the old man's home. I turned and looked at El Sayed.

"Very impressive!" I said.

El Sayed smiled, "Yes, it is." He replied, "It puts me in the mind of ancient evenings. It's magical."

"It is!" I agreed with a smile.

El Sayed shook his head slowly, "No, you don't understand, Christopher. It truly is magical."

I tilted my head to one side and looked at the old man, "I don't understand," I said, "What do you mean?"

 CHILLERS

"I mean that my sarcophagus has metaphysical properties," he said. My eyes must have betrayed that I thought he was talking nonsense because he stepped toward me and continued, "I understand you don't believe me, but it's true. You see me. I'm broken down and spent. I'm decrepit. You don't have to feel the need to be polite. I know how I look. But I'm actually even older than I appear to be. This sarcophagus has healing powers. It energizes you and revitalizes you. It's just … magical."

"You're serious, aren't you?" I asked.

El Sayed nodded, "I'm dead serious. When you stand in that sarcophagus you can feel the energy of the Ages move through you. You can harness the power of space and time. It revitalizes me." Then, the old man spoke to Kek without taking his eyes off of me. "Kek, remove the mummy from his coffin." The servant immediately began to carry out the command.

I protested, "But the mummy could get damaged!"

El Sayed stopped me, "Don't worry, Christopher. He's more durable than he looks. And he's just a husk at this point, light as a feather." Before the old man had finished his statement, Kek had removed the mummy from the sarcophagus and propped it up against the wall on the opposite side of where the sarcophagus lid was leaning. I looked back at El Sayed and he raised his hand and pointed shakily. "Go ahead, step inside. Kek will assist you. Step into the sarcophagus. Stand inside it and feel its magic."

I hesitated for a moment and then took a deep breath and walked over to the sarcophagus. Kek was standing to the right of it in front of the mummy against the wall. He took me by the elbow to steady me. The step up into the coffin was only a couple of inches, but it was awkward to get into it and turn around. Kek assisted me and, once I was in place, I looked at El Sayed. He was smiling, but again, his smile seemed wicked and not the smile of the friendly old gentleman I'd met at the art museum.

He whispered, "Now, Christopher, take a deep breath and relax."

I did as he said, and El Sayed bowed his head and began murmuring something. I couldn't understand what he was saying but it sounded almost like a chant or a prayer. As he went on, I began to feel a warm tingling sensation fill my body. It felt good and I grinned.

"I can feel something!" I exclaimed.

Without looking up, El Sayed held up a boney finger to silence me and he continued murmuring. I did as he instructed and remained quiet. The tingling sensation continued to course through me as the old man went on with his muttering for another minute or so and then stopped. He looked up at me slowly, his face blanketed with shadows cast by the fires in the braziers, and as he did, I began to smell the stench of sizzling, burning hair. I was going to say something about it, but found I couldn't. I was unable to open my mouth to speak. Then, the tingling became an unbearable burning sensation and I began to feel numbness spread across the right side of my body. I tried to scream but couldn't.

By that time, El Sayed was looking directly into my eyes. But he was different. His eyes were more vibrant, more alive, and full of fire. As smoldering locks of my hair began to fall from my head and past my eyes, his hairline began to fill in. It crept down his forehead and, as it did, his snow-white hair became jet black. Within seconds, the wisp of a man had a full head of thick, black hair.

I attempted to gasp and raise my right hand to point and remark on his change, but my arm wouldn't move. It was paralyzed. And my right leg, too. Then, I realized that the left side of me had grown numb and gone dead as well. I tried to call for help, but I couldn't make a sound.

I couldn't move at all.

I could only stand in place and watch El Sayed as a total transformation took place over him. Within seconds, he was standing erect with no hint of the geriatric curvature of an old man's spine. His form filled in with muscle, and his shoulders and chest broadened, as the wrinkles disappeared from his face and hands. Within minutes, he had become a man of my age, young and vibrant. He filled out the robe that only minutes before had hung loosely to the point that it had seemed to weigh him down. He smiled at me again, and now that smile didn't appear out of place. It was authentically wicked. He made a motion with his hand and without a word being spoken, Kek obeyed his command as if he could read his mind. Kek picked up an ancient mirror, stepped in front of me, and held it up in front of my face so I could see myself.

I was horrified!

The face staring back at me from that mirror wasn't my face at all. Instead of seeing myself, I was looking at a skeletal monstrosity, with dull and yellowed skin that looked as though it had been stretched tightly over a skull. That parchment-like skin appeared to be so dry and brittle that even the slightest touch could shatter it. That dead face couldn't possibly be mine, but the longer I stared at it in the mirror, the more I recognized that it was. It most certainly was me, but a mummified version. My hair was totally gone and much of my nose was missing as well. They had fallen off me to the sand-covered floor in front of the sarcophagus. Worst of all was my mouth. My lips had receded and shrunk until they were pulled taut and wide open, exposing my teeth, which were yellowed and cracked. My mouth had been frozen in a tortured grimace of death.

After the initial feeling of horror I had upon seeing myself, the first thought I had was how could this be possible? How could this have happened to me? I was dead but remained aware of everything going on around me. Though my eyes appeared dead, I could see. I could think, but I couldn't move. I had become a prisoner in my own body. The next thought that I had was that I had been damaged beyond repair. What had happened to me couldn't be reversed. I couldn't be fixed. I would be like this until I was truly dead.

Kek then removed the mirror from in front of my face and again, without a word being said, went about doing El Sayed's bidding. First, he reached into my jacket pocket and removed the golden scarab I had stolen in the study and gave it back to El Sayed. Next, he took a chair from against the wall and placed it behind where El Sayed was standing. With that wicked smile still on his face, El Sayed casually sat down. He watched as Kek approached me again and produced a pair of scissors from his jacket pocket and began to cut my clothing from my body. Once he had stripped me of all of my clothes, he removed the bandages from the mummy against the wall and wrapped them around me. The process seemed to take hours, as the servant meticulously went about the task of making me look like an ancient mummy.

Once the process was complete, Kek gathered up my shredded clothing and disposed of it. He then took his place standing at the left side of the seated El Sayed. El Sayed studied me for several long minutes and then finally nodded his head in approval. Kek had completed his task well. El Sayed was satisfied that I looked like an authentic mummy. The moment El Sayed nodded that the job was done, Kek began to change. The powerful looking black man shrank and grew fur. He continued to change until he was no longer a man at all. He became that same black cat that had rushed past my feet and startled me in El Sayed's study. Once he had completely changed into the cat, he leaped up onto El Sayed's lap, shot one more accusatory look at me with his bright green eyes, and then stretched and curled up on El Sayed's lap to take a nap.

El Sayed sat staring at me for what seemed like forever. As he did, he stroked the sleeping cat on his lap with one hand, while rolling the golden scarab around in the other. Then, he stopped fondling the scarab and placed it on the arm of his chair. He took a case and lighter out of his robe and removed and lit a cigarette. He sat up straight and took a slow drag off the cigarette, which expanded his broad chest. Then, he exhaled slowly, relaxed, and finally spoke.

"I suppose, young man," he said, "I owe you an explanation. Especially considering all you have just given me. As you can see, things aren't quite what they appear to be here. To begin with, Kek is not a man; he was a gift that was bestowed to me by the goddess, Bast. You would recognize her as The Cat Goddess. And my name is not Akil El Sayed; it is Imhotep. I am nearly five thousand years old, and am quite accomplished. I have been a highly regarded patrician, physician, and magician. I devised the hieroglyphic language that was so bastardized and riddled with 21st Dynasty slang on the sarcophagus we saw in the art museum. I was the first architect and designed The Step Pyramids at Saqqara for the Pharaoh Djoser. I was the vizier and governor of Egypt under that same Pharaoh Djoser and ascended to take his place as Pharaoh after his death. There were questions about his death and my rule was … brief. But my greatest accomplishment was as a High Priest of the Temple of Ra. In that position I became a familiar of the gods.

"I was taken by the goddess Isis, as her mortal lover, and it was she who gave the coffin that you stand in, my coffin, the power of rejuvenation. It has kept me alive for millennia in wait of her return."

El Sayed paused and took a drag off his cigarette and continued, "I have walked the Earth for centuries and have been present for every great event in the history of mankind. I have known the famous and the infamous. Many of them have called me *friend*. You have seen the works of some of my friends. The priceless works of art by Rembrandt and da Vinci and so many others that you haven't seen were purchased directly from them, often for not much more than the price of the canvas and paint that created them. And the portraits that you recognized as being the same man were in fact the same man. They were all portraits of me. And you, my little dullard, should have known that if Leonardo da Vinci and Rembrandt knew the same man something had to be awry because they lived in completely different centuries with a hundred years separating their lives. And you claimed to have a serious interest in art and history."

He grinned wickedly again and took another drag off his cigarette. "And now, we come to your life, you filthy thief. For the rest of what would have been your natural life you will stand there, in my place, in my coffin. Every breath I take will be thanks to you. Every beat of my heart will be yours. And at the end of your life, when my breaths grow short and the borrowed beats of my heart grow weak, I will simply replace you with another parasite just as I have with all of your predecessors."

Imhotep held up his cigarette for punctuation as he said, "Remember what I told you, young man? Always see the value in something and buy it cheap. I bought you with a promise of plunder and a cup of coffee."

Then, Imhotep laughed a low and evil laugh. He finished his cigarette and crushed it out in the sand beneath his feet. He continued laughing as he gingerly removed Kek from his lap and rose and walked to the doorway. There, he placed his finger on the light switch and stopped and turned his head to speak to me over his shoulder. "Now if you'll excuse me, Christopher Allen, I have some living to do."

With that he turned off the lights in his tomb. Or, more accurately, he turned off the lights in my tomb. Only the flames from the braziers lit the room casting shadows across the paintings of his Egyptian gods on the walls. Kek ran out of the room, past his master's feet, and Imhotep turned, smiled one more time, and then shut the door behind him.

Not long after Imhotep left the room, Kek returned. He was once again a man. He collected the mummy whose place I had taken from beside the sar-

CHILLERS

cophagus and placed it on the funeral bier in the center of the room. There, he began to ritualistically dismember the body into tiny pieces and burn them bit-by-bit in the flames of the still burning braziers. The final piece was the mummy's head, which he placed intact into one of the braziers. I tried to close my eyes but couldn't. I had to watch as its skin ignited like flash paper and its skull burned like balsa wood.

Once Kek had finished disposing of the body he turned and glared at me. It was only then that I realized that he had the same bright green eyes that he had in his feline form. He smirked in silence as if he was telling me that the same fate awaited me. That someday I would burn in the flames of the braziers. As if to punctuate that thought, he picked up my nose from where it had fallen to the sand at my feet and crossed to the nearest brazier and dropped it into the flames.

My God! He burned my nose!

He turned to look at me as he did this and laughed. Then, he extinguished the flames in the braziers and exited the room, leaving me in total darkness.

Over the months that followed Kek would visit me daily and play a sadistic game. He would hold that mirror up in front of my face to show me what I had become. He was telling me what I had known from the start; I was broken, ruined, and could never be fixed. Then he would yowl and laugh and leave me in the tomb alone again. But after a while Kek got tired of his game of cat and mouse and his daily visits ended.

Time passed. I was starving but could not eat. Worse, I could not die of starvation. That would have been a blessing, but the spell that had been cast over me wouldn't allow me to die. Eventually, after months or maybe even years, I stopped feeling the pangs of hunger. That was when I could feel my internal organs start to die, one by one. What was worse was I could smell them dying. The rotting stench was horrible. My organs died but my senses remained intact; I was aware of my situation and could see, hear, and smell everything. Even without a nose, I could smell everything.

As bad as that was, my remaining sense of touch was even worse. There were times I would get an itch and couldn't do anything to relieve it. I would feel the tingling sensation of the itching and, being paralyzed, couldn't execute the simple act of scratching. Even the mildest itch could seem like a maddening case of poison ivy.

I soon lost count of the days and months. Initially, the only means I had to gauge the passage of time was the change of the seasons. I could feel the change on my body, or what was left of it. Just as a wooden door will expand in the summer and contract in the winter, the barometric changes in the seasons were doing the same thing to the dead flesh of my body and the husk of skin that stretched over it. Over time my dried out body had expanded and contracted so much that my skin had cracked and pieces of me fell off into the sand.

I felt alone in the darkness of the tomb for what had to be years at a stretch. The only indication of the passage of time was the rare glimpses I got of Imhotep himself. On the occasion that he did make a visit to the tomb, I could estimate how long I had been standing inert by how much he had aged. I observed as he moved past his youthful twenties and thirties into his fifties and sixties. I was sure that I had stood in his sarcophagus for over forty years.

Then, finally came the day that Imhotep and Kek entered the room with another young man. The lights in the room were turned on and the long-haired boy gasped and looked around the tomb just as I had on that autumn Saturday in 1939. He giggled at the relics in the tomb and explained that they were just the kind of props he needed for the stage show for his band. He said that the artifacts in the tomb would make a woman bandleader named Alice Cooper green with envy. Then, he looked at me, grimaced, and commented that I looked like something out of an old Boris Karloff movie.

Imhotep smiled, listened to the boy, and assured him that he had plenty of things he could use for his band's show. Then, he bade Kek to light the braziers around the room and began to tell the long-haired young man about the magical properties of the sarcophagus I was standing in.

It was almost over for me. It was the end of the line. As I came to that realization one thought crossed my mind;

The kid was going to be an easy mark.

About the Author:
Bob Kokai has written for print, radio, and television. As an actor he has worked on the stage and television where he hosted horror movies as Count Dracula. He and his alter ego, Drac, were inducted into The Horror Host Hall of Fame in 2019. Kokai lives in Chippewa Lake, Ohio, with his canine best friend and confidant, Watson, a shifty black cat named Professor Moriarty, and a Chuckle Monkey named Stefanie.

MONOGRAM PICTURES Presents
BELA LUGOSI
BOWERY AT MIDNIGHT
with JOHN ARCHER · WANDA McKAY
PRODUCED BY SAM KATZMAN AND JACK DIETZ
DIRECTED BY WALLACE FOX
ORIGINAL SCREENPLAY BY GERALD SCHNITZER

CHILLERS

An Ending for Bowery at Midnight

by Todd Shiba

{Author's Note: If you've ever seen *Bowery at Midnight*, the 1942 Monogram Pictures film, you know that this movie is somewhat of a nonsensical jumble of half-coherent gibberish. And when it gets to the end of the last reel, the movie just … sort of … stops, like suddenly the filmmakers threw their hands up and said, "Nuts to this, let's just end the movie here so we can all go home."

This short story gives the movie a conclusion—or tries to, any-way—and it also tries to make some of the rest of the movie make sense, relatively speaking. This story might make more sense if you've seen the movie, but pretty much everyone who finishes watching *Bowery at Midnight* promptly says, "Well, that was certainly a bunch of people doing things in front of a camera," and then blots it out of their memory while wishing that they could get the last 62 minutes of their life back. The point is, if you've seen the movie, you might understand this short story a little bit more than if you haven't, but if you haven't ever seen *Bowery at Midnight*—well, lucky you, and stay that way.}

Sure, Doc Brooks was old and decrepit, but there was nothing wrong with his ears. He could hear every bit of the commotion that was going on upstairs. There he was, in the Friendly Mission's basement, which happened to be his bedroom, his kitchen, and also his laboratory, though he liked to think of the basement as a subterranean efficiency apartment, because it was better than thinking of it as the prison that it actually was.

The floorboards above Brooks' head shook and rattled and dropped dust in his hair as the heavy footsteps of the policemen closed in on Karl Wagner, the notorious crime boss who looked just like that Bela Lugosi fellow from the horror pictures, also known as the kindly proprietor of the Friendly Mission, who looked just like that Bela Lugosi fellow from the horror pictures, and also known as Frederick Brenner, the kindly University of New Califyorkia psychology professor who looked just like that Bela Lugosi fellow from the horror pictures, but with pince-nez spectacles.

Brooks wanted to revel in the police finally figuring it all out, but at that particular moment, Wagner's hatchet man Frankie Mills was standing in Brooks' basement pointing a gun at Judy Malvern, that idealistic young blonde who worked upstairs in the Friendly Mission's soup kitchen, New Califyorkia's finest culinary establishment for transients, where she handed out Wonder

Bread and Band-Aids and fended off advances from perverts. Frankie Mills was a stone-cold killer—Brooks had seen Mills shoot a man dead at point-blank range and then smirk and say cinematic one-liners afterwards—and Brooks was afraid that Miss Judy would be Mills' next victim.

Brooks heard the police break down the door to Wagner's office upstairs, and he heard Wagner open the secret door that led to the hidden staircase that led to the basement. Moments later, Wagner came rushing down the stairs.

"Police!" Wagner said to Mills. Wagner grabbed Miss Judy and dragged her over to the wall at the far end of the room, where he turned a switch that made a door slide open to reveal a secret room. Wagner threw Miss Judy in there and closed the door. Then he and Mills dashed to the other end of the basement and hurried up a different staircase that led to another secret door that led to the back alley.

Wagner opened that door, and saw too late that some policemen were patrolling the alley. They shot and killed Frankie Mills. Wagner slammed the door shut before the policemen could get him, then he turned and ran back downstairs.

Brooks saw the whole thing. He was waiting for Wagner at the bottom of the steps. Brooks had never seen Wagner look so panicked before. Wagner must have known that he was trapped, like a victim in a Bela Lugosi movie.

Brooks seized an opportunity that he hadn't expected would ever come. He took Wagner's arm and said, "I know the very place for you to hide, where no one will ever find you. Come with me."

Brooks led Wagner to the far end of the basement and opened the door to the secret room that held Miss Judy. This room had a dirt floor that held the graves of Wagner's lackeys who had outlived their use—the men that Wagner murdered so that they wouldn't tell on him.

Wagner had forced Brooks to dig the graves and make the grave markers. Now, as Brooks and Wagner hurried inside the room, Brooks glanced at the names that he had painted on the wooden crosses: Taylor, Robinson, Weston, Hilton, Stratton … and Dennison, poor Richard Dennison, Miss Judy's innocent boyfriend, who had just happened to stumble into the wrong place at the wrong time and paid a fatal price.

From the corner of his eye, Brooks saw Miss Judy slip out and go upstairs to the police. He breathed a sigh that she was safe now.

Brooks went to Hilton's grave. "I've prepared this for just such an occasion," Brooks said. He pushed Hilton's gravemarker toward the ground. A hidden door, covered in dirt, swung open like a coffin lid.

It wasn't a coffin lid, though, it was a hatch with a staircase that descended to a secret sub-basement room. Wagner descended the stairs into the sub-basement … that held the zombies that Doc Brooks was keeping a secret from everyone. The zombies swarmed Wagner and tore him apart.

 CHILLERS

Brooks laughed maniacally.

He hadn't meant to be so dramatically hammy, but the situation seemed to call for it.

Judy followed the policemen downstairs. When she'd escaped the dirt room, she dashed upstairs and found Detective Crawford and an entire squad of policemen trying to figure out where Wagner had disappeared to. "Quick, they're down below!" Judy had told them, and they all rushed downstairs to where Doc Brooks was standing. They got there just as the zombies dragged Wagner farther into the sub-basement and out of sight.

"Well, that takes care of the professor," Detective Crawford said.

Judy looked down into the sub-basement, and saw the most horrible thing she had ever seen in her life. "Richard!" she cried. Richard Dennison was clearly dead—and, also, clearly alive. What the minced oath? Judy thought. She knew it wasn't proper to use such foul profanity, even in the privacy of one's own head, but she was a modern girl, and this was 1942, the very definition of a modern year, and what other term was there to use when you suddenly see that your boyfriend has turned into a stark-raving whatever it was that he had turned into?

"What's wrong with him?" she asked Brooks.

"My remedy didn't work," Brooks said.

"Can you fix him?" Judy asked.

"That's what I've been trying to do," Brooks said.

Crawford pointed into the sub-basement. "Who are those people you're keeping down there? They just ripped the professor to pieces."

"Those people down there?" Brooks asked. "Well, they aren't really people."

Crawford looked baffled. "What do you mean?"

"They belong to me," Brooks said. "I take care of them. They're kind of like my pets."

"What do you mean?" Crawford asked again, looking even more baffled.

"You won't believe me," Brooks said.

"Try me," Crawford said.

Judy was trying to figure out what in the name of green barneymugging heck Doc was talking about. Not really people? What on earth was going on?

Doc Brooks didn't want to think about any of it. If he did, all the memories would come back, and he was tired of hurting from the memories.

But Brooks also wanted the police to know his story. So, as quickly as he could, he spilled everything to Detective Crawford. It had all started years ago, back when Brooks was a professor at the University of New Califyorkia. He taught biology classes in the daytime, and went home to his beloved wife Marguerite in the evenings, where they ate dinner and then retreated to bed and did passionately stentorian things to each other now that Abigail, their daughter, had grown up and moved out of the house. And after Brooks kissed Marguerite and she went to sleep, Brooks went to his secret laboratory on the university campus. What looked like a brick wall in the back of a disused utility closet in the science building was actually a secret door of Brooks' own devising, which led to a secret room where Brooks did his secret research that involved bringing the dead back to life. Brooks developed remedies in his laboratory and injected them into the bodies of dead college students, of which he had a ready supply. They were always doing stupid things like overdosing or hazing each other to death or hanging themselves because they got bad grades. They all ended up in the morgue of the University of New Califyorkia Hospital; it was quite easy enough for Brooks to borrow any number of bodies for a few hours.

For 10 years, all of Brooks' experiments failed: Remedies Able through Pup were terrible flops. But Brooks kept at it, and one day he developed Remedy Quack, which he was sure would succeed. All he had to do was try it on a body—but lately there had been an healthy epidemic among all the students.

When a body did turn up, it was Brooks' worst nightmare. One afternoon, Marguerite climbed an apricot tree in their backyard to pick a ripe fruit. She slipped and fell backwards, shattered her neck, and died.

Brooks found her body when he got home. It was nighttime by then, and the science building was deserted, so he brought Marguerite's body to his secret laboratory. He gently put her broken neck in a brace, strapped her body to the operating table, and carefully injected her with Remedy Quack. According to his calculations, it would make its way through her system in exactly 31 minutes—and then she should wake up, alive and breathing, as though she had never died at all.

But after 31 minutes, Marguerite hadn't awakened. Brooks waited an hour, then two, then a whole day, then two days, all without leaving her side. Marguerite remained cold and inert.

Brooks broke down. His beloved wife was gone forever, and Remedy Quack was a failure, just as all the others had been. It was just as well, because even if it had been a success, he wouldn't have been able to get more of the ingredients; it contained, among other things, his last containers of passenger pigeon oviducts, distilled quagga spinal fluid, and essence of Falls-of-the-Ohio scurfpea.

Brooks held himself together long enough to see his wife's casket buried in the cemetery. And then he boarded up his secret laboratory, abandoned his research, and tried to drink himself to death.

Not long after that, Brooks was fired from the university, and his house fell into foreclosure. He went to live with Abigail, his daughter, who welcomed him with open arms.

   CHILLERS

But Brooks kept drinking. One Sunday afternoon, when Abigail was having a lunch party with some friends, Brooks staggered into the dining room, drunk, and accidentally threw up all over the buffet table.

"I'm so sorry," Brooks said. He tried to wipe up the mess with the table runner, but then he realized that everyone was looking at him with a horrible mix of anger and pity. Later that evening, Brooks packed his few belongings into his suitcase. "I can see I'm an embarrassment to you," he remembered saying to Abigail.

"You don't have to go away, Dad," Abigail had said. "You just need to get some help."

But Brooks, not wanting to be a burden, grabbed his suitcase and headed to the front door.

On his way out, he heard Abigail say, "Dad?"

Brooks turned around.

"If you ever change your mind, Dad, I'll always be here," she said.

Brooks nodded, and then he walked away and disappeared from her life.

Brooks had nowhere to go, so he ended up at the Friendly Mission in the Bowery of New Califyorkia, where he ran into his old colleague Frederick Brenner, who, it turned out, was running the mission in his spare time under an assumed name. "Call me Karl Wagner from now on," Brenner said. "I use that false name," he explained, "because I don't want the tramps to visit me at the university." Brenner—Wagner—let Brooks move into the basement.

After a few months of living at the mission, Brooks realized that the mission was a front for a criminal organization, and that Wagner was the leader. Wagner admitted that it was all true. Then Wagner made Brooks his prisoner, but warned Brooks not to tell anyone. "I know you have a daughter," Wagner told Brooks. "And if you disobey me, I'll do … things … to her."

So Brooks did as he was told. As far as everyone at the mission was concerned, Brooks was merely Wagner's unhinged old friend—in Wagner's own dismissive words, Brooks "once was a great doctor, now just a human derelict" that had fallen on hard times, did odd jobs around the mission in exchange for a place to sleep and a jug of wine to crawl into, and preferred to keep to himself. Wagner mostly left Brooks alone—Wagner was usually away robbing jewelry stores and writing psychology books and throwing hapless stool pigeons off of high rooftops—so Brooks spent a lot of time by himself in his basement. His only true friend was a stray black cat that wandered into the mission one day; Wagner grudgingly allowed Brooks to keep it.

Then, one day, a few years later, Wagner brought one of his business partners down into the basement—and shot him to death, right in front of Brooks.

"He became … unnecessary," Wagner explained. He handed Brooks a crowbar and a shovel and told him to pull up the floorboards in the far corner of the basement and bury the body in the dirt beneath.

As Brooks dug the grave, he realized that this was his chance to continue his secret research. He stole some Petri dishes and chemicals from the mission's first aid room. He wished he had his old notebooks, but they were entombed in the laboratory he had left behind so long ago. Brooks carried on with his experiments anyway, hiding his equipment under the floorboards so that Wagner wouldn't find it.

Every so often Wagner would bring another of his associates down to the dank basement, kick Brooks' cat out of the way, murder the unwary associate, and leave it in Brooks' hands to bury the corpse; Brooks had plenty of fresh bodies at his disposal. When Brooks wasn't doing his research, he mostly played with his cat and made lots of coffee in the hope that the smell of arabica beans would cover up the smell of rotting corpses. When it finally became too unbearable, Brooks asked Wagner for some lumber and plaster and tools, and Brooks designed and built a wall with a nifty sliding door to hide that dreaded area of the basement.

Wagner was pleased to learn that Brooks possessed this skill, and he instructed Brooks to build some hidden rooms and secret entrances in and out of the mission, to give the hideout some pizazz. Brooks didn't mind; it gave him something to do. Even secret research into bringing back the dead can't fill all of your time when all you do is hang around a soup kitchen all day.

Brooks soon developed Remedy Rush out of some household chemicals and some mail-order items from a Sears-Roebuck catalog. This time, he was successful—sort of. Unfortunately, Remedy Rush didn't bring the bodies fully back to life; it turned them into vicious zombies who wanted to tear him apart. Brooks made modifications and tried Remedy Sail on Wagner's next victim, but the same thing happened. With each new victim, his new remedies turned them into zombies.

Brooks hid the zombies from Wagner—he knew that if Wagner knew about them, Wagner would want Brooks to build him an army of zombies to take over the world, and Brooks wanted no part of that. Brooks knew, deep down, that he was still a great doctor, and all he wanted was to figure out how to return the zombies back into the living beings that they used to be. He hollowed out a room underneath the basement and disguised a secret entrance as one of the graves, and hid his zombies there so no one could find them. Not even Wagner had known about that room.

Well, until just a few minutes ago, anyway.

And now Crawford was looking at Brooks like Brooks was out of his mind.

"I told you that you wouldn't believe me," Brooks said.

"Let's say I do believe you," Crawford said. "How do we help Miss Malvern's boyfriend?"

"Well, I'd like to visit my old lab at the university, but—" Brooks faltered. There were secrets there that he didn't want the police to discover.

On the other hand, Brooks surmised, if he had access to his old notebooks, he could review his research and figure out where he went wrong. He knew he could bring Richard back to life.

In the end, Brooks decided that he had no choice. Saving a life outweighed the chance that he might get in trouble for what the police would find in his lab.

"But what?" Crawford asked.

"Oh, nothing," Brooks said. "Can we go?"

"All right, Doc," Crawford said. "I'll give you a lift." He turned to Judy. "Miss Malvern, would you like to come along too?"

Judy wasn't an idiot; she knew that this detective was flirting with her. What a joke this guy was, making like he wanted to help Richard, when all he really wanted was to get in her lacy step-ins. It had annoyed her at first, but now that she had gotten a good look at Crawford, she realized that he looked just like Captain Midnight, the dashing crime-fighting pilot in that film serial that she liked to see on Saturday afternoons.

Crawford told his men to look after the mission, then drove Brooks and Judy to the university. Brooks led them to the science building, where they walked through a maze of corridors, until Brooks stopped at a utility closet. Brooks made sure nobody was watching, then he opened the closet door.

Before Brooks went in, he turned to Crawford and Judy. "Detective? Miss Judy? Would you mind staying outside here for a moment, please?"

"Why?" Crawford asked.

"I want to make sure it's safe before anybody else comes in."

Crawford looked at Judy, and then said, "All right, Doc."

Brooks went in and closed the door behind him. Judy and Crawford stood there in uncomfortable silence. She was looking at the floor, but she could feel the detective looking at her like he had a big stack of nickels and knew exactly which slot he wanted to insert them into.

"I admire the work you're doing, Miss Malvern," Crawford said.

"Thank you," Judy said politely.

"Do you think this doctor is telling the truth?"

"Yes," Judy said. "He's an honest man. Of course, I thought Karl Wagner was an honest man, so what do I know?"

"Do you think the doctor will be able to save your boyfriend?" Crawford asked.

"Who, Richard? I wouldn't exactly call him my boyfriend." Judy had decided to flirt with Crawford, because, well, he looked like Captain Midnight, and sometimes Judy was shallower than she liked to admit to herself.

Crawford's eyes brightened. "Oh? He's not your boyfriend?"

"Well, I've been doing some thinking about that," Judy said. The truth was that she was tired of Richard Denning, because he was a misogynistic rich boy, and she couldn't fathom why she had ever been attracted to him in the first place. And, the truth was, a little part of her wouldn't mind going out with this detective who looked like Captain Midnight. Maybe, if he were lucky, she would even invite him up to her apartment, as long as he agreed beforehand to wear a leather flight helmet and some goggles and didn't speak to her.

Crawford smiled. "Say, would you like to have dinner with me sometime?"

"You're very subtle, aren't you?" Judy asked.

"Now that I've been promoted to Detective," Crawford said, "I'm going to buy a little place in the country."

"That sounds lovely," Judy said.

"And work in the garden on my days off."

"That sounds lovely," Judy said.

"And have a dozen kids," Crawford said.

"Well, we just met, let's not rush things."

"How I love kids," Crawford said, with a wistful look in his eyes.

Judy rolled her eyes. She liked kids well enough, but she had plans for her life; she wasn't going to be anybody's baby-dispensing automat. Not even for a detective with a big stack of nickels who looked like Captain Midnight.

The secret door at the back of the closet still worked perfectly. Brooks never thought he would be in his laboratory again. He turned on the light switch and looked around. Everything was just as he had left it 10 years earlier, except more cobwebby. Marguerite's body was still there, strapped to the operating table. Brooks couldn't stand the thought of her being buried or cremated, so he had laid her to rest in his laboratory, and all of their friends and relatives went to the cemetery and paid their respects to a casket full of sandbags. That was why he had told Crawford to wait outside a minute; he didn't want the police asking why there was a dead body in his lab. Before Brooks let the detective in, he needed to hide Marguerite.

Her body was emaciated, yet well preserved, almost like she had been mummified. The air in the lab must have been warm and dry all those years.

Marguerite's neck was still in the brace that Brooks had put on her. No point in keeping it on now. Brooks unbuckled it and slipped it off so that he could gaze at her unencumbered face. He bent over and kissed her dusty forehead.

And then Marguerite's eyes opened.

Brooks shrieked and jumped back, his heart leaped out of his throat. "Marguerite?" he whispered.

Marguerite turned her gaze towards Brooks. Her mouth opened, the skin around the lips cracking as it moved. "Doc?" she asked weakly. Doc Brooks' eyes began to tear up.

Crawford and Judy came rushing into the room.

"We heard a yell!" Crawford said. "What happened?"

Marguerite craned her head slowly in their direction. Brooks could hear the bones and tendons creaking in Marguerite's neck.

Crawford and Judy stood there looking shell-shocked. Marguerite stared at them, then slowly turned her head back to Brooks. In a scratchy whisper, Marguerite asked, "Doc, why did you leave me all alone in here for so long?"

"Have you been awake … all this time?" Brooks asked.

Marguerite closed her eyes. "I lost track of how long it's been," she said.

Brooks felt like he wanted to throw up, and he wasn't even completely drunk this time. His mind was filled with sickening thoughts about what all those years must have been like for Marguerite—scared, all alone in the dark, unable to move. She had been there for 10 years, strapped to the operating table, unable to eat or drink—and yet she was still alive.

At the same time, Brooks was also quite pleased to know that Remedy Quack had apparently worked after all—in fact, even better than he'd thought it would. She had been there strapped to the operating table, unable to eat or drink—and yet she was still alive.

"Why did you leave me here?" Marguerite asked again.

"I'm sorry, my love," Brooks said through tears. "I didn't know. But I'll make it up to you now. We can start again."

Brooks suddenly had the future figured out. Now that he was back with his beloved Marguerite, he felt young again. He decided that he would quit drinking. He would clear his good name with the police, and nurse Marguerite back to health, and then he would go to his daughter's home and ask if she would forgive him for his having been such a deadbeat boozehound. He hoped after all these years that Abigail would still welcome him back into her life—in fact, he knew in his heart that she would, because she was a sweet girl who unconditionally loved all the people in her life. Also, she would probably be surprised and grateful to see her mother back among the living once again. The three of them would be reunited at last. Maybe Abigail was married and had a family of her own now? If that was true, then Brooks would find a place where they could all live together, a nice big house in the country with a wraparound porch, a garden and a Packard sedan in the garage, and live happily ever after.

Brooks unbuckled Marguerite's body. "Let me examine you," he said— surely she must have healed by now? He ran his fingers along her stringy neck. "Does it hurt?" he asked.

Marguerite moved her head around. Everything seemed in working order. "I'm thirsty," she said.

"I'll get you some water," Brooks said. "Do you think you can you sit up?"

Marguerite began to rise. "Slowly, now," Brooks said. He put a hand behind Marguerite's head to steady it. She sat upright, then turned slowly and dangled her legs off the operating table.

Brooks smiled. "That's it, darling! How do you feel?"

Marguerite opened her mouth to speak—but, to Brooks' horror, Marguerite's dehydrated, sunken body suddenly broke apart, all at once, like charcoal that had turned to ash. Her legs crumbled at the knees, her shoulders toppled into themselves, her neck fragmented and collapsed into her torso, and her head fell onto the operating table and broke apart in a cloud of human dust.

Crawford's mouth fell open. Judy screamed.

Brooks tried to scream, but he couldn't seem to make any noise. He saw Marguerite's disembodied, disemheaded face looking up at him with confused eyes, like she was trying to figure out what had just happened. And then her eyes, her beautiful eyes, went lifeless.

Brooks choked back anguished sobs, and kicked himself for being so optimistic about the future. Up yours to the future, Brooks thought; what he really needed was a stiff drink.

And yet, he realized that Remedy Quack had worked even better than he thought possible: it kept people alive forever, or at least until the brain no longer received oxygen. Now Brooks knew that he could truly bring Richard back to life. He searched his workbench and found enough Remedy Quack to fill two vials: one for Richard, and one for a rainy day.

Brooks held up a vial. "Miss Judy, I can save your boyfriend with this. Let's go back to the mission."

The three of them returned to the car, and Detective Crawford sped to the mission. When they got back, Crawford learned that his men had figured out that a shot to the head would kill the zombies. Only one zombie was still alive—fortunately, it was Richard Dennison.

"Hold your fire," Crawford told his men. He tackled Richard and held him down while Brooks injected Remedy Quack into the young man's arm.

Richard immediately went limp.

"How long until he gets better?" Judy asked.

"No telling," Brooks said. "Two days wasn't enough for Marguerite."

After only 45 minutes, though, the color returned to Richard's face. Brooks felt for a pulse—Richard was breathing normally again. Why had Marguerite taken so long to revive? Maybe it was because Marguerite was older than Richard. Maybe Remedy Yoke, which had zombified Richard, had started a chain reaction that Remedy Quack finished. Maybe it was something else Brooks hadn't thought of. Clearly there was much more research he had to do.

Richard opened his eyes and looked around. "What happened?" he asked.

Brooks felt Richard's forehead. "How you do feel, young man?"

"Like I was just reborn," Richard said, smiling.

Oh, great, Judy thought. Now he's going to have a Jesus complex. Goody gumdrops.

CHILLERS

Richard looked at Judy. "Take me home, please, sweetheart," he said.

"Your mother will be happy to see you," Judy said. She took him by the arm, and they went upstairs to hail a taxi.

Brooks put the last vial of Remedy Quack in a drawer. Crawford patted him on the shoulder.

"Well, done, Doc," Crawford said. He looked around at the dead zombies scattered all over the floor. "Can you bring these fellows back to life, too?"

Brooks shook his head.

"Oh, that's a shame," Crawford said. "I'd have liked to see these men brought back to life and given a trial so we could find them guilty and execute them for their crimes. Oh well. I'll send for a clean-up crew."

"Am I free to go, Detective?" Brooks asked.

"You know, Doc, I've been trying to think of something I could arrest you for. But seeing as you're as much a victim in this as anyone else, I guess you're free to go, yeah."

Brooks sighed with relief. Wagner was dead. Mills was dead. The police didn't want him. He was a free man at last. And he still had one thing in his life that was worth living for.

"Can you do something for me, Detective?" Brooks asked. "Can you take me to my daughter? I'm ready to see her again."

Crawford drove Brooks to Abigail's house. Brooks knocked on the front door, but nobody answered.

"Maybe she moved away?" Crawford asked. "It's been years since the last time you were here, hasn't it?"

"She loved this place," Brooks said. "But maybe you're right." His spirits fell. If Abigail had moved, he didn't know how to find her.

They went to a window and peered inside. Brooks saw framed photographs on the walls, photographs of Abigail and a handsome man and an adorable little girl—all smiling, all happy. Brooks smiled along with them. Not only was this still Abigail's house, but Brooks had guessed correctly: Abigail had a family! A husband and a daughter!

Brooks had a granddaughter!

He perked up, and imagined himself bouncing his little granddaughter on his leg like she was riding a galloping horsey, the way he used to do with Abigail when she was little.

"I guess they're not home right now," Crawford said.

"I'll go around and check the back, just in case," Brooks said. When he got there, he noticed that the back door was ajar. Brooks pushed open the door and looked inside—and what he saw chilled him to his core.

Abigail was lying on the kitchen floor in a pool of congealed blood. Brooks could see her face; there was no mistaking her identity. The man and the little girl from the photographs were splayed out next to Abigail, also in pools of blood.

"Detective!" Brooks cried out.

Crawford came rushing around the corner. He saw what Brooks was looking at.

All three of them—Abigail, the man, and the little girl—had been shot in the back of the head, execution-style. Brains were splattered all over the kitchen cabinets. There was no way Brooks could use his last vial of Remedy Quack on any of them. He had invented a miracle potion, but the body—the head, at least—needed to be intact for it to work.

Brooks fell to his knees and sobbed.

Judy was in Richard's bedroom, arranging some flowers in a vase on the dresser. Richard seemed to be fully recovered. He was lying on the bed, casually reading a magazine.

"I've gotta hand it to that doc," Dennison said. "I feel as good as new."

"You look as good as new," Judy had to admit.

"Now, Judy," Richard said, "you've got to go away with me. And, we'll be married."

"Yes, Richard," Judy said, though what she was thinking was: Oh, really? And you decided this unilaterally, you insufferable abercrombie?

"And you can do your social work anywhere but the Bowery," Richard said.

And you can shove your head up your keister, Judy thought. "Yes, Richard," she said sweetly.

"We'll have six kids—three boys, and three girls," Richard said.

"Yes, Richard," Judy said, wondering if science had developed to the point that Richard could go assemble in general congress with himself and give birth to sextuplets.

Richard put his magazine down and smiled at Judy. "Come here," he said. Judy sat on the bed. They held hands. "Can't you do anything besides say, 'Yes, Richard'?" he asked.

You can go jump in a lake made of my isochronal blood, Judy thought. "Yes, Richard," she said coyly.

They kissed. Judy really didn't want to kiss him all that much, but it was no skin off her nose, and she figured it would make a nice parting gift for him, even though he didn't deserve it.

Then Judy pulled away. "You know what else I can say, Richard? I can say that it's over between us, because you said that my job was silly. You said that saving humanity is ridiculous."

"But, Judy, I'm rich! And I'm college-educated! Who are you going to find who's better than me?"

Judy thought about Detective Crawford and the dozen kids that he said he wanted to have. Why did all the men she met want to have enough children to conquer Manchuria with?

And then Judy thought about the Friendly Mission and her social work, and also her electric massage vibrator. All of that would have to do for now, at least until she found a man who was worth getting excited about.

Judy stood up. "Goodbye, Richard," she said on her way out.

Doc Brooks sat in his laboratory in the basement of the Friendly Mission. Before the police clean-up crew had gotten there, Brooks had gathered up the remains of Karl Wagner for safekeeping. The zombies had torn off Wagner's arms and legs, and all that was left of him was a head and torso with ragged stumps where his limbs used to be. Now, at his workbench, Brooks attached Wagner's broken body to tubes and a machine that would circulate blood through his organs. Then he injected Wagner with his last vial of Remedy Quack.

An hour later, Wagner opened his eyes, blinked, and looked around. "What happened? Where am I?" he asked.

Brooks looked into Wagner's eyes. "Did you murder my daughter?"

"Murder?" Wagner said, looking confused.

"Yes, murder," Brooks said. "You know, that thing you like to do."

Brooks' cat jumped on the workbench and rubbed its head on Brooks' arm.

"Hello, my friend," Brooks said to the cat. He scratched its head.

"I can't feel my legs," Wagner said.

"Did you murder my family?" Brooks asked Wagner.

"I can't move," Wagner said, with a touch of frantic hysteria in his voice.

Brooks stuck a pushpin into the tip of Wagner's nose. Wagner screamed.

"Why did you murder my family?" Brooks asked.

"Murder your family?" Wagner scoffed. "I don't remember doing that."

Obviously, Remedy Quack hadn't entirely revived Wagner's brain yet. "Maybe this will help you to remember," Brooks told Wagner. He forced little steel rings into Wagner's eyelids to keep them open, then he sprinkled catnip into Wagner's eyes and watched as his cat licked Wagner's eyeballs with its sandpapery tongue.

"That's a good girl," Brooks said, as he listened to the melodious tones of Wagner's pained squalling. "And I'm still a great doctor," he told Wagner, who seemed too preoccupied to listen to anything that Brooks had to say. Brooks laughed maniacally. He might have lost everything—his wife, his daughter, his career, the son-in-law and granddaughter that he never knew—but at least he still had his basement. And his cat.

The End

About the Author:
Todd Shiba lives in Northern Virginia with a simulation-modeling aeri-alist, a giant metal chicken, the friendly spirits of two housecats, and every edition of *Bowery at Midnight* that's been released on home video.

CHILLERS

Dracula Never Dies
A Dedication to Bela Lugosi
by Christopher R. Gauthier

{Author's Note: Being an avid fan of Bela Lugosi, I've done my best to honor his memory throughout my years. I have been part of many classic horror-themed groups and clubs, but I felt in my heart I could do more … not because these groups aren't worthy, but because I felt a passion to honor my hero in my own way. So, I took it upon myself to start the Facebook group *A Celebration of the Life and Art of Bela Lugosi*. In its short existence, my group has garnered over 4000 members, making it one of the largest sites dedicated to the immortal king of horror cinema, Bela Lugosi.

Furthermore, what you are about to read shows my love and dedication to Bela. This short story is but a small part of my novel that will be published in the distant future. It's entitled *Dracula Never Dies: The Revenge of Bela Vorlock*. The novel takes place in Mr. Lugosi's latter days, and captures the powerful emotions of exhilaration, sadness and everything in between.

I do hope you will like this excerpt and find it a fitting dedication to the legacy of our immortal Bela Lugosi.

I wish to thank those (including classic film scholar Gary D. Rhodes) who have inspired me and taken the time to listen to my novel and give me feedback, and of course Bela Lugosi for the inspiration and love, the father to all the lost children of the night. Brad A. Braddock as well, for being a dear friend, and without him, this would not be possible.

But most importantly I wish to thank my dear mother, who has always encouraged me and listened to my poems and stories. Without her inspiration, I would not have the artistic mind that I have today. CRG}

Bela Vorlock grabbed his flask of Hungarian plum brandy that rested alongside his sterling silver cigarette case. A short sketch of lines he'd been told to review for this evening's theatrical performance rested on the dresser before him. He now acted in slum-encrusted theaters, something he certainly was not accustomed to while a young man on the Budapest stage. Why, he had played Romeo on stage, and the women loved him … he was a far cry from his handsome youth in the now waning days of 1956.

The brandy soothed his tingling throat as it swam down his parched canal, almost bringing him back to peace, the deception that only alcohol could give.

He gazed deep into the mirror before him, which brought him back to his reality, and he sipped his brandy again to calm his jagged nerves.

He searched for peace … the one true human emotion that he needed the most. His soul, now a lost and mangled dream, strived to crush his torment. It was just a slice of peace in the last mournful days of his life.

Even still, despite all the saddened rage and vengeful malice flowing through his veins as a raging torrent of fire, he acknowledged the fact that he was still a brilliant actor, a loyal artist of the macabre film and stage. The monsters of the '30s and '40s were somewhat now forgotten, and Bela Vorlock was prisoner in the present age that catered to box-office crazed science fiction. Large bugs, moon-men and creatures from the black lagoon were now Hollywood cinema. Even though Bela did his best to keep his dignity and pride as an actor and profound man of his vast abilities.

Bela Vorlock pressed his hand across the satin darkness of his hair. He formed a perfect V, the widows peak on his forehead, and a gargoyle's smile projected, and squinted eyes formed in the mirror before him. He still embodied all the Hungarian aristocratic charm that had left him immortal in the minds of his fans and on the 1931 silver screen. His distinct and piercing blue eyes of a Gypsy's blazing bonfire still evoked and revealed to the world their unearthly and ageless hypnotic power that beheld a mystical allure to the thousands of women who had fallen under his spell.

His eyes were almost supernatural, unearthly as a breathtaking Transylvanian forest. His mystique, his Siamese cat-like facial features embellished his eerily handsome structure of Gothic beauty. Bela rubbed his cleft chin and grinned as he was almost ready for tonight's performance.

"I am, Dracula," he projected, as he slowly stood and stared wildly into the mirror before him. His blood red lips creased into a stormy grin. Bela Vorlock was still tall and gallant, even in his elder years.

He was ready to shine that evening as the vampire garbed in his infamous Count Dracula cape. Its velvet darkness was as smooth as a bat. He wrapped it around him as a sheltered blanket of death, before popping the collar. He stood a little taller when he wore that cape, coming alive in the vibrant crimson, like that of the sanctified blood he had drawn from the throats of so many of his unsuspecting victims on the silver screen. His suit and tails, trimmed for a king in the divine elegance of onyx and ivory, only beautified his crest medallion, engraved with the unholy pendant effigy of the vampire bat that dangled from a silk sash below his bowtie. Now dressed, he lingered in the musty shadows of his shoddy dressing room, waiting to stage the inevitable performance he not only loved, but loathed.

A tranquil but stormy wind gusted through the shattered glass window of his dressing room, calming Bela with its cool breeze. Then came a stronger gust, and the ill-scripted ramblings for the evening's midnight performance be-

 CHILLERS

came scattered, and some of the papers went soaring into the trashcan, while others covered the floor. Bela thought to pick up the script but stopped himself. He had done this stage act many a time before and, although he was particular to the memorization of his each and every line, tonight he would ad-lib if he must. He took his flask and once more the plum brandy eased down his throat. It was then he readied to commit the remains of his time to this evening's public hell.

Upon entering the movie theater, the riotous howls of teenage laughter ushered in the live entertainment. Youthful sweethearts, clenching hands and necking in the dusk of the theater would never come to appreciate the innovative horror that Bela had evoked in each of his astounding performances.

The crowds of people sweltering through the cinema were no more than kids, who just wanted to have fun and stay out late. Teenage fools who were there solely for the privacy of the darkness and not for the crowned-king of horror, Bela Vorlock. But rather to exorcize their throbbing teenage hormones in the luxury of seclusion, far away from their overly protective parents, something that Bela Vorlock had never known as a teen.

Bela Vorlock would have a distinguished entrance that night, once he emerged from the threshold backstage. He was always on time for whatever theatrical contract he had been provided. The rustling curtains that hid the movie screen also hid Bela as he lingered backstage, out of sight from the crude eyes of the public. The curtain served as a divide from his hell, as well as his earthly purgatory, and was the only shield left to protect him from his ceaseless nightmare. Too soon, the curtain would open, and he would be thrown before the soul-killing, feeble-minded tyrants of his life that felt more like death.

The teens were like a monstrous breed that only reciprocated to tasteless dialogue and phony cheap gimmicks. They would poke fun at his once thought brilliant character, the role of the greatest vampire king, Count Dracula.

Bela was truly doomed at this time, in the atomic age of science fiction fascination that had invaded the nation like some bodysnatching alien creature from another world. Its growing popularity had foreshadowed Bela Vorlock as a typecast horror icon. In turn, his style of mythological and supernatural horror films was no longer requested in public demand. He had been reduced to these small, frivolous public appearances.

This evening was a rarity for Bela, during this decade when classic horror had been widely discarded by the entertainment public. For that night they were showing Bela Vorlock's timeless classic *Dracula* with his earnest hope that it would perhaps resurrect interest in the eyes of its young beholders.

Bela looked to his right; there lurked from the shadows the sluggish and drunken fellow who would wear the ridiculously fake-looking ape costume that night. He came to him in a staggering midnight waltz with a bottle of whiskey clamped tightly in his hands.

Bela welcomed his colleague. "Good evening, my friend."

The stormy laughter that had bellowed from the teenagers had finally silenced when the lights of the cinema slowly dimmed. The curtains lifted to reveal the sight it had secretly hidden, an enormous movie screen, towering seventeen feet high, that left the youthful public in attentive bondage and this visionary sight chilled Bela to silence.

It had been many years since he had last seen one of his very own movies projected on such a glorious screen. Bela was then eager to observe the critical reactions that would come from the youth of 1956. Bela Vorlock, Hollywood's darkest theatrical count, wondered if they would understand the morbid poetry of his weird symphony. One he had mastered on stage and film, his poetic masterpiece of horror crafted while under the intoxication of his vampirical obsession with the dark world.

Would they acknowledge his brilliance and grasp his cinematic craft, or would they be very much like the rest of the teenage world that felt *Dracula* was nothing more than a leftover relic of the past?

Bela's eyes were two blue burning crystal embers and his sleek cryptic fingers caressed the velvet flesh of his monarch burial cape, anticipation rising. A curious smile of a Mephistophelian nature grew upon the shadows of his 74-year-old face as he turned to his now drunken ape companion.

The ape wished him a benevolent token of good fortune for the unfolding act of the evening. "Good luck, Bela." Those were the muffled words that came from the man behind the ape mask.

Bela could smell the whiskey on his breath, even behind the false face.

"Here, have a drink." The ape reached out to hand Bela the bottle of whiskey.

This would fulfill his needs and Bela did not refuse. The bootlegged American whiskey was not his favorite, but the alcohol itself would serve its duty and permit him to mask an inner rage that often crept back into his soul.

As Bela shared the whiskey with his ape companion, his fellow actor studied the count of the audience as he lifted up his mask.

He peeked out of the curtain from the side of the stage. He studied the mob of teens they had been paid to entertain before he said to Bela, "I've never seen you nervous, Bela. You have enthralled millions with your Count Dracula act. But tonight, I think you are consumed with stage fright!"

Bela Vorlock returned the whiskey with a glowering glance inscribed on his face, full of his eerily intriguing honesty. "Yes, I have enthralled millions in my days of magnificence long ago. And I am not in the least apprehensive in regards to this reprehensible theatrical evening. Although, given the circumstances of my current career placement and life … a life which has become some kind of endless hellish nightmare, I will enact revenge upon anyone who impedes my path with mayhem and murder!"

Bela's companion took another swig from his bottle as he stared at Bela oddly. He said no more.

A microphone was placed center stage, and a plump lobby man stood before it. He looked out at the audience with his sweaty hands behind his back, while grinning at the teens. The audience momentarily disciplined themselves to silence as he began to speak, causing an echo.

"Boils and ghouls, prepare to hold one another extra close tonight." The lobby man rolled his eyes before he continued, "Tonight we have in our company a 500-year-old vampire with us, a real bloodsucker of the night! One which refuses to die, despite being sick and lame, so please give a nice round of applause for the skeletal remains of what was once an actor, Bela Vorlock!"

Bela Vorlock could diagnose immediately the sarcastic tone of the lobby man, without the slightest doubt. The man had set Bela up as a spectacle to be scoffed at. They would laugh at him in unbalanced hysteria. They would laugh at his image and the theatrical objectives he had always maintained, keeping his character nobile.

Then, like a swooping midnight vampire bat, the graceful Bela Vorlock swayed his cape as he dashed from the shadows behind him and into his present public world.

The campy, recycled organ music played before Bela said, "Greetings, I am Dracula."

He continued with his dialog as the eerie music blasted from the speakers. The teens quickly lost interest in Bela's drowned out words, and they began to grow anxious in their seats.

"500-year-old vampire, my ass." One of the kids shouted.

Bela ignored it, before he continued, "You have all dared to venture out at the stroke of midnight and into the unknown darkness that cloaks this theater. You are brave, are you not? Yes, you are all brave. I must advise you though, as a warning, that tonight, your little eyes shall bare witness to the horrors that will plague you in sleeping dreams for many, many moons to come!"

The teen's laughter grew louder as they refused to come to a much-wanted halt. They were so loud that Bela's voice could no longer be heard above it.

An audaciously sinister idea began to linger in his distraught mind. The former legend of Hollywood horror wasted no time. He selectively singled out a beautiful young woman from the howling crowd. She remained inaudible and seated quaintly beside her obnoxious boyfriend, who was loving the chaos.

"You there!" Bela pointed at her. With his voice monotone, he said, "Come here."

The lobby man looked confused. At a distance, he skimmed through the pages of written text. Nowhere in the script could he find this scene. The beautiful young girl gazed deep into Bela's eyes, bedazzled by Bela Vorlock. She blushed before giving him a smile he had not seen the likes of in many years.

The deviously cunning Bela Vorlock raised his slender right hand and formed it into a beckoning talon claw. His pantomimed gesture moved rhythmically up and down. He pretended to hypnotize the young woman as he had done to his unwary victims on the motion picture screen. His sharp, white incisor teeth were drawn with hunger and an air of Satanism as he welcomed the shy young woman into the deep creeping darkness of his infamous cape.

Weary and hesitant, she obeyed his silent command and came into the lecherous fold of his opening arms. The insipid theatrical monologue and its gawking teenage patrons no longer concerned Bela Vorlock. He could care little for the humiliating embarrassment of being seen with a derelict man dressed as an ape that stood on stage beside him.

No, now the delicious vision of the young girl's panting, pulsating throat wisped his tormented brain with many dark thoughts of murder, death and the fresh scent of blood, which had been his unspeakable fantasy since his first discovery of the lucid vampire lurking in the depths of his soul. Bela longed to taste it, that precious fluid unlike any other found amid the boundless soils of the earth!

He hungered to become the fantastic character he had created on the glorious movie screen of a long bygone 1931, to become the lord vampire, the immortal, indestructible monarch of the undead world. How he wanted more than ever to replenish the hollow void within him and satisfy his howling for sinister nourishment. For that he would resume some means of revitalized redemption and peace through unleashing upon the world the savage beast that had always before been discreetly concealed within the ominous shadows of his forsaken soul. To leave behind this wretched existence of the daylight living world and thrive to become forever vengefully powerful with the exquisite beauty of blood to purify his lips, tongue, and soul. He would at last inflict a gruesome justification on the society that had long made him that vile creature of the night.

He stared at the crowd with a hypnotic gaze, demonically persuasive while submerged under the bright spotlights. His soul was inflamed with the powerful fury of hell for his degenerate blood lust to devour his living sacrificial victim. As she leaned toward him with her gentle figure interlaced in the velvet sea of his black cape, his sleek fingers swathed around her tender throat, and she could immediately tell that this embrace was no laughing matter.

In his grasping choke she could feel his sweltering hot breath tingling on her throat. She could hear the ghastly reptilian hissing sounds and the dark whisperings into her ear, the very seductive sounds of a foreign evil, in which he intended to seal her doom! The spectators were now in silent terror, they now noticed Bela's realistic lust for human blood upon his ageless face.

She suddenly became drunk with a convulsive fear she had never know or had ever dreamed of before in her short time on earth. She truly felt under the control of a living corpse, a maniacal creature who truly believed he was one of the nocturnal manifestations of the undead. Like the monsters of the night were depicted in the folklore of ancient ghost stories, and the legends exhumed from the dust of a hundred thousand years.

Before Bela Vorlock could live out his fantasy to its weird and awe-filled satisfaction, with his tapering white fangs nearly puncturing the young virgin's tender flesh, his eyes tumbled from the colossal pinnacle of his very own morbid pleasure to perceive the pompous lobby man beholding a disgustful gaze. It was an expression he had seen many times throughout his lifetime as a fallen Hollywood star, and one of the many things he yearned for the pits of hell to be without.

The lobby man shouted, "What the hell are you doing, you nut!"

The young woman couldn't maintain her silent terror any longer, as she cried out in true horror, looking up at the diabolical vampire tyrant. It was a fearsome symphony of haunted and fear-ridden screams. Reality and Bela Vorlock's extreme abhorrence for it had returned, as did the intolerable guttering echoes of the mimicking laughter of the teens.

Bela's eyes blinked rapidly, as if he was coming out of a trance. "My child," Bela spoke to the sobbing girl, while placing his hand gently on her naked shoulder. "I was merely under the conception that you were more than willing to perform alongside me in this evening's theatrical presentation. My dear little flower, I hope that you are not afraid of me. I speak to you in an honorable manner, my intentions were not ill."

Turning on his charismatic charm, Bela answered swiftly with cunning wisdom in the sly masquerade of what could have been considered a crime. Her angered boyfriend stormed the stage before punching Bela in the face. Bela stood silently before the boy, staring deep into his soul, before a rain of blood trickled from his nose. The young man took hold of his teenage lover and posed with a macho demeanor.

The audience once laughed at the tarnished actor, but now they hated him. In the midst of the chaos they began hurling their popcorn containers on stage, hitting Bela and his regal cloak. Beverages followed before Bela hissed like a serpent and twirled his magnificent cape to cover himself as he crouched upon one knee. He protected himself behind the dark armored sanctity of his black and red operatic cape, which became drenched with pools of bubbling foaming cola and the foul stench of popcorn.

"Damn you all!" he shouted before continuing, "In the names of heaven and hell!" he howled like a werewolf under an autumn full moon before continuing, "You have all disgraced me with your cruel actions!"

The teens calmed after Bela screamed, and refrained from furthering to badger the inflamed Hollywood Dracula. They took a few moments to think about his bloodthirsty, werewolf cry.

Bela continued, "May you all endure the wraths of forsaken devils and avenging gods!" He asked, "Is this to be my infernal damnation, to be scoffed at and belittled in the waning days of my life?"

It was then he had to face that he was not the immortal Count Dracula, but in truth he was nothing more than a mortal man. This reality was to him at times his blessing but ultimately his curse. As he dashed away from the small screening stage and its jeering audience, now behind him, he seized his alcohol backstage and guzzled a large quantity of its liquid gold, temporarily evading his living nightmare of full soul-crushing scorn.

A deep moaning growl came from the bowels deep within him. He swallowed the whiskey to calm the flames smoldering among his troubled seas.

"What came over you out there, if I may be so bold as to ask, Bela?" The man wearing the ape costume asked. He had removed his mask and was holding it under his arm.

Bela Vorlock returned his answer while drying his blood-leaking nose with his silk handkerchief. "I am Count Dracula and this vile world will never comprehend the dark answer to that question, Sir. I have expressed throughout the years that I am what Hollywood has made me, and this is no secret to taint me with their madness and sin. I have transformed into my most infamous creation in all of cinema and theater. I am a cadaverous body beneath the haunted moonlight, the undead Count Dracula. It is so complex that this world before us will never entirely come to grasp … that Dracula Never Dies!"

About the Author:

Christopher R. Gauthier has been writing since he was a young child. He lives in Montreal, Quebec, Canada, and will "write until the day I die."

Colin Clive as Henry Frankenstein and Valerie Hobson as Elizabeth from *Bride of Frankenstein*

The Puppets of Frankenstein
by Kurt McCoy

{Author's Note: Shortly after the end of *Bride of Frankenstein*, Henry and Elizabeth hide with a traveling carnival, posing as puppeteers.

This work uses concepts and characters from the unused *Return of Frankenstein* story treatment submitted by L. G. Blockman.

A couple of scenes and paragraphs are lifted almost entirely from that work, mostly the descriptions of the street carnival and the introductions of characters who would figure prominently in the movie treatment, and in the longer work for which this is an introductory piece, though I put them to entirely different uses than Mr. Blockman did.}

The traveling carnival rolled into Goldstadt two days ago, and today, just like the day before, the biggest attraction was the marvelous "Heinrich Puppets." Puppeteers Victor Heinrich and his wife Elsa worked out of the wagon that was their theater, their workshop, and their living quarters. A panel on the side folded out on struts to reveal the puppet stage. Children, and more than a few adults, crowded close to watch the amazingly life-like puppets go through their paces.

The story was fairly trivial, even cliché. There was a Queen who resisted the advances of her overly amorous King, while a beleaguered-looking Archbishop raced about flailing his arms and blowing a whistle trying to prevent the royal couple from consummating their union right there on the stage, in front of a crowd of impressionable children. The Devil stood off to one side, occasionally offering advice to the King and making droll observations.

Between acts a beautiful little Ballerina appeared and danced to Mendelssohn's *Spring Song*.

The story was inconsequential. What people crowded in to see were the puppets themselves. Exquisitely crafted, their features were so fine and detailed, their motions so unnervingly natural that onlookers would swear that they were actually alive, if it weren't for the visible wires attached to them and the occasional jerks and hops as they performed. That the Heinrichs did all the voices themselves was painfully obvious, but the crowd was willing to forgive their sometimes comically amateurish attempts at vocal characterizations, just to watch the puppets. Whoever created the puppets had been gifted with rare and wonderful genius.

Carnival workers plied the crowd with wicker baskets in hand, collecting donations from the crowd. The puppet show was taking in almost as much money as the whole rest of the carnival combined.

Eventually the King finally grabbed his Queen while the Archbishop buried his face in his hands and the Devil applauded. Curtains fell as the royal couple kissed. A side curtain opened with the Ballerina spinning through her dance for a couple of minutes, then that curtain closed, and the main curtains opened again. Now, though, the stage was filled with a glass tank full of real water. Inside, a perfectly formed little mermaid sat on the rocks waving at the crowd. Lights came on behind the glass tank and the slightly distorted faces of Victor and Elsa Heinrich appeared behind it. They beamed at the wildly applauding crowd and took their bows by nodding their heads. Elsa Heinrich waved a hand holding the marionette control rod, which made the Mermaid lift her arms and sway from side to side.

Then the light went out and the curtains closed for good on that day's performances.

The crowd roared their approval and the fare collectors were pelted by a veritable rain of coins. Eventually the crowd wandered off to check out the other attractions the carnival had to offer, lured by the smell of roasted nuts, fresh pretzels, and popcorn. The busy fare collectors dropped to their hands and knees to scour the ground for stray coins.

Henry Frankenstein and his wife Elizabeth laughed and hugged each other after the show, in the privacy of their caravan. The couple had been forced to go undercover, temporarily, to avoid the anger of the villagers from their hometown. Though the Baron and his wife had been as much the victims of Dr. Pretorius' mad vision and the Monster's cruel demands as anyone, the angry mob was not inclined to see it that way. It was Henry's idea to procure the jars with Dr. Pretorius' homunculi and go undercover as "puppeteers." The money their shows brought in bought the silence and complicity of Rudolph, the carnival's owner. The renegade couple stayed to themselves as much as possible and avoided the other carnival workers when they could, but they had made a few friends among the performers.

Working quickly with practiced hands, the couple untied and removed the wires that gave the illusion that they were controlling the homunculi on stage. However, Pretorius had created them; he'd made the miniature beings amazingly compliant. Their black little eyes gave little indication of intelligence or will. Left to their own devices, the homunculi would perform their own little charades endlessly, tirelessly. They only required being walked through the puppet show routines a couple of times, guided by wires and prods, before mastering the movements perfectly. They performed six shows a day flawlessly, unvaryingly, and they likely could have done it many more times if not for the limitations of the couple's vocal cords.

"He's torn her dress again!" Henry said, removing the wires from the little Queen's arms and legs.

Elizabeth sighed.

She was busy trying to fish the mermaid out of the large aquarium used for the show, to transfer her to the glass canister that was usually her home. Tonight, the little creature was being uncharacteristically willful and was not inclined to leave her more spacious surroundings. Elizabeth chased her around the tank with a long-handled aquarium net, but she kept evading capture, darting at remarkable speeds. The tiny being had a wickedly gleeful look on her little face and actually stuck her tongue out at Elizabeth on three occasions.

"Greta sewed up a replacement gown. It's on the shelf next to the spare curtains."

Henry nodded and plucked the tiny garment from the shelf. Gently, he scooped up the Queen, who went limp in his hands, eyes open staring blankly at the ceiling. With the nimble fingers of a trained surgeon, Henry deftly removed the torn dress, which was hanging off one bare shoulder.

Once again, he marveled at how exquisitely the little Queen's body was formed, perfect in every detail, the body of a beautiful woman rendered in a tiny simulacrum of flesh. Absentmindedly he ran a finger along her bare flank. The flesh was smooth and cool to the touch, its skin soft as a baby's.

"Do you need help with that?" Elizabeth asked, with a trace of bite in her voice.

Henry blushed and smiled sheepishly.

"Of course not."

He plucked up the new dress and pulled it over the Queen's head, gently lifting her limp arms to fit through the sleeves. The tiny body lying supine in his palm as he worked the dress down and over her hips. Tiny blank eyes still stared listlessly at the ceiling, but the Queen's lips were slightly parted. Her tiny heart fluttered like a bird beneath his thumb on her chest.

"All done!" he said with a boyish grin.

Elizabeth was staring at him with worried eyes.

The Mermaid, captured at last and hanging in the aquarium net, lolled about limply, all the fight and fierceness drained from her. She barely moved as Elizabeth dropped her into her water-filled canister. She floated like a drowning victim, arms slightly raised, hair spreading like a blonde stain through the water. The stare she gave Elizabeth was unblinking and utterly without emotion, but still somehow managed to seem like a glare.

"Sometimes, these things make my skin crawl." She said. "I'm not sure that being around them isn't tainting us with whatever unnatural Black Magic Pretorius used to create them."

"Alchemy, my dear."

"Hmmm?"

"Pretorius created them through Alchemy, not Black Magic."

Henry said the words with conviction, but his tone suggested that he harbored doubts about their origins as well.

"Still," he said with a smile. "They are keeping us fed and safe, so we owe them some measure of respect, even affection."

Elizabeth raised her eyebrow at the word "affection" but chose not to say anything out loud.

Outside, at the far end of the carnival, a barker shouted about the wonders contained within the main show tent. Gaudy banners writhed and snapped in the wind, advertising the presence of "Fifi the Giantess," "Heta and Greta, the Siamese Twins," and the prestidigitations of "Arnaldo the Magnificent." A stranger in a long black coat with the collar turned up to muffle his face and an expensive hat pulled down almost over his eyes slipped quietly through the crowd, patiently working his way to the barker's side. Once he reached his goal, the stranger stood silently, waiting for a lull in the press of passing patrons.

"Is Henry Frankenstein with you?"

The stranger's voice was an urgent whisper.

The barker stared at the stranger in shock, before shaking his head.

"Don't know nobody by that name." The barker said in a hoarse whisper.

The stranger stared at him for several uncomfortable seconds before turning away with a shrug.

The man stalked through the streets, his rigid posture and imperious bearing in stark contrast to the rough and tumble peasants thronging through the street fair around him. He ignored the food stands where others crowded in thick clusters. In the background a steam calliope wheezed through a barely recognizable rendition of *The Blue Danube Waltz*. Nearby a Trigane violinist fiddled soulfully, if discordantly, and a horse-faced spieler harangued the murmuring crowds about the extraordinary pliancy of "Egyptian" dancers. The stranger paused to whisper with Emma the Lion Tamer, who paced restlessly in front of cages in which lions sprawled languidly, already bored with the stares of passersby. The course-faced woman with close-cropped sandy hair laughed harshly and swiped playfully at him with her wound-up whip. The man frowned but continued on his way.

Next the stranger grabbed a young blonde woman in pink silk tights by the shoulders, questioning her insistently. The young woman, Sari by name, was on her way to be sawn in half by the magician Arnaldo and had no time for his questions.

Hans, the small bespectacled calliope player, who looked absolutely tiny at the keyboard of his huge steam piano, was more than happy to talk while he played, but the stranger could barely make out his words over the wheezing and skirling of the machine. In frustration, he turned abruptly and walked away. Hans kept talking for several minutes, unaware that his listener had left.

The stranger paused in front of a garish, flare-lighted banner announcing the Heinrich Marionettes. Crude puppet characters painted on canvas seemed to almost dance as the wind rippled the banner. He stood there, a dark shape framed by sputtering white glare for several minutes before coming to some sort of decision.

Checking to see that he was unobserved, the stranger slipped between carnival caravans parked along the square until he reached the one with Heinrich's Marionettes painted along the sides. He knocked on the door, calling, "Henry! Henry Frankenstein!"

Inside Henry and Elizabeth were hooking the threads of their marionette wands to tiny cleats in the top of the puppet stage. They looked at each other, eyes wide in alarm. The stranger continued to knock and call Henry's name.

Henry Frankenstein cleared his throat nervously, then answered using one of the voices he affected for the show.

"There's no one here by that name!" He said, without opening the door. "Have the decency to let us get some rest, whoever you are."

The stranger on the other side laughed.

"It's Victor, Henry. Victor Moritz! Isn't that the same voice you used to use when mocking that pompous windbag, Professor Gorman? C'mon, Henry, open the door!"

Elizabeth let out a sigh of relief and covered her mouth to suppress giggles.

Slowly, Henry cracked the door open and peeked out.

Victor was standing there, eyebrow raised, hat held aloft in one hand.

"I've come to talk to you about appropriating my name, 'Victor Heinrich!'"

Henry laughed, despite himself. He threw open the door.

"Come in, Victor. But for God's sake hurry and be quiet!"

Moritz stepped into the caravan cabin, clasping first Henry then Elizabeth in heart-felt embraces.

"Victor, however did you find us?"

"You don't think I'd let my dearest friend disappear without making every effort to find him?" Victor replied.

He spoke to Henry, but his eyes were on Elizabeth.

She blushed but gave him a grateful smile.

"I hope you don't think," said Henry with a prickling of wounded pride, "that my flight was from cowardice. I'm not the sort of man to let a pack of villagers drive me from my home."

"I understand." Victor said hastily. "It was on account of Elizabeth. You did it to keep her safe. It's the smartest and noblest thing you've ever done, Henry, and I respect you for that, I truly do."

Henry sighed, then sat on the bed wearily.

"She'd already been through so much, on my account. I couldn't see her suffer any more for my obsessions."

He then explained about his old professor, Septimus Pretorius and how the eccentric fellow had first proposed that they construct a mate for The Monster. Then how The Monster showed up, *speaking*, and demanded that he cooperate, or face losing his own mate. How Elizabeth had been kidnapped and hidden from him in a dank cave, bound and helpless, and he had been forced to return once more to the art of sewing corpses together and calling the Spark of Life out of angry clouds.

People died, and horrible unnatural evils were spawned. The watchtower with the secret laboratory blew to bits in a horrific explosion, killing all inside, while he and Elizabeth barely escaped with their lives.

Henry and Elizabeth watched the mob of villagers boiling through the trees toward the Frankenstein manor, torches in hand, an angry, seething flood of hatred raised against the couple, who had themselves been victims of madmen and monsters. They'd had no alternative but to escape out the back, down a brush-clogged gully and flee into the night.

In the days that followed, the couple retrieved Pretorius' living dolls and set themselves up as puppeteers, though neither of them knew a thing about actually staging marionette shows.

"My God, Henry! I had no idea."

Victor stared in fascination at the "marionettes," which were once again ensconced in their glass storage jars. The tiny beings stared back at him with their unblinking, expressionless eyes.

Henry pulled a bottle out of a hamper and uncorked it.

Elizabeth caught the cue and searched around until she found three clean glasses.

"Frankenstein 1885." Said Henry. "I managed to salvage two bottles when we left home. I've been saving them for a special occasion, like this."

The three friends drank long into the night, while the sounds of the carnival around them slowly died down, then fell silent.

Later that night, Elizabeth woke in the dark, her eyes wide in the moonlight, a thick blanket wrapped around her naked shoulders. Henry lies face down beside her, his bareback exposed by the blanket Elizabeth had wound about her in her sleep.

Victor long ago said his good nights and retired to the rooms he'd rented at Goldstadt's finest hotel. The couple declined his suggestion of relocating to similar lodgings in favor of their cozy caravan quarters.

With Victor gone, Henry had been in quite high spirits and more passionate than usual. Elizabeth smiled and ran playful fingers through his dark hair.

An odd prickling sensation rippled across her skin. Suddenly she was quite sure that she was being watched. Nervously she glanced around the moonlit cabin. She spotted the little King homunculus, who had somehow worked its way out of its covered glass canister and was standing on the edge of the shelf staring fixedly at her. The King slowly rubbed his fat belly, his round, bearded face devoid of any expression.

     CHILLERS

A cold chill rushed down her back and pooled in her belly. She pulled the blanket tighter around her, suddenly feeling painfully, vulnerably naked. The rotund homunculus quaked mirthfully and made odd squeaky little sounds that might have been chuckles.

Frantically, Elizabeth looked around the cabin, hunting for anything that could be used to swat the miniature lecher. By chance she caught sight of a roughly whiskered dirty face peering in through the caravan window. Bleary, drunken eyes were fixed upon her. A coarse tongue licked cracked lips.

Horrible memories from her first, abortive wedding night came flooding back to her.

Elizabeth shrieked.

Henry Frankenstein woke to the sound of his wife screaming and bounded out of bed, naked with clenched fists before he was even aware of his surroundings. A bestial mad snarl erupted on his lips, his eyes glittered dangerously.

"What's wrong? What is it? Has it come back?" He shouted.

A calming white hand touched him gingerly on the shoulder.

"There was a face, at the window. One of the carnival workers, I think." Elizabeth tried to sound calm, even though her heart was racing, and terror was still prickling across her skin, pinching at her exposed chest.

"Carnival worker?" Henry asked, blinking. "Which one? I'll teach that peasant swine a thing or two!"

Elizabeth shook her head, but Henry insisted on pulling on a robe and stalking about outside the caravan to ensure that no one was there. Elizabeth looked back to the shelf where she'd spotted the King watching her, but there was no sign of the homunculus. The shelf was bare, the canisters were all lined up in a row with their black satin covers in place. For just a second, Elizabeth thought she heard squeaky whispering among the canisters and maybe a satin cover rippled in an unseen breeze. But she might have imagined it. Her nerves were still jangling like struck cymbals and the memory of a horrible, leering gray face, an inhuman face, leaning in toward hers was burnt across the inside of her eyes.

She felt cold, dead hands gripping her shoulders. She was helpless, utterly helpless, pinned beneath a heavy dark shape. The grip on her shoulder ached in her skin, a tactile echo of a trauma months gone by. She couldn't shake the feeling of being completely helpless, of having no control, the violation of her will almost as bad as the ravishing of her flesh. The cabin spun lazily to one side and shadows were closing in around her.

Then Victor was back, holding her, whispering comforting words in her ear. She melted into his embrace.

No!

Not Victor. Henry. Henry was her husband. Victor wasn't here. She'd chosen Henry.

She buried herself in that embrace and lied to herself that it was the one she wanted.

The next day Elizabeth was left alone in the caravan while Henry and Victor went to settle some business about salvaging Henry's estate, while they remained in hiding. She busied herself tidying up the cabin and tending to the spare costumes for their "puppets." Her fingers weren't as nimble and her stitches not as tiny and precise as Greta's, the carnival worker who crafted the miniature costumes, but she sewed well enough to manage repairs and the work relaxed her.

While she worked, sewing up split seams and embroidering designs, she took the glass jars containing the homunculi and sat them on the workbench next to the window. She removed their black satin covers so the little creatures could get some sunshine and fresh air.

Henry told her to leave them covered, in darkness, as much as possible to keep them dormant and manageable. But Elizabeth thought it cruel to deny the little ones what semblance of a life they could enjoy. So much of their own safety depended on the performances of the "puppets," Elizabeth felt that they owed the creatures the occasional free time in the sun.

The little Ballerina twirled and danced tirelessly, performing to the music from a music box that Elizabeth sat near her canister. The Mermaid came to the front of her jar to bask in the sunlight. She endlessly brushed her platinum blonde hair and swam upside down, so she could stare at the clouds with her unreadable glittering eyes. The little Queen and the King fanned themselves, squawking and squeaking at each other through the glass walls of their canisters. The King alternated between impassioned oratory and banging on the glass in frustration. The Queen smiled serenely and feigned indifference.

Elizabeth laughed at their antics, amused by the imitation of amour Pretorius had succeeded in creating.

The Archbishop and the Devil engaged in what Elizabeth had to assume was an impassioned debate on matters theological.

The only one of the homunculi that Elizabeth left on the shelf, in the darkness under its cover, was the Baby. She hated to admit it, but the only one of the little creatures that truly disturbed her was the Baby. Half the size of the others, the Baby was perched upon a miniature high chair. Its little arms and legs could barely support it. The Baby was dressed in swaddling and a bonnet, but the face that stared out from under the frills was disturbingly adult in appearance. Sometimes the Baby would laugh and play with its tiny rattles, but more often it just squalled incessantly, crying itself red-faced while watching her with beady, passionless eyes.

The Baby gave her the creeps. Elizabeth was happy to leave it covered and silent, and out of sight. It was the only one of the homunculi that she and

Henry were in unspoken agreement that they were never to use in any of their shows.

Elizabeth was so focused on her sewing and amused by the little creatures that she did not hear the cabin door creep open. First a dirty hand reached inside, easing the door wider, slowly, silently. Then a rough featured, stubble covered face peered inside. The carnival worker's eyes were not bleary with drink now, but were sharp and glittering, the eyes of a predator. A smile that was more than half sneer crept onto his lips.

The dirty ruffian was one of many who attached themselves to the carnival for a short time, paying for transportation from one town to another with hard work. Rudolph, the carnival owner, never asked questions of such men. He took them on as needed, paid them little, and just shrugged when they eventually wandered off. This particular man joined the carnival in Reigelsberg and Rudolph was unaware he was wanted by the police for rape and murder.

Now, with practiced ease, the Reigelsberg Ripper slid across the floor until he was nearly in arm's reach of his prey. Elizabeth's first warning of approaching peril came from the sour body odor that wafted off the man. She wrinkled her nose at the smell and started to turn around. One calloused hand clamped over her mouth while the other grabbed her by the shoulders.

Her eyes went wide, but her scream was muffled.

"Hello, Pretty." Crooned her assailant.

Elizabeth immediately began to thrash and kick, the memory of The Monster's assault on what was supposed to be her wedding night rose like a blister in her mind. Her foot crashed against the workbench, spilling the canisters with their squeaking contents on the floor. Her assailant was momentarily caught off guard by the ferocity of her resistance, but with gritted teeth and grunts of exertion, he managed to pin her on the caravan floor.

She went limp and uttered a banshee wail of such utter terror and hopelessness that the hardened murderer's blood ran cold. He had no way of knowing that his victim's eyes were seeing a face even more grotesque and monstrous than his own, a face with dead gray skin and hooded lids, with an angry snarl twisted by more pain than any human could ever know.

The Reigelsberg Ripper paused in his assault, clamping both hands over Elizabeth's mouth to try to stifle that blood-curdling wail. He didn't feel the first few drops of liquid pattering down on his back. It was only after the dripping became a steady cold stream in the middle of his shirt, soaking through the fabric to his skin beneath, that he paid any heed to it.

"What the Devil?" He growled.

Crashing Elizabeth's head against the floor to stun her, he turned around to see where the spill was coming from.

An uncorked flask of lantern oil lies on its side on a shelf above him. To his horror, a tiny figure with wicked features, dressed in a black suit with a red satin lined cape, stood next to the bottle. The little figure smiled sardonically and bowed.

There was a scratch to his left. The murderer turned to look.

The tiny Archbishop was standing on a nearby stool with a lit wooden match in his hands. He held it like a staff, mad glee beaming from his face.

The homunculus let out a squeaky, screech that was almost discernible as the words, "Burn, Sinner! Burn!"

Then the creature hurled its wooden match like a spear.

It landed square in the center of the man's back and immediately set his oil-drenched shirt alight. The man screamed and clawed at his back, trying to pull the flaming shirt off. Elizabeth, his intended victim, was wholly forgotten.

In seconds the flames from the furiously burning shirt set his hair ablaze as well.

The Reigelsberg Ripper leaped to his feet and staggered across the cabin and out the door, howling in agony and leaving a hazy trail of blue smoke in his wake.

The Devil looked across at the Archbishop, who still gesticulated wildly in a squealy fit of righteous indignation and applauded in admiration.

Elizabeth moaned from the floor, slowly recovering from the horrific flashback that had gripped her. She grabbed a sharp tool off the floor and began to look around for her assailant.

Quickly, the two tiny homunculi scurried for cover and disappeared before she could spot them.

Carnival workers arrived at the door, calling out for her. Heta and Greta, the Siamese Twins, pushed through the door sideways and rushed to her side. Four hands helped her to her feet and brushed at her hair, and two voices squeaked in dismay at the blood on the back of her head. Heta cried with distress while Greta murmured consoling words.

The twins waited with her along with a couple of other carnival workers the Heinrichs had become friends with, until Henry came rushing back, pushing frantically through the crowd of fair-goers in the streets outside.

Calls and alarms went out, soon a mob of angry carnival workers and townspeople were combing the streets for the would-be murderer, but no sign of him was found.

The Reigelsberg Ripper left only a charred shirt and the smell of burnt flesh behind him as he fled the town.

About the Author:

Kurt McCoy is a moderately prolific writer of fan fiction, mostly based on the Universal Monsters canon. He has posted on several sites, of which Archive of Our Own has the most complete selection of his work, 127,609 words worth. He has published two fiction books, *The Werewolf's Heart*, a Weird

Western novella based on the very first Werewolf movie ever made (a 1913 Silent film), and *Monster Beach Party*, a dark humor send up of '60s Beach Monster movies that also features nearly the whole crew of Classic Monsters, all on the island where they were last seen.

He is best known for *White Things: West Virginia's Weird White Monsters*, a minor classic in the Paranormal/Cryptid field.

He'd love to hear from anyone who's read his work, or even just shares his enthusiasm for the Classic Horror genre and can be reached at: E-mail: OguaBooks@yahoo.com; or mail: Kurt McCoy, P.O. Box 1631, Morgantown, W.V. 26507

Helen Chandler as Mina and Bela Lugosi as Count Dracula from Universal's 1931 production of *Dracula*

CHILLERS

The Open Window
by Stefanie Kokai

{Author's Note: As a life-long fan of horror movies and a devotee of Bela Lugosi and *Dracula*, I have examined both the film and novel in depth. I have often wondered what I would do if I had been faced with the predicaments and choices that Lucy and Mina had to deal with. In *The Open Window*, my nameless Victorian heroine is faced with making those very choices.

Across the sill of *The Open Window* comes both fear and affection. It is across this narrow, isolated, space that my heroine must come to grips with her feelings. Like the moth she is drawn to the call of the very flame that could extinguish her. She dreads the call but cannot resist. Like so many women she is attracted to the thing that hurts her, but also comforts her with much needed love and companionship. She is fulfilled by the attention that is given to her by that which will most certainly kill her. What does my heroine do when that line between brutality and passion tests her moral character? Nietzsche said, "That which does not kill us makes us stronger." But what happens when that which does kill us fulfills us?

I hope you read my story with an open mind, but not an open window, and ask yourself if my heroine makes the choices that you would make. Then you can decide if you want to open your window or not.}

Does it take more bravery to live or to die? Tonight I must decide that very thing. I've never been a courageous soul but, as of late, I've been feeling more so than ever. I suppose death, the fear and reality of it, makes one muster up courage they never knew they possessed. When something so precious as your own life hangs in the balance one tends to find out all sorts of surprising things about themselves.

It was on a chilly October night when it all began. The air was filled with an eerie stillness and everything seemed enveloped in a weighty darkness. I had been hard-pressed with boredom all day and had spent my evening reading soliloquies and poems from various books I had yet to finish. The rest of the house had already retired and I was just preparing for sleep. I glanced out of the window which stood opposite my bed and searched for a glimpse of the moon, but in vain. Before retreating to bed I opened the window a couple of inches allowing some of the night air to permeate into the room. Just as I turned a gentle breeze brushed across my pale blue nightgown forcing a few waves of my auburn hair to graze across my face.

After settling into bed, before turning out the table lamp, I said a quick prayer and then wrapped myself tightly in a cocoon of blankets. I fell into sleep rather quickly, but it wasn't long before an icy breeze blowing over my face awakened me. At first, still not fully conscious, I merely covered my face in attempt to escape the chill, but then I realized something wasn't right. The large window at the far end of the room was sitting wide open. I sat up, still holding tight to the blankets that were wrapped around me and watched as another gust of cold air blew the drapes to and fro. I started to get out of bed but at that moment I suddenly became aware of a dark figure standing at the far left corner of the room. My heart leapt in my chest so violently that I felt as though I may faint. I gasped for a breath and fell back onto my pillows, pulling the covers over me instinctively.

The icy gusts coming from the window coupled with my immense fear left my body rigid. I glanced out to the pitch-black sky from behind my tightly clutched blanket and gathered up the courage to look at the mysterious figure again. As soon as my eyes landed upon it another jolt of fear burst through my body and I felt faint. At that moment the figure shifted forward, still remaining enshrouded in the heavy darkness that filled the room. I pulled my blanket up over my mouth as I saw the figure come another step closer, and then another. I felt the need to scream but I was too terrified to make a sound. I sat motionless as I watched the shadowed figure inch closer and closer. Finally it halted a few paces from the bed.

The moon at last made its way from behind the clouds, illuminating the room with a pale light, and it was then that I could see that the mysterious figure was a man heavily garbed in black. He was tall and of average build. The cape that he kept wrapped around his body made him look that much more imposing. His face still remained in the shadows, though the longer I stared the more my vision adjusted to the darkness and I began to make out his eyes—two black holes within pools of grey.

His right hand rose rather slowly upward, his fingers extended starkly in a claw-like fashion. As his hand rose inch by inch, the lamp by the bed began to glow dimly—illuminating the room no more than a single candle. His hand continued to slowly move up, increasing the intensity of the lamplight until it offered a glow that made the entire room visible to me. At that moment he suddenly halted, his hand recoiling into a bony fist, and it was then that I finally got a good look at my silent intruder. He was dressed in black from head to foot with a black silk cape hanging around his shoulders, falling just below his knees. In the light he seemed even taller than I had at first thought him to be. His pallid skin was so fair that it almost seemed to glow. His features were severe, his nose aquiline, his mouth taut and his lips were a deep red, which appeared almost ebony in the present light. And his eyes—those overpowering pools of black—took on a strange iridescence as I stared at them, becoming at first a brilliant orange and then shifting to a fiery red before returning to their original caliginous hue.

He stared at me with an animalistic intensity, much like a cat transfixed by its prey. His gaze entranced me so greatly that I could not look away. Our eyes remained locked on one another for several minutes longer before he shifted his weight and took another step toward me. This broke the trance he had cast over me and I started to rise from the bed in attempt to escape. As he took another step, however, his eyes still locked intently on mine; I lost my courage to run. He halted as he reached the foot of the bed and, at that moment, I let out a barely audible gasp and fell back onto the bed. Upon hearing my utterance the intensity in his eyes dissipated and his gaze shifted to that of determination, rather than primal hunger.

He placed his right hand on the bed and leaned over my feet, raising and resting his left knee upon the plush, silken coverlet and moving forward so that his body was now positioned over my legs. His movements were like that of a snake gliding up and over me until his face reached the level of my throat. My heart was beating madly but I couldn't move. I shut my eyes tight out of desperation, unable to cry for help. He had cast his spell over me. I was entirely at his mercy.

I felt him exhale, his warm breath hitting the left side of my throat and sending a rush of numbness through my body, which lingered for a long while. I felt his right hand glide up the side of my arm, his fingertips grazing ever so lightly across my flesh. My heart continued beating rapidly and my breaths increased as his fingers intertwined with locks of my hair and he brought his face down and nestled in it. I could hear him inhale slow and deeply, lingering there a moment before he brought his mouth over against my neck once again, letting out another warm breath which made me grow numb all over again.

He took hold of my right arm just below the elbow and gripped me firmly; he then did the same with my other arm and held me against the mattress. He exhaled again and I could feel his mouth gape slightly, his sharp teeth running along my sentient flesh, sending a jolt of terror down my spine. He rested them on the side of my neck and I could hear him begin to salivate as another warm breath numbed me, but this time the sensation was restricted to that single spot.

The pressure of his teeth on my throat increased, and I could feel little else. He made a low, deep groan as he gripped my arms tighter and buried his face into the crease of my neck. Suddenly I felt something warm flowing down my throat and onto my left shoulder blade. He continued to grip my arms tighter, pressing his face deeper into my neck again and again, almost rhythmically.

I began feeling tired, as though I were about to fall asleep, and at that moment he removed his hand from my right arm and began caressing my torso over and over again, clutching my waist after every few strokes. The numbness that resided on the side of my throat was dissipating now and I realized then that he was latched on to me like a leech. I felt a gush of blood spill down my neck and on to my sheets, pooling under my shoulder as he broke from me momentarily.

I opened my eyes and glanced over at him just as he raised himself. His lips were stained with blood, and his expression was solemn yet still hardened with determination. I felt sick and drained. My eyes fluttered again as I began to lose consciousness. In the last moments before I passed out, I felt him clutch my torso again and through hazed vision saw him lower his face nearer to mine. As my eyes closed and consciousness left me, I heard him speak in a deep, ominous tone, "My beauty—my lovely, little fountain of life ..." All slipped into blackness at that moment.

In the days that followed I kept to my room as much as possible and dared not speak of my encounter with anyone. I was too terrified, shocked, and ashamed to tell what had happened to me. I managed to hide the blood-soaked bed sheets in my laundry until I could dispose of them the following evening, after everyone had gone to bed. But, not surprisingly, even with all my efforts to hide what had happened, it wasn't long before my parents took notice that something was wrong. My pallid complexion, lethargy, and frequent desire to be left in seclusion alerted them. In an attempt to remedy this, my parents required that I spend several hours each day out in the sunroom so that I could hopefully regain some color and my cheerful demeanor, but nothing improved my condition.

More time passed and I remained lethargic and listless. Friends called for me but I had no interest in seeing anyone. I was so terribly lonely and unhappy but I didn't wish to see anyone or discuss my condition. Mercifully, my parents caught on and allowed me to have most afternoons and evenings to myself in my room. That is where I felt most comfortable—alone in my room with only the dim lamplight and my books to keep me company.

With all that time to let my mind wander, my thoughts returned every so often to my encounter with the cloaked intruder. The wounds on my neck had healed but I could feel the sensations just as strongly as when they had occurred. Part of me was deathly afraid of his return, and yet part of me hoped that he would. Something in his eyes—in the way he had looked at me with such intensity and tenderness—and in his voice had touched me deep inside. I wanted to see him again. I wanted to feel his touch, feel his breath on my flesh, and hear his deep, lustful voice. Another week passed, and I continued to reside very much in solitude, fearing and yet anticipating his return.

It was the eve of All Saint's Day, and my family convinced me to go with them for a trip into the countryside. Somewhat unwillingly I agreed to go, but I did so with great disinterest. We spent the day with friends and took a ride through the forest on my uncle's wagon, and then we returned home just before the sunset. My parents went to Mass but they permitted me to stay home and rest. This was the first time I would be left entirely alone since the encounter. Before leaving, my father kissed me goodbye and reminded me to relax until they returned. I assured him that I would and explained that I needed the time to recuperate from our earlier excursion.

At the stroke of 10 I decided to retire to my room. I changed into my nightgown and turned down the bed. Just then the moon peered out from behind a mass of clouds, illuminating the room with a pale, golden light. I looked out and watched the moon for a moment as a few wisps of clouds brushed along the lower half of it. My mind traveled back to the night of my encounter with the intruder. I peered down to the grounds below, which were mostly shadowed in darkness, and then I glanced again at the moon. Something deep within urged me to open my window, letting in a steady gust of cold night air as I did. I then retreated to my bed, huddled up tightly under my blankets, and attempted to sleep.

Unbeknownst to me, at a little past midnight, my nocturnal visitor arrived by way of the open window and made his way over to my bed where I was deep in sleep. I became aware of his presence only after he had positioned himself next to me and had begun running his fingers through my hair. Somewhat startled but not yet fully conscious, I opened my eyes slowly and, as they adjusted to the darkness, I finally focused on the face hovering above my own. I took a deep breath and let out a whimper, but even before the sound had fully exited my lips, he placed his hand to my mouth in an effort to hush me.

I stared up into his eyes, overcome with fear but also a secret anticipation. He kept his gaze fixed on me, exuding a hunger that seemed more sensual than before. He continued running his fingers along my hair and at one point lowered his face down next to my ear. I could hear him inhale deeply as he nestled himself in the crease of my neck, just as he had done before. His breaths were heavy and hit my flesh in bursts, which sent a flood of warmth coursing through my body. And then in a low, resonant tone he spoke, "My beauty ..."

I felt his lips glide across my neck and pause just below my right ear. He took hold of my arms, slowly sliding his hands down to my forearms and gripping them firmly. He moved down to the center of my throat and I could feel his teeth press into my skin. My body tensed. I clenched my hands and shut my eyes as I grew fearful again, but the feeling was short-lived.

Obviously sensing my apprehension, he raised himself up, prompting me to open my eyes. He was gazing down at me with a staid expression. His eyes were staring deeply into mine and I saw them again change from dark to a flaming red, then yellow and orange. His eyes entranced me and I felt my body relaxing once again. My arms grew limp and my heartbeat slowed. A clever grin appeared slowly on his face and as he lowered his parted lips back down to my neck I heard him recite again, "My beauty—my lovely, little fountain of life ..." before latching onto my throat and beginning his ritual. I felt a short jolt of pain as his teeth punctured my flesh but then I seemed to grow numb.

I could hear him lapping up blood as it flowed steadily out of the wound he had bestowed upon me. The few times that he broke his hold on my throat I could feel a warm stream of blood flow down my neck and pool beside my head, which caused me to feel somewhat nauseous. I did my best to keep the disturbing reality of what was happening out of my mind. With each passing moment my thoughts continued to grow foggier and my body became more relaxed. At last when he was done devouring his portion of blood, he pulled a handkerchief from his pocket and dabbed away what lingered on his lips.

I lay motionless; my breathing was rapid, excited, and shallow. At this point I was only half-conscious. I watched him look me over with great intent. He began running his hand up along my left hip and waist as he stared at me with the same intense avidity. His fingertips seemed to grow warmer as they traveled up my body until finally, once he had reached my ribcage, it felt as though they might burn right through my nightgown. I managed to muster the strength to jerk away from his touch but, just as quickly, he took hold of my arms again and pinned me to the bed. His eyes grew inflamed, changing from red to orange in quick succession as he glared at me.

My heart began beating faster—his expression alarmed me and I grew desperate to escape his grasp. I tried to pull away from him but it was useless. His strength was so much greater than mine and I feared what would happen if I tried him any further. He gripped my arms tighter and tighter until I felt his nails cut into my flesh and blood began rising out of the wounds. He glared at me a moment longer before turning his attention to the new source of trickling blood, slowly lowering himself down to partake of it. I dared not move but my fear and disgust forced an involuntarily moan to erupt from deep within me. He seemed to take notice of my utterance, but showed little reaction until he had finished lapping up the last of the free-flowing blood.

A shooting pain traveled up my left arm where the open wounds were still pulsating with fresh blood. His attention turned back to my face and his expression changed once again to one of solemnity. The longer he looked at me, the calmer I became. Those dark eyes of his seemed to cause an all-enfolding peace to wash over me. He brushed his hand across the wounds on my arm and suddenly I could no longer feel them. He then brought his left hand up and touched the side of my neck, easing the throbbing pain from that spot, as well.

Slowly, he lowered himself down until his lips were within mere inches of mine. I shut my eyes tight and felt as he touched his lips to my cheek and gently led up to my temple. He released the firm grip that he had on my left arm and began again to caress locks of my hair. In a near whisper he broke the silence, repeating tenderly, "My beauty ..." exhaling a deep breath to punctuate his words. My eyes fluttered open for a brief moment before closing again as he continued to tousle my hair and gently run his hand over me. I sighed and turned my face from his in submission. It wasn't long before all faded to black, and I lost consciousness.

Another two weeks passed without any excitement and without another visit from my mysterious intruder—or should I call him a companion at this point, for that is what he had inevitably and unavoidably become to me. I had seen him only twice and already I felt such a need for him whenever he was absent. Was it some sort of spell he had cast on me that made me feel as I did? Perhaps, but I preferred to think my feelings, however strange, were genuine.

My parents, particularly my father, continued to voice concern over my pale complexion and chronic listlessness. I made excuses and assured them that I was quite all right and that another few weeks of rest and recuperation would fix everything. They were obviously skeptical but they made little mention of my condition from then on. Truth be told, I too was concerned and fearful of what was happening within me. I felt tired and lethargic every hour of the day and had no desire to eat, but my mother ensured that I got nourishment enough. The wounds on my arm and neck still looked as fresh as on the night he had inflicted them, but I kept them well hidden from sight and they caused me no discomfort at all.

Week after week, I continued to endure each day, waiting for the blessed night when I could retreat to my bedroom and watch the moon rise. It was the only time that I really began to feel like myself. My body seemed to thrive at night, and my mood also seemed so much more improved during those hours alone in my room.

Most evenings, after everyone else had gone to bed, I would stand at my window and watch the moon slowly make its way through the star-littered sky. Every so often I would see a carriage far in the distance, its lamps—small burning orbs of gold—the only things visible as it ventured sedately through the overwhelming blackness. Bats would hover occasionally overhead, swooping in for a brief moment before going out of sight again. Oftentimes, I spent half the night or more watching the moon, watching the bats come and go, always secretly yearning for my elusive companion to return again.

More days elapsed and I began to grow wearier than ever. My body, while it seemed to be revived during the night hours, seemed ever frailer during the day. My mind seemed in a fog most all of the time. I had trouble distinguishing reality from illusions. I began taking meals in my room, partaking only of a few morsels of bread, which is all that I could stand to ingest. I tossed the rest of my food out the back window, into the flowerbed below, where our four wolf-hounds would quickly dispose of it.

I was becoming tormented, I must admit. My body was shutting down and the still-present wounds I hid so well had begun to cause me great pain. On top of all that, my heart was aching for the very person that was causing all of my pain and duress. My mind, still seeming in a constant fog, was being lost to hallucinations, daydreams, and a thousand worries and torments that affected my brain at a quickening rate. I knew I couldn't endure it all much longer.

The second week in December, unknown to me, my father sent for a doctor to examine my condition. The elderly physician took my temperature, questioned me about my mental state, and then looked me over from top to bottom, which allowed him to discover the wounds I had been hiding. When questioned, I made up a hokum excuse for how I had acquired them, which I could tell didn't deceive the doctor. In the end, he prescribed a mild sedative which I was to take every evening before bed, and plenty of valerian tea—I was to drink five cups of it a day.

After the doctor had gone, my parents immediately began implementing his suggested treatment. They had me drink two cups of valerian root tea, got me settled into bed, and my mother carefully administered the first sedative. Within a short while, I had fallen asleep.

At around 11 I awoke somewhat startled. I looked around my room, which was completely dark, and took a long deep breath to relax myself before laying my head back down on the pillow. I shut my eyes again but almost immediately opened them to glance over to the window. I took another deep breath, got out of bed, and put on the dressing gown that was lying across the chair next to my vanity. I walked slowly over to the window and glanced down over the landscape—there was no movement, no dim lanterns crossing the distant roadways.

I felt an overwhelming, weighty loneliness fall over me as I glanced up at the sky, searching for the moon or even a single star. But to my disappointment, the sky was fully blanketed in a large cloud, which offered no relief from the constricting darkness. I looked out at the nearly undetectable horizon for a few moments longer and started to return to bed, but then a thought came to me. I put my hand on the window latch, pausing to think over what I was about to do, and then opened the window a couple of inches. I then returned to bed, pulling the covers up over my face to shield myself from the chilling air, and went to sleep.

I do not know how long I managed to sleep before being awakened, but I would assume it was an hour or so judging by the still thick darkness that pervaded everywhere. The open window was just as I had left it, but I noticed one of the curtains had gotten hung on the armchair beside it. Then, I suddenly became aware of something moving toward my bed just a few feet away—it was him.

CHILLERS

A tinge of fear raced through my core and I watched as he arrived at my bedside and leaned over me. I looked up into his eyes, which were blazing like tiny flames, and in a whisper I confided, "I hoped that you would come back."

He reached over and took hold of both sides of my head, his fingers interlacing with strands of my hair, and he brought his face down until it was resting on the right side of mine. I could hear him breathing heavily, his mouth mere inches from my ear. Gradually he moved his face down to my cheek, his lips grazing across my jaw. As he halted at the top of my neck, I could feel his teeth resting on my flesh.

As he exhaled another breath, the warmth hit against my throat with such a burst that it startled me. My body grew tense and in that same moment he tightened his grip on me as though to keep me still. As my body began to relax so did his hands on either side of my head. He rose up so that he was now peering down at me again with that intent, fiery gaze. I reached my left hand up from under my blanket and attempted to touch him, but he caught hold of my arm before I made contact.

He stared down at me a moment longer until finally turning his attention to my arm—to the wounds on it. He ran his hand up the length of my forearm and over the injured spot, caressing it gently. As he did this, I could feel the sharp pain that had resided there begin to subside, and with another brush of his hand he caused the wounds to disappear entirely.

Next, he turned his attention to my throat and the place where he had bitten me all those weeks ago. Here too he caressed away the discomfort and all traces of the wound. Leaning down once again to rest his face next to mine I heard him whisper, "My beauty ..." which stirred me inside and made me feel slightly faint. He was still caressing my arm, but eventually I felt his hand begin to travel down my body, slowly gliding over every inch of me, while his other hand still gripped my hair. I kept expecting him to make a move but for an hour or more he did little else than hold me and look me over again and again, occasionally running his mouth along my neck or the edge of my face.

Another hour or more elapsed and I attempted again to bring my hand up to touch him, but again he prevented me. Grabbing my wrist he brought my hand to his mouth and seemed to become transfixed by it. He ran his mouth along the underside of my wrist and let out another heavy breath, sending a jolt of numbness through my body. Before I realized, he had opened a vein in my arm and, as he continued running his lips up and down, began lapping up all the blood that trickled out. I felt nothing, but the sight of it forced me to cringe and close my eyes until I felt him take a final draw from my vein and run his hand over the open sore.

I got up the courage to open my eyes and survey what was done. The wound in my arm had vanished and he was again peering down at me with a mixture of hunger and satisfaction. There was still some blood present on his lips, which he quickly wiped away. He leaned down so that his mouth rested just next to my ear and in a low, deep tone told me, "You will soon be just as I—a creature of the night. Soon, your mortal body shall die and you will be reborn—immortal. The pain will last only a short time, and then you shall be mine for all eternity." With that, he waved his hand slowly over my face, forcing sleep to overtake me once again.

The following day, I felt so drained that I couldn't get out of bed. I turned away each meal that was offered and tried to sleep as much as possible. My body ached and I found it hard to take each breath. My mind ventured to the night before, to him, and the decision that had been laid at my feet. As night arrived once again I both dreaded and anticipated it. I feared seeing that figure appear in my room again, and yet I yearned for him. My heart was torn and my mind was ridden with confusion. I had to make a decision soon. This frail body of mine was ready to die, but I didn't know if I could face it under such terms.

At midnight, I lay awake and peered out the window, stubbornly remaining in bed. I knew that if I ventured to that window and opened it, my lifeless companion would appear within the hour and his will would be done. Every part of me ached to see him, to feel him, but my mind prevented me from making a move. I had enough of my faculties left that I could still rationalize that much.

The night passed and I managed to sleep on and off until the daybreak, then I faced another day and the onset of another night. I spent much of the time pondering what I should do to resolve this dire situation in which I found myself. By that evening I had come to a final conclusion. I was afraid and, truth be told, my heart was not fully in it, but I knew it was really the only choice I could make. Tonight I would leave my window open, retreat to my bed, and hope that he took advantage of the invitation.

I was reasonably nervous all evening, and even when I tried to sleep, it evaded me. I lay awake and thought about what I was about to do, what that meant for he and I, and for everyone involved. I grew afraid and then managed to conjure up a bit of confidence again. Over and over the fight went on in my brain. Finally it grew to be midnight. I lay awake, waiting for him to arrive.

Hours passed and I began to grow impatient. Just when I was about to give up and let sleep take hold, I heard a rustling through the trees and a strong, icy breeze flowed through the room and over my bed. A moment later, I saw him materialize beside the window and creep steadily toward me. His hand was extended in front of him, ready to grip me as soon as I came into reach. I sat up in bed and removed the covers, exposing my entire frail form.

As he reached the edge of the bed he lowered his hand and stood glaring at me for a long while. I looked up at him—our eyes remaining locked onto one another—with a mixture of fear and anticipation lingering on my face. At last he reached out his right hand and placed it on the left side of my head, petting me a few times as he looked me over. I lowered my gaze and reminded myself of what was about to happen, attempting to bolster my confidence and muster up some bravery.

Keeping my eyes looking downward, I leaned forward as my strength began to wane. My forehead made contact with his right hip and I rested there as I searched the depths of my soul for another boost of courage. With his hand still on my head, he continued to pet me gently, eventually moving his hand down to my shoulder and moving me back away from him a few inches. I glanced up at him again and saw his eyes transition to a dark orange and then to a crimson red. A clever grin appeared on his lips as he broke the silence, stating triumphantly, "Very soon, you shall be mine forever. This frail and delicate body of yours cannot resist death much longer."

He laid me back onto the bed and sat down beside me, beginning to run his hand along my upper body as he looked me over with great avidity. I placed my right hand underneath the massive pillow on which I was lying and turned my face away from him, shutting my eyes. I felt him lean down against me, his chest pressing against mine, and then I felt him place his lips on the side of my neck and exhale a long, heated breath. His teeth pressed into my throat, closing down upon my flesh. I felt his warm, wet tongue glide over my skin and his teeth bit down tighter, pulling my flesh into his mouth. A mixture of pain and elation mingled and erupted from the wound and travelled through my body.

At that moment, I regained a small fraction of courage and opened my eyes. I quickly brought my hand up from beneath the pillow, opening the vial I had retrieved from under it in a swift motion, and doused my auspicious mate's face with holy water. Immediately he cowered back and let out a loud, excruciating growl. He looked at me as he moved away from the bed, a confused mixture of hate, disgust, and shock upon his face. He then staggered toward the open window, making it only half the distance before dissolving into a plume of gray smoke which was expelled out of my room and into the cold December night.

I sat up and stared at the spot from where he had disappeared; waiting to be sure he was really gone. After a few minutes, satisfied that he wasn't going to reappear, I got up, closed the window, and retreated back to my bed. I huddled under the covers and buried my face in them, taking a deep breath to relax myself. I placed my hand on my neck and rubbed it for a moment. Not long after that sleep mercifully overtook me.

It's been almost 40 years since I last encountered my immortal intruder. I still reside at the same house where my parents and I lived all those years ago. They have since passed on and I now live here alone. I never married.

I have made my living as an author, writing novels—primarily of a romantic nature. I have been very fortunate in life—I've accumulated great wealth over the years—but money and possessions can only satisfy one so much. I battle loneliness and declining health more and more frequently these days.

It is the eve of All Saint's Day. For the first time in 38 years I will be absent from this evening's Mass at St. Anthony of Padua's Cathedral. There is to be a full moon tonight and I feel rather compelled to sit in bed and watch it rise. And I'll leave the window open a few inches, just in case an intruder wishes to accept the invitation.

About the Author:

Stefanie Kokai holds degrees in nursing and culinary arts with an additional concentration in the fine arts. She enjoys writing and painting. Stefanie is from Greenup, Kentucky, and currently shares a home in Chippewa Lake, Ohio, with Count Dracula, aka Bob Kokai.

In this publicity shot from *Dracula*, Dracula(Bela Lugosi) carries Mina (Helen Chandler) as Dracula's stooge Renfield (Dwight Frye) looks on.

**Vincent Price as Frederick Loren stalks both ghosts and people in the
House on Haunted Hill.**

The Ghost Beater

by Brian Carney

{Author's Note: I love Haunted House movies, but one thing always irritates me—haunted house movies where there aren't any ghosts in the haunted houses! Oh, I enjoy the atmosphere well enough, though. I'm a fan of the whole Dark House mystery thing, but I want GHOSTS in my haunted house movies, damn it!

This story is inspired by one of my favorite haunted house movies, *House on Haunted Hill*, a fine film, with a house that damn well does have ghosts, even if they're ultimately not what the movie is about.}

"You shouldn't have come here. I shouldn't open the door for you, Mr. Brogan. None of this is supposed to be happening. If you're wise, you'll leave now and forget that you ever even heard of this house," Mr. Watson Pritchard said.

The man peeping out from the open crack of the door was deathly pale, white. His forehead was furrowed by worry lines, his eyes were wide and dull and filled with fear. On the phone, his voice had sounded faint, as if he were speaking from far away. In person, it wasn't very different. This looked promising!

"Yeah. But I am here," Mr. Ike Brogan retorted. "You did open the door. And I ain't going nowhere until I get a look around. So, open up, Mr. Pritchard."

A wide, knowing particularly un-pretty smile appeared on Mr. Brogan's face. He fished around in the pocket of his rumpled suit and pulled out a fistful of crumpled bills, "This ought to make it all easier to do," he said.

Pritchard stared down at the crinkled paper, almost as if he didn't know what it was. The door creaked open and he extended both hands, cupped together.

Brogan dumped the bills in his hands and winked, "There, see how easy that was?"

Brogan pulled the door open and shouldered his way past the worried looking little man. The first thing that struck Brogan was how cold and dark the inside of the house was. Outside, it was a blazingly hot Southern California summer day. Ninety degrees and no humidity.

Inside, the house was cool enough that Brogan pulled his sports coat closed and buttoned it. He could almost see his breath in the murky entry hall. The air was not only cold; it was dank, and almost dripping. He could smell the mold that was growing on the carpets and the drapes.

"Got the AC cranked up pretty high, don't you, Mr. Pritchard," Brogan remarked.

The little man was still frowning down at the balled-up bills in his hands, poking at them with one finger, and rolling them around. "There isn't any air conditioning, Mr. Brogan. It was never installed," Mr. Pritchard said.

"No AC? Are you crazy?" Brogan replied.

Brogan walked about, staring up at the shadowy ceiling and the ornate antique chandelier hanging from it. His footsteps echoed hollowly in the dark corridor, "How'd you get it so cold in here, then?"

Pritchard looked up, eyebrows arched over beady little eyes, and mouth pursed in an almost petulant pout, "Oh … that would be the ghosts."

"Ghosts?"

"Yes, the house is full of them. You can hear them whispering to each other, if you listen carefully."

"Fantastic!" Brogan laughed.

He cupped his hand to his mouth, shouting, "Wake up! Wake up, wherever you are!"

Harsh echoes of his shout rippled about the hallway, ringing out of empty rooms, and rolling down long corridors.

Pritchard looked down at his feet, wincing, "You shouldn't do that," he whispered, "You shouldn't mock them. They will find you soon enough. You don't want them to be angry when they do."

Brogan laughed, and harsh barking laughs came bouncing back at him from the shadows, "So … you gonna give me the grand tour, or what?"

"Oh, no!" Pritchard said, head snapping up in dismay, "It's almost night-fall. I never stay in the house after dark."

"Not even for 10 thousand dollars, Mr. Pritchard?"

Mr. Pritchard pursed his lips and shook his head, "I stayed here one night for that amount. I'll never do it again. Not for a hundred times that!"

Brogan laughed and rubbed his nose. A hundred times that is about what he hoped to clear for this job, if half the stories he'd heard about this place were true. His employer, Plato Zorba, would pay him at least that if he could bring back proof that there were real ghosts in the house.

"Suit yourself, Mr. Pritchard. Just hand me the key and go," Brogan said.

Pritchard shook his head, "There is no key, Mr. Brogan. The doors are on an automatic locking system these days. Once they close after sundown, they can't be unlocked again until after sunrise the next day. The Loren Estate insisted on the change when they leased the house."

"Like a bank vault, eh?" Brogan winced, but that news didn't particularly bother him. He planned to stay the night in any event.

"Yes, like a bank vault. It keeps the curious out. Maybe, with luck, it can keep *them* inside as well."

"Unless you open the door during the day, then some curious soul might wander in," Brogan observed with a wink.

 CHILLERS

"I'm not supposed to do that," Pritchard looked stricken. His face contorted into a wrinkled mask of guilt and fear, "They must have made me do that. They must want you here for some reason. You shouldn't be here!"

"You've been paid," Brogan growled.

Mr. Pritchard's hand grabbed Brogan by the arm. His fingers were icy-cold, even through the sleeves of Brogan's suit.

"It's not too late, Mr. Brogan! You can leave with me. Forget that you ever heard of this place. Go far away. It's not too late … for you."

The little man looked pleadingly at Brogan with a tiny spark of hope gleaming in his eyes.

That gleam guttered and died out as Brogan waved goodbye and purposefully shut the door. Moments later, there was a buzz and a loud *thunk* as the locking system engaged.

The sun went down, and night rolled in like a dark, purple wave. Streetlights winked on down in the valley. High on Haunted Hill, the strange angular house, looking like a Cubist pile of rectangles, was engulfed in blackness.

Crumpled 100-dollar bills blew across the yard, scuttling in the wind like husks of dead beetles, discarded and forgotten.

Brogan was a ghost beater and he was on safari. Dr. Zorba's "ghost beaters" were like the beaters who accompanied hunts, thrashing the brush to flush out wild game. Zorba hired men like Brogan to hunt for haunted houses, to spend nights in them and try to rouse any ghosts that might be lurking there. When a genuine haunting was found, Zorba was notified and came to trap the specters for his personal collection. The beaters were paid exorbitant bounties, if they could come up with the real thing. Brogan didn't particularly believe in ghosts, but he wanted to believe. He wanted to believe about a million bucks worth.

Brogan pulled a flashlight from his suit pocket and shined it around as he slowly ambled through the house. The house was pitch black but for his one circle of white light, flicking about. There was electricity, but only a few rooms were properly wired for it. The gas, which might have fed Victorian light fixtures on the walls, had been turned off long ago. Brogan passed some candles that he might have lit, but he preferred to rely on his trusty Maglite, and he didn't want to risk starting a fire and burning down his ticket to a fortune.

The downstairs was not extraordinary. It featured a large entry hall and foyer, a neatly appointed living room and study, dining room, kitchen, and a bathroom tucked in a cramped diagonal space under the staircase. There was a door that led to the basement, but that was firmly locked. Everything was remarkably clean. There wasn't even a hint of dust on any of the surfaces. All the furniture was covered with crisp, white sheets.

Brogan didn't expect to find much downstairs. According to his research, almost all the murders had been committed in the house. There had been quite a few and they had taken place upstairs.

Despite having spent many a night in reputedly haunted houses, and having seen many things he could not explain, things that most men have never even had nightmares of, Brogan's heart was pounding as he crept up the stairs. This house's reputation was especially brutal. Its ghosts were reputedly malevolent to the extreme.

His flashlight beam twitched from one side to the other. Brogan scrutinized the upstairs landing and hallway, scanning for any sign of movement or any out of place shadow. The long halls ate his flashlight beam, drawing it out like a white piece of taffy until it shone feebly against the heavy drapes that curtained off the side halls, to cut down on drafts. Faint motes of dust swirled in the beam, like a light snow drifting down from the ceiling.

When he reached the landing without incident, he let out a sigh of relief. He chuckled ruefully and ran a hand through his thinning hair.

The sun had barely set, and he was already feeling spooked. While that seemed ridiculous, it was actually a promising sign. Brogan had good instincts when it came to hauntings. If he were already this on edge, despite having seen nothing out of the ordinary, it was likely that there were unseen presences around him, pressing in, triggering nerves that were honed to respond to the uncanny.

"I think Plato Zorba is going to love this place."

Brogan poked his head into an upstairs sitting room and flashed his light about. The circle of white light zipped and zagged, sweeping over the sheet-covered tables and chairs. The room was cold. There was an odd, coppery smell in the air, along with a faint stench of rotted meat.

"Hello!" Brogan murmured excitedly, "Something is going on here."

He stepped into the room, with a big grin on his face.

"Come out! Come out! Wherever you are! Here ghostie, ghostie, ghostie!"

Brogan made the shout like a pig call.

Something dark fell past his face. Hot liquid drops splattered on the back of his hand.

"What the hell?"

He shined his flashlight to the back of his hand and witnessed glistening red drops spread across his knuckles. The liquid, whatever it was, was hot and sticky, thicker than water, but thinner than paint.

"Fantastic," Brogan whispered.

The night had barely begun, and he already had something to show Zorba. No doubt that the fluid would prove to be blood. He pulled out a handkerchief and wiped the back of his hand. To his surprise, the liquid was impossible to wipe off. It smeared around, spreading thin, but wouldn't come off his skin.

Finally, he dabbed the handkerchief over the drops and held it in place. Slowly, the liquid soaked into the cloth, staining it bright red.

The back of his hand was stained a light red, like spilled ink partly soaked into the skin.

"Marked," he whispered with a chill.

There was something about that in his research, too. Those who were marked by the Ghosts of Haunted Hill were destined to join them, or some such rot.

"Give it your best shot, spookies," Brogan snarled.

This was not his first spectral rodeo. He came prepared. Salt. Chalk. Stubby little candles shoplifted from a church. Water and oil blessed by a bishop. Sutras painted on rice paper by a snaggle-toothed spirit wrangler with wrinkled parchment skin that he'd found in Chinatown. He even carried a dagger with a solid silver blade. That one was really supposed to be for werewolves, but Brogan believed in being prepared.

Nothing else out of the ordinary turned up during his first tour of the house. He broke into each of the bathrooms and tried the faucets. Water was running, but there was an odd color to it, not quite red, not quite brown. A few of the rooms were wired for electricity, but Brogan left the lights off. The wiring in this place just couldn't be up to spec.

It was a strange house. The interior was dark and felt worn, aged, while the outside seemed hideously modern—despite having been constructed a hundred years ago. It was a brutally Cubist cage built up around a Victorian heart that was half-rotted with age.

Brogan shrugged. He didn't understand architecture. All he knew about the house was that it was more than a 100 years old. The outside walls had been constructed from pieces of a ruined Central American temple that the wealthy retired archaeologist who commissioned it brought back from his expeditions, stone by stone. The weirdly quasi-Mayan antique pile had inspired Frank Lloyd Wright, who based one of his own designs on it. This made the house important enough to be on historic registers and therefore prevent it from being torn down, despite the fervent wishes of most who had owned it over the years.

Having tramped around the inside of the house without much success, Brogan decided to settle into one of the bedrooms and wait for the ghosts to come to him.

Brogan lit a brace of candles and plopped down on a bed, happily resting mud-spattered shoes on the antique coverlet. He pulled several pages of notes from a pocket inside his suit-jacket. The pages were heavily creased, folded and refolded with finger smudges on the carbon copy print. There were stains from mustard and spilled beer on a couple since he had been looking them over during lunch.

The notes were Zorba's research on the Pritchard House and its history. It was a sordid story. At least nine murders were known to have been committed in the house, along with an unknown number of disappearances, and several deaths by natural causes under very suspicious circumstances. Some of the murders were spectacularly brutal: Dismemberments, decapitations, disembowelments and at least one that involved skin flaying and vivisection. Something about this house seemed to bring out the most violent of urges.

Brogan was beginning to feel an urge or two of his own. He scratched his balls through his pants and yawned, tipping his hat over his eyes. The pages of research wound up scattered across the bedspread and spilled onto the floor. Brogan snored, very loudly. The echoes rumbled down the hall, stirring up whispers in their wake.

Shortly after midnight, Brogan was awoken by the sound of whispering voices nearby.

"I want to bite him."

"I know."

"I just want to sink my teeth in and chew a bit."

"You always do."

"Is he waking up?"

"I think so, shh!"

The voices went silent as Brogan opened his eyes.

Something rustled in the wall beside his head, like rats scuttling around between the boards.

Brogan frowned and put his ear against the wall. Something stirred on the other side, in the wall cavity. Broken plaster rattled. Something scraped across wood.

"I think he's listening to us."

There was a long silence, some barely audible sibilant whispers, and something like teeth chattering.

"I'm going to BITE him!"

Something slammed against the wall right next to his ear.

Brogan jumped back, hat falling off, with one hand against his ear.

There was muffled laughter and scuttling inside the walls.

The heads were never found. Words from the police report on the murder of Pritchard's brother and his wife's sister.

Brogan grimaced and slapped the wall with his hand.

"It'll take more than a couple of talking melons to scare me!"

Something hissed like an angry rat. There were more bumps and rustlings from inside the walls.

Brogan laughed and lit up a cigarette.

The disturbance started with a distant scream of a female voice shrieking in terror.

 CHILLERS

Heavy chains rattled and clanked. There were groans of pain. Most unsettling was the slow, steady thump of a heartbeat.

Brogan stabbed out his cigarette with a grin.

"That's more like it!" he laughed, "Gimme something that'll make Zorba's mouth water."

The sounds all abruptly ended.

Brogan frowned.

The eerie cacophony was replaced by the sound of heavy footsteps coming up the stairs from the first floor. The chains rattled again, but more quietly this time, as if the thing carrying them was trying not to attract attention. The footsteps reached the top of the landing and began to clump down the hall, coming toward Brogan's room.

Brogan eased off the bed and crossed to the door. The footsteps kept coming nearer. There was nothing spectral about them. The floorboards beneath his shoes shuddered with each heavy step.

Brogan flicked on his flashlight, took a deep breath, and then flung open the door. He stepped into the hallway, shining his light toward the approaching footsteps.

He expected to see an empty hall or perhaps a startled human hoaxer. Instead, he saw a living nightmare.

The Shape revealed in the circle of his flash beam was pure corruption in vaguely human form. It was glistening wet, white and lumpy like milk curds, with patches of bristly black hair. Rusted chains hung from two long arms. Its wet face writhed and split open, revealing yellowed, fang-like teeth. The eyes that glittered in the flash beam neither blinked nor squinted but stared back at Brogan with sheer mad hatred.

The Thing that killed her was not human. That is what the servants in the house at the time insisted. The coroner agreed in his report, saying that nothing human could have torn a woman limb from limb like that. Pieces were scattered all about the room. The original owner of the house hunted the Sisimite in Central America. Perhaps he found one?

A passage from the research notes that Brogan had read earlier that evening.

"Oh God!"

Brogan ducked back into the room, slammed the door shut and threw the bolt. He slid a chair over and propped it under the doorknob for good measure.

"No, please no!"

The footsteps came to just outside the door and stopped. Chains rattled.

There was a horrible stench of spoiled meat and wet rot.

The doorknob twisted slowly.

The thumping heartbeat sound returned, and Brogan could hear coarse breathing from the other side of the door.

The door shuddered as a heavy weight slammed against it.

Brogan backed up, light trained on the door. The beam flickered and stuttered. Brogan's hand was shaking, and the batteries were failing.

The door shuddered again; the wood creaked but did not break.

Everything went silent.

Brogan was breathing hard.

A wet stain appeared on the oak door. Something clear and syrupy seeped through the wood grain. The smell of rotten meat became so intense that Brogan covered his mouth, with vomit clawing up his throat.

Bubbles rose from the wet stain.

Blood-red liquid began to weep through and trickle down to the floor.

The bubbles grew, lengthened, and then became the tips of thick fingers, pushing through the wood. A hairy, wet arm emerged from the seeping stain and began to feel around the door. The fingers found the bolt and slid it open. Next, they scrabbled down until they found the doorknob. The knob turned, and the door creaked, but it didn't open, thanks to the chair propped against it.

The arm began to swing about fingers stretching blindly, seeking the obstruction.

"Oh, God," Brogan whispered.

There was no other way out of the room. The window was open but blocked by steel bars.

In desperation, Brogan opened the closet door and backed in. He pulled the door shut after him.

The chalk in his pocket and the holy water didn't seem like enough protection to even occur to him.

The chair rocked, and then clattered to the floor. There was a creak as the door opened.

Brogan covered his mouth with both hands and tried not to breathe. Heavy footsteps entered the bedroom. Furniture began to scrape across the floor. The heartbeat sound returned, so loudly that it hurt Brogan's ears.

Brogan backed all the way to the back of the closet. His shoulders pressed against the wall.

There was a hollow thump. A hidden panel swung open and Brogan stumbled backwards onto a narrow landing, almost tumbling down a rickety flight of stairs that disappeared into the darkness below.

Without hesitation, Brogan pushed the panel shut and quickly crept down the stairs.

The secret stairway led to the basement. Brogan stepped out onto a stone floor. The air was full of mold and an acrid, nose-itching smell not unlike bleach or chlorine.

The flashlight swept around the room. There were huge keg vats on trestles and several doors. In the center of the room was a rectangular pool of oily black fluid with white bubbles scudding across its surface. He recognized the

CHILLERS

room from the notes he'd read. This was once Ambrose Norton's wine cellar. The vat in the middle was filled with acid. Norton had murdered his wife by throwing her into it. Two other people had also died there, much more recently.

Brogan tried one door and found a wine rack filled with dusty bottles. Ambrose Norton had failed as a vintner. The wine he made turned out bitter and earthy, more black than red, and was barely a step away from vinegar. His wife spat it out and laughed at him. Norton's experiment was a failure, but ironically, whether from connoisseurs who found the bitter flavor to their liking, or more likely from the notoriety that accrued from Norton's murder of his unappreciative wife, the few bottles of Norton Black Grape that showed up on the market went for astronomical prices at auction.

Brogan took one of the bottles out of the rack and worked the cork out with his teeth. One quick sip affirmed that the wine inside was indeed from Norton's batch. The strong, bitter flavor with its almost gritty aftertaste was very distinctive.

A quick count of bottles in the rack multiplied by the most recent auction prices equaled … Brogan let out a low whistle.

There was a fortune's worth of rare vintage on the rack. Though, if so many bottles were to enter the market at the same time, the price would crash, rendering the lot practically worthless.

"Pritchard, you devil!" Brogan said with a grin. The twitchy little man had probably been selling just a bottle or two a year and raking in a tidy income, one that was guaranteed to keep coming for many years.

Brogan took a long, slow draw from the bottle, wincing at the sour flavor. In a glass, at a restaurant, that swig would probably have cost hundreds of dollars. Brogan took another and grinned.

He made a mental note to help himself to a couple of bottles on the way out. He would come out of this night richer, whether Zorba came through with his ghost bounty or not!

He continued to drink from the bottle as he explored the basement.

Brogan was about to open another door when he heard a sound from the other side. Cautiously, he put his ear to the door before turning the knob.

He heard a woman sobbing.

With a quick yank, he pulled the door open and shined his flashlight into the room beyond.

A remarkably beautiful woman in a flimsy negligee was curled up against the far wall. Her feet and long, slender legs were streaked with dirt. Her eyes were red, and her cheeks were covered with tear tracks. At first, with his light shining in her face, she cringed in terror, but as he stood watching, she slowly unwound. A hopeful look dawned upon her pale face.

"You're not him, are you?" she asked timidly.

"No, Ma'am," Brogan choked out.

She was truly a classic beauty. She had a long aristocratic nose, highly defined cheekbones, and slightly oval eyes. Her mouth was a delectable little pink blossom above a small chin. Her hair was honey blonde, curled loosely, but disheveled by mishandling. A stray lock curled down across a blinking blue eye.

"Oh, thank God!" she gasped. She leaped to her feet and threw herself against him, arms locking around his shoulders. She pressed a very soft, shivering cold body against him.

Mr. Brogan took immediate notice.

She registered his sudden interest and hesitated a moment before pressing even more tightly to him. Her hips ground against his crotch with hungry intensity.

"Please!" she whispered hoarsely in his ear, "Get me out of here and I'll give you anything you want. In any way you want it. Please."

She began to cover his cheek and neck with quick, fierce kisses.

Embarrassed by her intensity, Brogan stepped back from her and held her at arm's length.

A look of dismay covered her face. Her eyes met his, pleadingly. She bit her lip to keep from begging. She seemed terrified that she'd scared him away.

He patted her shoulder reassuringly, "Who are you? How did you get here?" Brogan asked.

He looked around the dark basement, shuddering at the sudden chill he felt, "What's going on here?"

She stood, shivering, arms hugging her chest, one leg half raised across the other instinctively covering her womanhood, which was dimly visible through the gauzy fabric of her negligee.

"They do this because," she explained bitterly, "it amuses them. The Loren Estate thrives on picking people who need money very badly. They offer them a sum of 10 thousand dollars to spend a single night in this horrible house. They pick people who desperately need the money, who won't ask too many questions."

"Why?"

"I don't know. Most of them are never seen again. My … boyfriend took the challenge. I never saw him again. I wanted to know what happened to him so I … so I …"

She broke down into uncontrollable sobbing again, covering her face with both hands and shaking her head.

"Hey! It's okay," Brogan said, taking her in his arms again, "I'll take care of you. I'll get you out of this place."

She gazed up at him with wide, pleading eyes.

"Promise?" she asked, barely daring to breathe the word.

Mr. Brogan promised, pulsing with sincerity.

Her mouth melted into a sultry smile. She put her face against his chest.

CHILLERS

"Anything you want," she whispered, nibbling at his chest through his shirt, "Any way you want it."

Overcome by the feel of her softness pressing against him, by the brine and flower smell of her, Brogan wrapped her in a bear hug, his heart beating like a jackhammer in his broad chest. She turned her face, nestling one ear against his chest. The sound of his heartbeat seemed to excite her. She moaned.

One knee slid up his thigh as her leg twined around his.

"You're so warm!" she purred, "so goddamn warm!"

The negligee she wore seemed to melt away, tattering and dissolving like cotton candy in your mouth. Soon, she was wearing nothing but sticky strands like spider webs. Her skin was smooth, silky soft, and cold as ice.

A shiver ran through Brogan's body. Somewhere in the darkness around him a man's voice chuckled.

Brogan started, "Who's that?" he asked suspiciously.

"Never mind him," she whispered.

She playfully bit his pec through his shirt. Her fingers dug into his back, painfully sharp. Her hips ground against him, the points of her pelvis surprisingly sharp.

"That's just my husband," she explained with a laugh, "He used to be insanely jealous, but now he just likes to watch."

"What?"

This whole scene was starting to feel very weird, very wrong.

Brogan tried to pull away, but the woman clung to him as tenaciously as a spider clutching a fly.

"I don't think ..." he started.

She took his hand and planted it against her breast. Her skin was icy-cold, but her breast was firm and her soft nipple was as hard as tire rubber under his palm.

A pale, white face floated out of the darkness ... a distinguished looking man with saturnine features and a pencil thin moustache over smirking lips. The man's eyebrows rose in wry arches. His clear, piercing eyes combined amusement, mockery, and pity into one look.

Brogan shivered, suddenly chilled to the bone. It was as if all the heat in his body was leeching out, into the icy-cold softness pressing against him. Most of it flowed from his boiling loins into her undulating hips.

The breast he was squeezing turned spongy and squishy under his hand. The skin on her back was sticky and soft as tar, and his fingers sank into it.

"What the hell?"

Brogan tried to pull away from her, but she stuck to him like glue.

"Don't leave me! Don't let me go!" she cried.

Sharp fingers gouged at his back, snatched at his hair. He felt the bones of her pelvis jabbing into his thighs as she writhed sensuously against him.

"You can do anything you want," she whispered with her breath cold and stinking like spoiled milk.

"Do it to me now, Mr. Brogan! Before it's too late. Please!"

Her skin melted away, turning into something like drippy mud, and thinning into a greasy gruel. Her breast came off in his hand, and then melted through his fingers, dripping like tallow.

The man in the dark began to chuckle; the man must have been wearing a black suit, because Brogan could only see his head and his face. The man then laughed a harsh and mocking laugh that sounded more than a little mad.

Brogan felt like he was spinning, and like the world was spinning around him. Everything became a dark, dizzy whirl of movement. His feet stumbled across the stone floor, which suddenly seemed slick as ice.

The flesh of the woman in his arms turned completely liquid and splashed onto the floor. Sticky drops dripped from hard bone. Soon, the thing he held in his arms was a hard, brittle skeleton that still moved, grinding and clutching and squirming against him. It was light as a feather but had a grip like steel.

"I want you inside me," whispered the skull, looking up at him, "I want to feel you warm and alive, filling me with your life. I want to feel you on my vertebras! I'm as open as any woman has ever been for you. Be one with me!"

Mr. Brogan was not at all interested.

There was a lurch and Brogan found himself falling sideways, dizzy and disoriented.

He heard a loud splash first, then scalding hot liquid washed over him, stinging and burning and …

"Oh … goddamn it!"

Brogan ended his life with an obscenity in a pool of oily, black liquid.

About the Author:

Brian Carney lives in a trailer outside Cameron, WV but he spends most of his time in the garage, which is twice as big, trying to make vintage motorcycles run again. He's a bad-tempered, beer-swilling, bike-riding piece of rough trade who collects '70's pin-ups of biker babes and Men's Pulp novels from the '50s and '60s. He's especially fond of haunted house movies, having grown up in an old, rambling, thoroughly haunted farmhouse that—thankfully—burned to the ground ages ago.

Even servants Howard Huffman and Leona Anderson appear demonic in *House on Haunted Hill.*

In a dynamic shot from *Son of Frankenstein*, Inspector Krogh (Lionel Atwill) has his arm ripped off for a second time (this time a prosthesis) by the Monster (Boris Karloff).

The Abominable Inspector Krogh

by Dwight Kemper

{Author's Note: Having written a mystery novel titled *Who Framed Boris Karloff?*—a fictional account of a murder that takes place on the set of *Son of Frankenstein*—I had to watch that film many, many times. And each time I kept asking myself the same question. As Lionel Atwill tells of his encounter with the Monster when he was a mere boy, I kept wondering how in the hell he had survived having his arm ripped off. Such an insult to the boy's body would have led to shock and instant death. This eventually inspired the story you're about to read. It's not the only possible explanation, but it's one that satisfies me. And hopefully, will satisfy you as well. May all your crimes be perfect ones—DK}

The firelight gave Inspector Krogh's face the look of Satan himself. Lit from below, Baron Wolf Von Frankenstein found the village inspector's visage quite intimidating. His face was square, his mustache a black slash across his upper lip. Angular black eyebrows served to give each word a punctuation that inspired wariness in whomever those piercing gray eyes happened upon.

Nevertheless, Wolf feigned confidence. After all, Inspector Krogh assured him his visit was one of "protection." Ever since Frankenstein came to the village named after his family, he, his wife, and young son had been received with both fear and underlying contempt.

Inspector Krogh came straight to the point. "I've reassured the villagers that I would ... keep an eye on you."

Wolf took a sip of his brandy and stood erect. "Really, Inspector?"

"You've inspired fear amongst the villagers." Krogh reached for his right arm, which was nothing more than a wooden prosthesis. He bent the elbow with his left hand, making a clicking ratchet noise at the joint. He twisted the hand until the fingers were in a perfect position to hold the monocle that he removed from his right eye. He set it in the black-gloved wooden fingers, and then removed a handkerchief from the prosthesis' sleeve and set to nonchalantly polishing the lens. "Oh, I think I can assure your safety," he blew hot breath on the lens, fogging it, "but beware, Baron, fear is a powerful motivator for violence."

"I see," Wolf said coolly. "And what precisely are they frightened of?"

"Your name. You are, after all, a Frankenstein."

"Do you suggest I change it to something like, say, 'Smith'?"

"You can change your name, but not erase the brand. It's indelible. And need I remind you that your father's abomination is often referred to as 'Frankenstein'?"

Wolf bristled but tried to keep his composure. Still, he couldn't help pacing the rug as firelight danced in his eyes. "My dear Inspector, the fact that my father breathed life into a corpse is unquestionably true, but I feel that this poor creature's menace has been so exaggerated in the telling and the retelling, that it is now seen as the most fiendish monster to ever walk the earth!"

Krogh smirked as he reinserted his monocle. "As if there were other such monsters."

Wolf was taken aback by the Inspector's wit. "Well, yes. You know what I mean." He waved the matter off and continued his pacing. "Can you list even one horrible act this poor creature committed?" He stopped and stared intently at the Inspector. "Have you ever even seen him?" he challenged.

Inspector Krogh's gaze took on a faraway look, as if becoming lost in some past tragedy. Finally, he said, "It's the most vivid recollection of my life." He turned and stared into the dancing flames illuminating the huge fireplace. "I was a mere child at the time, about the age of your own son ..."

As the Inspector reminisced about the horror, he felt as if the flames themselves were conjuring up images from those dark, early days of his boyhood ...

"Bang! Bang!" a five-year-old Krogh said, as he fired his cap pistol at the imaginary enemy. He had sought cover behind the living room couch, imagining his father was a battalion of soldiers about to raid his tin soldier stronghold. Krogh was the general leading his men to victory! It was his fondest ambition to be a soldier, even at his tender age. His father saw Krogh had an instinctive understanding of military strategy, a soldier of the Great War himself, who had seen bloody combat up close; the father now enjoyed a career as the village Inspector. He encouraged his son to take up chess, to hone his skills with strategy and being four moves ahead of his opponents. But Krogh was, after all, only a little boy. Better to teach him such things with toy soldiers instead of chess pieces. Krogh's father was puffing on a meerschaum pipe and reading the paper, snug and safely wrapped in a warm blanket. His son began his imaginary assault. The cap pistol, one Krogh's father had ordered from America, emitted loud snaps followed by the scent of burnt gunpowder. At last the father grabbed his chest and feigned the pain of having been shot. "Oh, you've gotten me!" Krogh's father put down his pipe so better to pretend dying on the rug without setting the house on fire.

"I won! I won!" the young man exalted. Doing a dance around his toy soldiers.

Krogh's father chuckled and sat up. Grabbing his boy in a bearhug, he said, "Indeed you did, General Krogh! Indeed, you did!"

It was then that the front door was assaulted by a fearsome pounding so powerful that the heavy wooden barrier and iron hinges instantly gave way to the irresistible force. It was then that they saw him, or rather, *it*. The Monster lurched through the doorway, pausing as if for dramatic effect. Its features were hideous, a gaunt, square head with hair scorched by licking flames. Heavily-lidded eyes surveyed the scene. The yellow, watery eyes fell upon the father. The Monster snarled.

Krogh's father gasped as he stood between the boy and the Monster. In one quick movement, he reached for his hunting rifle and aimed for the Monster's chest. The Monster, more than familiar with what such firearms can do, growled menacingly as he both grabbed the gun and sent the father hurtling into a corner, with one swift, superhuman motion.

Krogh's father slumped to the floor with a gasp of pain.

Little Inspector Krogh eyed the Monster narrowly. Being a mere boy, he thought his plaything was a real weapon to defend his father with. He aimed at the Monster and fired his cap pistol until curls of burnt paper issued forth from the striking hammer.

Not knowing the difference between a toy gun and a real gun, the Monster assumed he was about to be harmed. He had already been shot many times that day, once while saving a shepherdess from drowning, and again while escaping a jail. He did not like the burning pain and refused to allow it again. In one swift motion, the Monster grabbed the toy gun and the boy's arm. He yanked. As easily as one tears off a turkey leg, there was a scream from the child as the tiny white branch that was his arm came away from the shoulder. The scene devolved into a cacophony of screams, blood, and finally death.

The little boy's body lay there in a pool of spreading blood, looking like the caricature of a broken doll. The Monster stood frozen with confusion. He looked at the arm that dangled from his clutch, the tiny hand still holding the toy cap pistol. Suddenly filled with revulsion, the Monster threw the arm aside. He looked down at his stone white hands. They were colored with stains of red. He remembered another time, another child, a little girl that showed him kindness and invited him to play with her. He remembered daisies, a lake, and a tiny scream, "No, you're hurting me! NO!" … and then the splash of water. The Monster remembered how her cherubic face sank beneath the water, her dead eyes filled with fear. He ran through the woods then, stopping to look down at his murdering hands. He cursed those hands then, and now …

The boy's body twitched slightly as life ebbed swiftly from him.

The Monster tried to wipe off the blood on his tattered, muddy clothes, but it didn't wipe away the sudden feelings of guilt and regret. He looked at the tiny discarded arm and the toy gun. He pried the gun from the spastic fingers of the severed arm and examined it. The Monster fingered the trigger. A cap was ignited, but no bullets issued forth. It was little more than a crude noisemaker. It was no danger to him, or anyone else. This made the Monster regret his actions even more. He had killed another child, and for no good reason. The creature threw the gun away, snarled, then with increasing anxiety looked this way and that to try and think of what to do next. The blind hermit had taught him to speak. He muttered, "Bad, bad, bad," in his deep, guttural snarl. He wanted to flee, escape before more men with torches and guns came for him. He turned towards the door, ready to run, to blend into the night, when a spark of something like a conscience stopped him. He turned and looked back at the boy. He was dead. He was nothing but a dead body.

And then he remembered what one of two hunters seeking sanctuary in the blind hermit's hut has said; "He isn't human," referring to the Monster, "Frankenstein made him out of *dead bodies!*"

Those words echoed in the Monster's mind now. The boy was a dead body. *He, the Monster himself,* was many dead bodies.

Inspired by an idea, the monster lumbered to the chair, took the blanket that had once given comfort to the boy's father, and wrapped the boy's limp, red-stained body in it. Cradling the horrible bundle in his massive arms, the Monster strode with purpose through the front door and into the night, strode towards the home of the one man who could fix this. The castle of Henry Frankenstein, his creator!

Henry Frankenstein stared into the fire that crackled in the hearth. He clutched his silk bathrobe to stave off a chill of horror. The Baron contemplated the flames, seeing his many sins played out in the dancing firelight. The graves he had robbed, the body parts he had sewn together, the life he had raised with his unholy super ultra violet ray. He ran his fingers through his thick, slicked back hair, his handsome face contorted into a mask of regret. He had breathed life into a being that, through no fault of its own, had murdered and maimed and killed. It would prey upon his own conscience on that fateful day when he himself would face his own creator. How would God judge Henry when all was said and done? Henry Frankenstein had abandoned his own Monster. Perhaps there was a special place in hell for anyone who forsakes his own creation.

There was a knock at the study door that sent a chill down Henry's spine. "Yes?" he said.

Elizabeth entered. She wore a filmy blue negligee and transparent dressing gown. Her beautiful young body was barely hidden by the folds of diaphanous material. "Henry? It is our wedding eve. Will you not come to bed?"

How could Henry even think of satisfying his lust for his bride while the Monster was still roaming the countryside, maiming, killing? "I am sorry, darling," he said, despair in his voice, "but I must contemplate the horrors that I have let loose upon the world."

 CHILLERS

"Darling," she said, "surely tonight of all nights, you should attend to your responsibilities as my husband and lover."

She entered the chamber, her hips swaying seductively; her very presence the personification of lust. She stood before the fireplace, draping her arms on the mantle, in full view of her husband's gaze, allowing the firelight to silhouette her naked body. "Take me, darling," she said. "Together we shall create life. A life from our union as husband and wife."

Henry groaned with anxiety as he turned away from Elizabeth's lovely image. His hands worked feverishly, one hand massaging the balled-up fist of the other. "I can't think of our happiness, darling. Not while my horrible creation is still loose upon the countryside. I've had a terrible lesson. And Pretorius ..."

Elizabeth was not so easily put off. She undid the ties on her nightgown and let her clothing fall to the floor revealing her naked body in all its sensual glory. Her alabaster skin, her dark flowing hair, all served to create an enticing visage to tempt Henry Frankenstein from his despair.

"Henry," she said, her voice breathy with desire. "Look upon your bride."

Henry Frankenstein wiped his parched lips. He gazed upon her, noted every curve and how the firelight made Elizabeth a supernatural being of orange dancing flames and curves.

"Take me, Henry," she implored.

Even though his mind was plagued with guilt, his rising lust was greater. Throwing back his robes, tearing away at his pajamas, he took Elizabeth there on the carpet, before the roaring fire, while the heavens blast the night outside.

What Henry did not know was a pair of eyes that he had chosen were watching from the large window. The Monster saw his creator take his bride. The lightning had erased most of the Monster's memory. When he first encountered Elizabeth, he wanted to tear off her wedding gown and do .... something. He couldn't remember what it was he wanted to do to her. He felt the heat of lust. But he had no idea how to satisfy it.

He watched as his creator satisfied that lust. Together they were a mass of writhing flesh and plunging hips. It made the Monster yearn for something, for a mate ... a bride!

Then he watched as both Henry and Elizabeth cried out in passion, which enflamed the Monster's own desires to be lusted after by a being much like himself. He saw Henry embrace his bride and it was in that moment that the Monster knew he would not be happy until he felt such passion.

He looked down at the small bloody bundle in his arms and remembered why he was there. He wanted Henry Frankenstein to bring the boy back to life. He would not accept "no" for an answer! He hesitated. A part of him did not want to interrupt Henry's enjoyment of his bride's young succulent body. In a way, the Monster found the acts of lovemaking ... beautiful. Perhaps, even sacred.

Long after they fell into each other's embrace, Elizabeth gathered up her filmy gowns and clutched them to her. "Don't leave me waiting, darling," she teased. And then left Henry alone in the study.

Henry covered his nakedness with his robe and drank some brandy, exhausted from his dalliance with his wife's body. It was then that the Monster could wait no longer and opened the study window. Henry turned and saw, illuminated by a flash of lightning, his creation lurching into the room.

"Frank-en-stein," it said.

"You fiend," Henry gasped, amazed his creation could talk. "Why are you here? What do you want?"

The Monster held up the horrible bundle and shoved it in his creator's arms. "FIX!" the Monster insisted.

Taken aback, Henry took the bundle and opened the blanket, finding the boy's remains. He examined the extent of the damage. "You want me to ...?

"FIX!" the Monster insisted.

At first, Henry wondered what he meant. Then, slowly, he began to understand. "You killed this boy, and you want me ... to bring him back to life?"

"FIX!!!" the Monster snarled.

"I shall have no hand in such a thing!" Frankenstein protested.

"Yes, must!" insisted the Monster.

Frankenstein paused. What if he could indeed breathe fresh life into the boy's mangled body? Would that not vindicate him? Would not such an act prove his theory that life could be restored, and mankind could benefit from such a discovery?

He took the boy's body to the sofa and made a more thorough examination of the damage. "Do you have the arm?" Henry asked his Monster.

The Monster grew agitated. He had left the white, soft cylinder of flesh back at the boy's home. All he could do was gesture vaguely and make a guttural moan. Henry noted those stone white pleading hands, a gesture he saw once before when the Monster wanted the light back after Henry had shut the blinds overhead. "I see," Henry said at last. "How did it happen?"

The Monster looked away. "Gun. Grabbed. Pulled. Not real gun. Boy die."

Henry gazed at his creation. "You feel genuine regret, don't you?"

The Monster looked at Henry with tears forming in his heavy-lidded eyes. "Make boy live again." He searched for the right words. "Please," he said.

A new life stirred within Henry. Yes, he would bring the boy back. He would be as he was before. Not a monster, not a re-animated corpse, but as the boy he was, or used to be. His eyes grew cold with steely determination. "Follow me," he commanded. Henry bundled up the corpse and strode purposefully toward a bookcase near the fireplace. Bending down, he found the secret lever in the molding and pressed. The bookcase opened inward, revealing a secret passage. "Come with me!" Henry ordered.

     CHILLERS

The Monster obeyed.

Through corridors of jagged stone lit by burning torches, Henry and his Monster wended their way toward the laboratory that sat on the crest of a volcanic crater just across the ravine. It was a domed structure, filled with equipment equal to that of the watchtower where Henry had set up his distant laboratory. But this was the prototype. It was built over a bubbling sulphur pit. Steam from the pit rose up and filled the domed chamber with the stench of rotting eggs. The pair made their way through the ancestral crypts, up the well-worn stone steps, past a heavy brick and mortar door, and into the laboratory proper.

As Henry laid the boy's corpse upon an operating table, he said, "Bring me that tray of instruments!"

The Monster did as he was told. On a wheeled metal cart were an array of operating tools, forceps, scalpels, retractors, sponges, and more. He picked up one of the scalpels and remembered how the old man, Professor Waldman, tried to dissect him with a similar little knife, and how he strangled the old man when he listened to the Monster's chest.

"Don't touch them!" Frankenstein scolded. "They're sterile!" He pushed the Monster. "Oh, go away and let me work!"

The Monster staggered back, feeling a bit put out by his creator's reaction. He could have crushed Frankenstein with his bare hands, but there was something about the man that the Monster liked. He had passion, not only for his woman, but for his work. *He* was *his* work!

Henry examined the wound at the right shoulder. The Monster had literally torn the arm out by the roots. Had he only had sense enough to bring the arm with him ... No, there would have been too many questions about *how* the arm had been reattached. As far as Henry was concerned, the fewer questions the better. If he succeeded, it would be in the boy's best interest never to know of his resurrection!

Scrubbing up and slipping into his surgical attire and a pair of rubber gloves, Henry began his work. First, he would do a common amputation, bringing the torn flesh together to form a proper stump. The boy would be without his right arm, but he would be alive. Next, Henry infused the body with his own artificially created blood, the very same blood that flowed in the Monster's veins. He prayed the boy would never have to have his blood typed and cross-matched. Imagine the horror experienced by any doctor to see blood cells that battle one another!

Then the boy's body was wrapped in bandages. All the while the Monster watched as Henry performed his feats of near magic. The boy was strapped to the table, electrode plates placed at the temples, readings taken about the levels of electricity in the air due to the thunderstorm. With headset in place, Henry heard the crackling sounds inspired by the heavenly display of cosmic fury. "The storm is at its peak but just may not be enough." Henry examined the switches that fed power from the condensers into his ultra violet ray projectors. "There may be enough stored up energy to compensate." Henry pointed at a bank of levers. "You! Pull those levers as I call them out to you. I can't do this alone!"

The Monster quickly obeyed, staffing the bank of levers, and waiting for Frankenstein's instructions. Overhead, the lightening rolled and boomed. There was a flash and a tumbling down of sparks from the cosmic diffuser.

Frankenstein threw a switch and the table upon which the boy's corpse rested was elevated into the chimney of the domed roof. There was a shower of St. Elmo's fire as the super ultra violet rays were aimed at the lifeless body. The Monster looked at Frankenstein. The man's chiseled features were a mask of deep shadows and frightening grimaces in the flickering light of the lightning!

When at last the spectacle was over, Frankenstein lowered the operating table, and grabbing a stethoscope, he placed the bell over the boy's heart and listened with burning anticipation. Finally, he proclaimed, "He's alive! Alive!"

Reaching for a pair of bandage scissors, Frankenstein cut away the gauze that covered the boy's eyes. They were open! They were aware!

The boy reached up with his left arm, and as he did, he murmured a long, ghostly moan. Working quickly, Frankenstein cut away the bandages covering the boy's head. It revealed dark hair and a plump face, a pink plump face, not stone white as the Monster's had been. To anyone looking at the boy, the child would seem perfectly normal!

"Do you know who you are?" Frankenstein asked the resurrected boy.

There was a hesitation. Then, slowly, he said, "K-Krogh. W-Wilhelm Krogh." Adding with a child's anxiety, and with a peculiar lisp that would have been cute under different circumstances, "Where'th my daddy?"

"You've been sick," Henry said. "But I'm a doctor. I've made you well again." He gestured for the boy to embrace him. "Come. I will take you to your daddy."

"I ... want ... my ... daddy," Krogh said.

"And who is your daddy, child?" Henry asked.

"Inspector Adolf Krogh."

Henry was rocked. The thought of the village Inspector inquiring about the miraculous healing of his son, and far too many subsequent questions about Henry's other experiments, fed the scientist's growing anxiety. It then occurred to Henry that he had seen so much horror, it was good to see something could still sour his stomach.

Fortunately for the boy, Henry, being the Baron of the village, knew the address of the Inspector well.

Henry reached for a bottle of chloroform. "I have something to help you relax." With his free hand, he grabbed a ball of cotton wool and upturned to bottle until the cotton was soaked. Just as he brought the cotton to the boy's face, he noticed the Monster lurking in the shadows, smiling gratefully that the boy was alive again. The cotton muffled the boy's scream and he fell into blissful unconsciousness.

Wearing a dark cloak to hide his face, Henry drove the coach-and-four while the boy was inside the cab, sedated and in the arms of the Monster. Nothing Henry could say could convince the Monster to leave the boy alone. The creature had taken a liking to the child, it seemed. It was rather encouraging that a Monster possessing a criminal brain could think of a boy's welfare above his own.

Over the crest of a hill, Henry pulled back on the reins and climbed down from the driver's seat.

Opening the door to the cab, Henry noted how the Monster was gently cradling the sleeping boy. "Come out of there," Henry commanded. "Leave the boy on the seat." He noted how the Monster hesitated. "Don't worry, I plan to return him to his father. Assuming you haven't killed him."

"No," the Monster grunted. "Man only sleep. Still breathes. Just sleep."

"For that child's sake, I hope you're right. Now get out here."

His creation reluctantly obeyed, leaving the boy bundled in a blanket and asleep in the passenger seat.

From the distance, the sound of angry villagers could be heard. The Monster's ears pricked up and he snarled with a gesture of defiance.

Henry grabbed the Monster's powerful arm and got his attention. "No, you fool! There are too many of them. They'll overwhelm and destroy you!" Henry pointed to a fence that hugged the dirt road. "There, just a few yards from here is a cemetery. Make your way to the catacombs! You'll be safe there!"

The Monster gestured at the boy in the coach. "But boy ..."

"I'll take him home! I'll come up with some convincing story. Or perhaps they'll be so relieved to see their son alive, they won't bother to ask too many questions." Henry could see firelight from torches over the crest of the far hill and through the branches of bare trees. "Now go! You will live! Go!"

The Monster studied Henry's intense face. "I not forget. You helped me. Friend."

"Enough talk. Go! Now!"

With a snarl of frustration, the Monster did as he was bidden. He hurried to the fence, easily climbed over it, and then headed off into darkness and the direction of the cemetery.

Placing the hood of his cloak over his head, Henry remounted the buckboard of the coach and took the reins. He was long gone before the angry townspeople poured into the road and beyond the fencing like a flood of humanity.

"Are you all right, Inspector?" Wolf Von Frankenstein asked as it seemed the Inspector was hypnotized by the blazing logs in the fireplace.

Warming his one good hand, Krogh said, "Do you ever have faint memories haunting you? Little fragments of images that make no sense, but still gnaw at you?"

"I can't say that I do." Wolf sipped his brandy. "Inspector, why are you so obsessed by this Mon—my father's work?"

Krogh's eyes narrowed. His monocled eye studied Wolf intensely. "I'll tell you why, Herr Baron. That creature your father made, he's an abomination, an insult to God. And I have sworn to find him and kill him! It is my right! For he is but a Monster, and I am an ordinary, living ... human being."

The Beginning

About the Author:

Dwight Kemper began his mystery writing career hosting mystery dinner theater shows for hotels like the former Sherwood Inn, Greene, N.Y. As Detective Chief Inspector Kemper of Scotland Yard, he performed up and down the East Coast and as far away as Bermuda, entertaining Sara Karloff and friends.

His first mystery novel, *Who Framed Boris Karloff?* was nominated for a Rondo Hatton Classic Horror Award. He has since written and illustrated two follow-up novels, *Bela Lugosi and the House of Doom* and *The Vampire's Tomb Mystery*, which is also available on Audible as an audiobook produced by Circle of Spears Productions.

On television, Kemper appears each Halloween on Michael Legge's *Dungeon of Dr. Dreck Halloween Specials* as Uncle Mess

Kemper has appeared in Legge's feature films, including, *Crawlers, The Brothers Dim,* and as the title character in Dre Boyd's *The Adventures of Jim Powers.*

Visit Dwight Kemper's Website: www.murdermysterytheater.com

The playful Inspector Krogh (Lionet Atwill) alongside the young Peter von Frankenstein (Donnie Dunagan), a boy very much like himself.

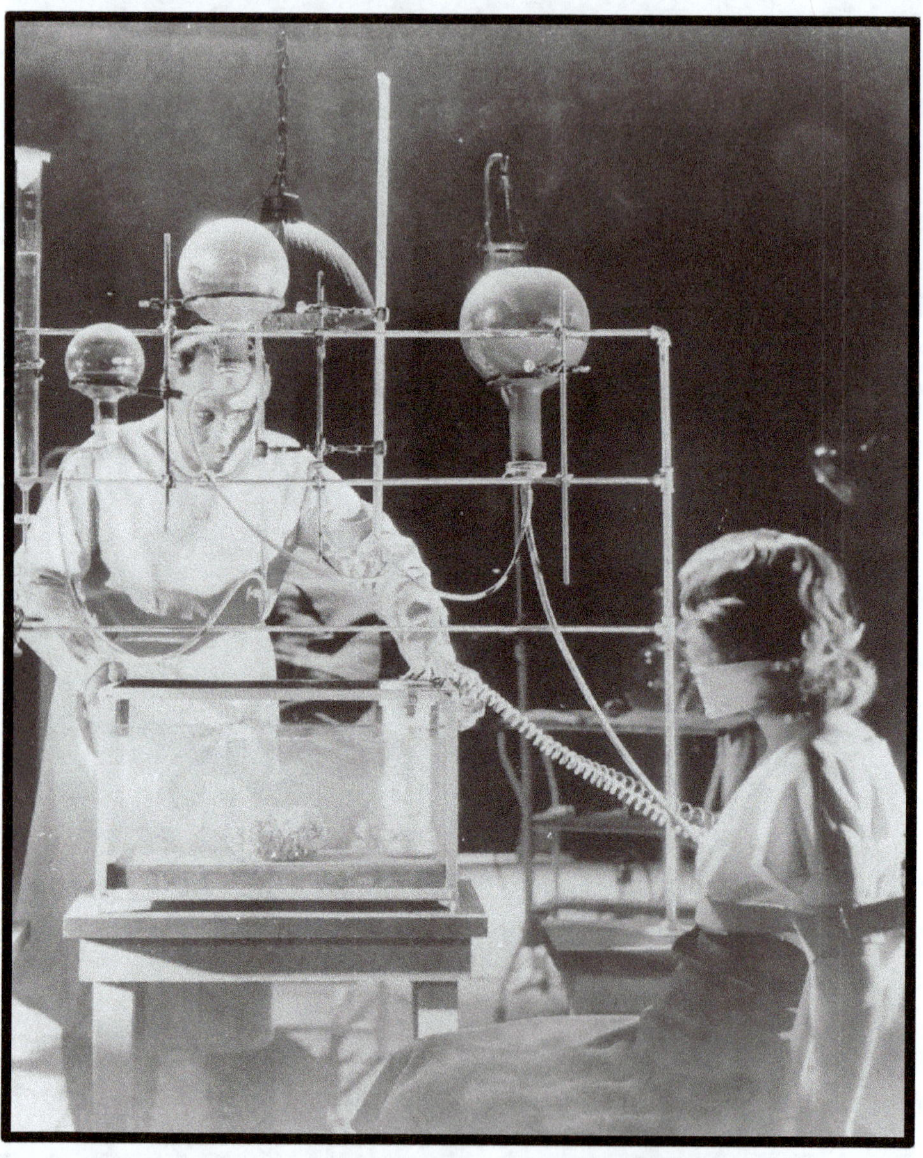

Dr. Otto Von Niemann (Lionet Atwill) experiments upon a helpless Ruth (Fay Wray) in *The Vampire Bat*.

The Vampire Bat Prelude
by Brad A. Braddock

{Author's Note: While watching Turner Classic Movies late one night, the wonderful Robert Osborne was just beginning his introduction to one of my favorite films, *White Zombie*, with Bela Lugosi. Of course, I'd seen the film too many times to count. I own the VHS, DVD, and Blu-ray … and of course, who doesn't?

To make a long story short, I thought to myself, why are writers not taking old films and embellishing them? Breathing new life into these undying classics? So shortly after, I began to write what became a prequel to *White Zombie*, titled *Memoirs of Murder*. I had so much fun creating that project that I wished to embellish further on classic horror.

Having enjoyed the 1933 film *The Vampire Bat* many times as well, I wished to offer a bit of a backstory, the struggle that is Emil Borst, played by the brilliant actor Robert Frazer. His part is not the largest in the film … in fact it's rather small, but as you watch Mr. Frazer standing in the shadowed background, there is a poetic sadness upon his face. This prelude gives a sort of backdrop to his struggles, and I certainly do hope that you will find it fitting … I know I do.}

The sweet smell of pipe smoke filled the dimly lit study, imprisoned deep in a dark and ominous castle. Doctor Von Niemann sat in his favorite chair by the crackling fire, coffee in hand at 10 p.m. sharp … *The witching hour,* as he would sometimes describe it to his servant, Emil Borst, with a sly, sadistic smirk upon his arrogant face.

Burgomaster Schoen had just departed from the good doctor's presence, after a rather rousing conversation on immortality, with brandy in hand. And, of a few of the fine maidens of the village that were soon to be of age. The doctor arose from his gilt-bronze upholstered chair and stood in front of the fire, his back to Emil. He gazed deep into the roaring fire that was surrounded by handcut stone, some of the finest and most prized of the land.

After a long deep breath, Von Niemann slowly turned his head to the left and peered over his shoulder at Emil, who stood in a dark corner, the faint candlelight flickering off his handsome face. Emil sometimes wondered how his life had come to this point, after being born into a family of wealth and riches. How he could have destroyed it so. How he now must abide unto the doctor's unholy game. Emil was torn, he felt this was his final redemption, his last chance to restore dignity to his name and family. But by which he might also etch his name in the enshrouded books of hell.

Emil gambled heavily upon this last chance …

Taking the hand-carved pipe from his lips, the doctor said, "Do you realize the possibilities to which I have laid ground? The creation of human tissue! Mad, is what some have said, those without my intellect, you see. They are mere doctors caught in a spider's web. But I, I am the spider." Von Niemann paused as an imperious simper flowed unto his face, like a warm breeze comforts a chilled babe. He then continued, "I will capture the blood of those who are caught in that web."

Emil moved from the dark corner, the flowered wallpaper now exposed where his body had hidden it. His expression was one of concern, as he gazed upon the floor. The hardwood creaked as Emil inched slowly to the doctor. Emil gradually raised his head to look upon Von Niemann.

Emil ran his fingers throughout his coal-colored hair. "Doctor," he began hesitantly, "we are talking about the murder of innocent villagers. How do we bear a crucifix upon the wall when we will carry the mark of the devil upon our chests? Branded, as if an ox unto the slaughter … as if a bird unto the snare …"

"… And he knows not it is for life." Von Niemann finished Emil's biblical quote. It was then, that the doctor became angered. He snuffed out his pipe with his right thumb, pressing hard and furiously upon the fiery tobacco as he stomped to Emil with the devil in his eyes.

The doctor gazed hypnotically, deep into Emil's eyes, and he spoke to him with a spellbinding tone, "What are a few lives," he asked, "when you and I will save the world?"

Emil's body wavered, as if drunk, and his eyes blinked rapidly. He stepped backwards and threw his left hand to the front of his face. His head shook slightly, his eyes wide as his lips pursed.

He felt woozy before saying, "I feel as though …"

The doctor finished for him, "… As though you've been touched by the grace of an angel, and all of your shortcomings and wrongdoings have at last come to their end." Von Niemann, spoke softly, grasped him tightly by his shoulders, and pulled him face to face. "This is your answer, to serve your fellow man in a way only God can … the creation of tissue! Do you understand what lies before us, Emil? We are in league with God!"

Emil stepped back from his master and dear friend for a moment to think before stating, "But to take the life of another, I will surely find my place in hell."

"My good man, you must think of the greater picture, the chance to rescue an entire race from the depths of despair!" The doctor paused and began to pace about the room with excitement before continuing, "Why, if a blacksmith would lose a hand while taming a blade, we may remedy this! Or, if a farmer accidentally lopped off a foot, or an arm, we could heal this! If a child were

CHILLERS

facing a heart condition that would be his or her demise, we could grow a new heart and save that babe and its mother's despair for a lifetime! The possibilities are endless!"

Emil gazed into Von Niemann's eyes, as if he could see the breathless wonders that the doctor controlled. "You are truly a genius doctor, one that I could never be. My thoughts on this are minor, for I will help you with this great task that you pursue." Emil paused and gazed deep into the roaring fire before asking, "But what of God's thoughts, Doctor Von Niemann?"

"My good man, why talk of God when we are doing what God will not?"

Emil took his ebony cloak that rested upon the hall tree by the front door. He swung it around his shoulders, his body now covered by the dark cape. He looked back at the doctor with stone-faced anxiety. The doctor's right eye twitched as he peered deep into his servant's eyes, reading his lost soul. Emil grabbed his top hat and placed it upon his head before slowly turning to the front door.

Von Niemann called out to his servant. "Do not fear your destiny, the beauty that has now been bestowed upon you." The doctor placed his hand on Emil's shoulder, as if to comfort him before continuing, "Let this be the beginning of a new era, one that heals the sick and cures the blind. *This* is our purpose. You may shudder in horror—so did I the first time. However, you will have no doubt from this moment forward."

Emil looked back into the doctor's icy glare and felt the command of a father that he had really never known. He reached for the handle and inched the door open quietly, wishing not to alert the doctor's servants.

Into the sticky, humid night, Emil drove his body up to the highest rooftops, lurking like a spider that was driven for blood. Not for self-gratification, but for the wishes and demands of a cause beyond his mind's powers, or so he perceived.

Resting for a moment against a cedar shake rooftop, he gazed at the full moon. Dark clouds streamed across it, before the wolves' eerie howls took hold of his body and soul. He thought about their bloodlust, now his was no different than theirs.

"Am I a vampire?" he whispered the question before continuing. "A wolf in the vast wilderness."

And we all knew that the blood is the life ...

It was then that Emil caught the sound of faint footsteps upon the cut stone walkways of a bygone village. He eased his body toward the edge of the rooftop, so that he might witness what beast, or devil, or soft soul that may be lurking about the village in these hushed hours of the devil's night.

Bracing his body with his right hand, he grabbed hold of the roof spouting, and eyed a slender man that looked back and forth with unease. As the dark shadows that betrayed the moonlight lessened, the pale glow exposed the trepidation of a thin man with a frail mind.

It was Herman Gleib. Emil found his presence out and about at such a witching hour rather strange. He gazed on to see his purpose and found him creeping to a familiar window. It was Ruth Bertin's house, and now, both Emil's and Herman's interest truly piqued.

Emil climbed down from the towering rooftop, the spider that he had become, and webbed himself into a dark shadow … one that would never tell. He had a close view of Herman, staring into the beautiful Ruth Bertin's window, a woman he also had lusted after. He knew of her beauty all too well.

She sat at her vanity, humming a simple comforting tune as she gazed into her mirror, combing her soft, cropped-curled hair. She was the dream of many a man in the tiny village, most notably Karl Breettschneider. Some whispered that they had shared a kiss under the boundless moonlight, and who knows, perhaps even more. Herman, with his frail mind, had heard the village ramblings, and couldn't help but gaze upon her heavenly beauty in awe. It was an innocent gaze, for he was infatuated with her attractiveness.

But, when a spider finds a weary insect in its web of deceit, the spider is judge and executioner, and Herman had laid his own trap.

"Herman!" A deep voice hissed in the darkness.

Herman quickly turned from the window and walked away.

"Herman Gleib!" Again, the voice called into the foggy night.

Herman paused, hunched his shoulders and began to rub his hands together nervously before asking, "Who wants Herman? Who's there?" His wild eyes and mad gaze were evident in the vast moonlight.

A shadowy figure slowly approached him, each footstep announced by the cut stone cobble walkways. He paused as he came close to Herman's body, and raised his head to look deep into his eyes.

Emil shook his head from side to side with disgust before saying, "How could you peek into the window of a woman? Why, you know Herman, your act will be frowned upon, and may conclude with swift action."

Herman was distraught and began to cry. He lunged forward and grabbed Emil by his ebony cloak, wiping his tears upon the coarse fabric.

"Herman no mean wrong."

Emil tilted his head upward and to the left, gazing down upon Herman with a cracked grin and a mad stare. "Perhaps, but I have no choice but to turn you in to the burgomaster. He and the other elders will deal with your wicked ways now."

"Oh please!" he cried and begged further before continuing, "I'll do anything! Please don't tell on Herman!"

Emil took a step backwards before gazing at an age-old church that was now vacant and left to the wilds of the night. Something terrible had happened

 CHILLERS

there, nearly a century ago. Now no one would go there. He pointed to the abandoned house of God and motioned that they must journey inside.

Opening the spider web filled doors, they made their way into the dark interior, flushing out squeaking rats that lie enshrouded in the night. To the distressed altar they descended, where Emil spoke with his deep, monotone command.

"Herman, with a heavy heart, I *must* give you up to the burgomaster. He will see your sins, whether I tell about you or not."

Herman again cried, he was embarrassed and ashamed, and fell to his knees at the altar. Not to serve God, but to serve his own purpose, so that he would not be exposed and shamed further than he already had.

It was then, that Emil heard a shrill squeaking from the rafters, followed by thunderous wings that began to descend from the darkness of the church. And he thought, *bats and blood* and his quest to claim the life force of the living! And what better creature to do so, or be blamed for such an act, than perhaps … a vampire!

His eyes went mad. "Herman, I will not give you up on one condition."

Herman wiped the tears away from his eyes and begged, "What must I do to keep you from telling?"

A presence in that darkened church seemed to whisper to Emil, to give him the words to speak. The bats swirled above, as if stirred by an unseen hand.

"You will learn to love *bats*. You will keep them upon your person. You will love them and cherish them." Emil paused for a moment before he sneered, "For they are soft and nice. You will show the villagers that you truly love them!"

"But Herman no like bats."

Emil peered upon Herman with a frightening and fearsome gaze before saying, "Would you prefer I tell of your ugly obsession with Ruth? Peeping Tom, doing God … knows … what?"

Herman looked to the floor where a bat had fallen. It was either old or sick, or perhaps it was being offered up by the darkness. It trembled and stared at him with the blackest eyes. At that moment, his dread of bats meant nothing to him if he could save what little name he had left.

He picked up the bat and petted it. "Herman like bat, they soft."

As he stroked the bat, he listened to the trilling sound it made, a gentle sound, almost a lullaby. The bat's fur was not stiff or oily or caked with dirt. It was soft as silk. Something shivered inside Herman. Here was something that loved him! Here was something that longed for his touch, the way Ruth never would.

A wicked, crazed smile bloomed on Herman's lips.

He'd said it once, to please the man in the dark cloak, but he repeated it now, feeling the truth of it burrowing within him.

"Herman like bat, they soft!" he whispered with conviction.

Emil's eyes gleamed.

Doctor Von Niemann had fallen asleep in his study by the crackling fire, now just a pit of cinders, as his mind wandered into the world of dreams and nightmares. His body twitched as his head rested on his left shoulder. His hands clinching one of his handcrafted pipes as his eyes sprung open. He took a long, exasperated breath before gazing at the clock that was about to strike 3 a.m.

Dong, dong, dong ... the clock tolled between the rhythmic pace of the *tick, tock*.

The doctor's heart raced, wondering of Emil and what he may have discovered among the darkness of the cold, brick streets. What he may have found lain rest in the ebony corners of bedchambers. This resting blood, awaiting a true purpose, one that would enlighten mankind for generations to come.

With mad eyes, he grabbed the arms of his resting chair and sprung through the dimly lit study. Anxious energy now drove him as he ran up the steps, and burst into Emil's room, unannounced.

Emil was startled, his heart unsteady as the moonlight shined down upon his eyes. Von Niemann beamed in his direction as he inched the creaky bedroom door closed, turning the handle so that the latch wouldn't make a sound. His footsteps were that of a predator, quiet and precise, as he stood with his back to the moon, that blasted its wonder through the bedroom window.

"Emil," the doctor hissed, "where is my blood?"

Emil sat up in bed before taking a deep breath. He whispered, "Doctor, I have not discovered our first blood. However, I have perhaps discovered something of far greater use."

Von Niemann was frustrated as he let out a long sigh. "Go on," he demanded.

"Doctor, I have planted a seed that will grow in any soil. The halfwit, Herman Gleib, I caught him peeking through Ruth Bertin's window this eve."

Von Niemann lit up as he kneeled by Emil's bed. "Yes, go on," he coaxed with excitement in his voice.

"And I told him I would give him up to the burgomaster unless he met my one request."

At that point, the doctor began to squirm. "Damn it, man ... what did you tell him?"

Emil leaned close to Von Niemann's face before answering softly, "I told him that if he didn't show his fascination for bats in front of the villagers, I would be forced to turn him in. In turn, he at last took one of the sickly bats and stroked it, comforting it, as a loving mother would do so for a babe."

The doctor gasped a deep breath before covering his mouth. Wide eyes followed before shouting, "A patsy!" Von Niemann grabbed Emil with an icy-cold grasp before continuing, "You are right, Emil. My God, man … when the villagers catch wind of the murders that will soon plague this village, we will have our patsy. Brilliant, I say!"

Emil replied, "Doctor, when the bell tower strikes midnight long after the sun has fallen, and the moon has set, I will be there for you and your work. You dream of a better world with no sickness; you dream of a better world without death. One where you will help God rid the evil that the devil has cast upon mankind. To heal the sick, cure the blind. We are doing and will continue God's work."

The next day Doctor Von Niemann was completing recommendations and theory for the Germanic world of science when he heard screams from the cobblestone streets below. He threw his spectacles on the desk and leaned his body upon the open window of his second floor office.

He could hear the young children screaming as he watched Herman Gleib run toward them with a bat in his hand, grinning and laughing madly.

His cries could be heard about the village. "Herman love bats. They soft and delicate."

Emil heard the cries and crept into the doctor's office. He stood quietly to Von Niemann's back. The doctor felt his energy, his presence, and slowly cocked his head to gaze upon his servant.

With an arrogant smirk, the doctor began, "Emil, my man. Look what you have done."

Emil peered with lifeless expression at the cuckoo clock that quickly approached the witching hour.

The doctor's time had at last come …

Dark cloak and top hat covered Emil as he found himself engulfed in another foggy night. The soles of his boots could faintly be heard on the brick paving as he prowled in the shadows, becoming ever more familiar with a darkness that was creeping deeper into his soul.

A lullaby came from an open window, and Emil was quick to discover it. He darted from shadow to shadow, at last pressing his body against the damp wooden wall of the cottage. He carefully peeked into the window to find a mother laying her child to rest. The young girl was asleep, and the mother was tired. Emil could see the weary condition in her eyes.

He heard her warm breath blow out the candelabra and watched as she tucked her child in for the night.

Emil heard her soft footsteps upon the hardwood as she walked, careful not to wake her slumbering babe.

With trembling hands, Emil eased the cracked window open and slipped his serpentine body through the gap. He was silent as he gazed down upon the child that slept softly in bed. He took the back of his hand and stroked the child's brow with a loving caress.

Here was blood, easy to take.

It was at that moment an expression overcame his face like he had been stabbed through his heart. The thought of murder entered his mind. Forever darkness. He knew that could not be. No matter how great the doctor's vision was. No matter how great the outcome might be. He would have to kill, and a killer of children, Emil was not.

He slowly backed from the bed and started for the window when his body suddenly quivered and stopped.

Emil heard the doctor's voice in his head. "Emil." Mad eyes gazed from a faraway darkness … a gaze gifted by the devil. "You will do as you promised. Emil, hear me now ... you will take her. The blood, Emil, is ours."

Emil came under an evil spell. He felt the doctor had a strange power over him at times. He struggled against it. However, this power he could no longer resist. He fought helplessly but his mind was taken, and he was soon under the doctor's supreme command.

Blood covered the walls of his black and white world, as if he had suddenly fallen under the influence of the devil. His body now succumbed to his reprobate thoughts.

"Emil … do this, now." A deep voice commanded. A deep voice rang from the shadows beyond.

Emil rolled the dark collar of his cloak around his neck and pulled the brim of his hat over his forehead. He crept from the child's room and found the young girl's mother asleep in bed. She was chilled, and had her quilt pulled up to her neck. Lavender and herbs hung from above, filling the room with soft, comforting scents.

Emil took his handkerchief and pulled a bottle of chloroform from his pocket. He doused the rag, as he tried to slow his anxious heart. To not breathe heavily, and under the doctor's spell, it was not an easy task.

As the wolves' howls grew greater, echoing from the woodland beyond, he pounced upon the mother and covered her mouth, stifling her breath. Her screams were muffled as she squirmed, as she strove desperately to fight back. But Emil's ungodly strength and the howling of the devil's children were too much. Her body at last gave way to limp helplessness.

Emil arranged her carefully in her bed, then gently pulled away the quilt that covered her neck. He took a deep breath before sitting in a rocking chair that sat by the mother's four-poster. He opened his coat pocket to reveal two sharp needles and six bottles that were strapped to the inside of his cloak.

He slowly punctured the jugular vein and inserted a long, rubber tube into the first flagon. Blood quickly flowed from the young mother's neck like water from a ruptured dam.

CHILLERS

She stirred restlessly, eyes flickering, as if struggling through some chloroform-flavored dream.

"I hope your dream is a pleasant one." He whispered as the blood gushed rhythmically into the glass bottles. "Because you will never wake from it."

At last her eyes flicked open and a desperate moan sounded in her throat. But it was too late. The last heartbeats of blood splashed out.

He reached over and gently closed her eyes.

Emil wept.

As the morning sun came, the young child gradually awakened. She stretched her arms and yawned, squinting her eyes, fighting back the morning sun. Gaining her wits, she looked to the window and found it open, which she felt was rather odd. Her mother was superstitious, and always closed the windows with worries of vampires and werewolves that could roam about the wicked shadows of the night.

Now that it was morning, she thought not to close it and ran for her mother's room to jump on her bed like she always did.

Yelling, the young girl dove upon her mother, shouting, "Mommy, oh Mommy … it is such a beautiful day. Won't you come look?" She asked as she pulled her mother by her arm.

But her mother didn't respond, never even twitched. The child became worried for a moment; then smiled, as she knew her mother was being silly, just playing a jest.

"Mommy," she laughed. "Get up, Mommy." She pinched her cheeks.

It was then that she noticed the pale complexion and the two bloody marks upon her neck. She began to panic, her heart now kicking inside her chest. She shook her mother harder to wake her, but there was nothing, and the reality began to take hold.

She let out a bloodcurdling cry that rang out of the bedroom window and into the village street. Burgomaster Schoen was taking a cigar as he walked with his old friend, Doctor Von Niemann, through the thoroughfare.

It was then they heard the young child's shriek.

He dropped his cigar before the two men quickly made way for the living quarters. Foregoing the knock for someone to let them in, Von Niemann thrust his body into the front door, breaking the latch.

"Where are you?" the doctor shouted.

"Help, please help!" a child's voice rang.

They ran up the steps and toward the clamor to find the frantic child, tears running down her face, dripping upon her mother, causing what little blood she had left to trickle from her neck and stain her white bedding.

"Oh, child!" The doctor rushed to her and swooped her from the tragic sight, out the bedroom door and away from the horror.

The burgomaster looked back to the now vacant doorway, then gazed back to the mother that was no doubt dead in her bed. He inched toward her with shattered nerves and a shaking hand. He grabbed her by her chin and rolled her head to the right, exposing the two puncture marks on her neck.

He didn't have to think long. He knew the devil's markings and quickly rebuked Satan and his evil horde that roamed the night, whispering frightened prayers.

Karl Breettschneider had been made aware of the situation and hurried to the scene as quickly as he could. Up the stairs he ran, where he found the burgomaster and Von Niemann studying the victim.

"Doctor, what do you make of it?"

"It's rather strange, Karl." The doctor looked upon him with unsure eyes. "Two markings upon the neck would indicate …"

"… Vampirism!" the burgomaster clamored.

Karl was silent as he looked cynically into the doctor's eyes. "Gentlemen, you surely cannot be serious?"

At that moment, there came shrillness from the street below, and strange laughter followed. Karl rushed to the window to find Herman chasing a young girl in the cobblestone streets with a dead bat.

"Herman!" Karl shouted. "You will stop that this instant!"

Herman shuddered before shouting, "Herman just having fun. Herman sorry."

"Well, for God's sake man, this surely is not the time." Karl scolded.

Herman ran off into an alley. He looked ready to cry.

Karl took a cigarette from his pack and lit it with a match that he struck off the wooden window frame. He took a long drag before blowing out the match and throwing it out the window. He turned back to the two men slowly before taking another elongated draw.

The burgomaster was ill, sick to his stomach. He held his belly before saying, "The doctor has indicated that this woman has been completely drained of her blood. Two marks upon her neck, and that freak is running around the streets with a bat! Question him, Karl, he must be our culprit."

Karl squinted his eyes before blowing smoke toward the dead body. "Herman has been in this village for years, and has never harmed anyone, has never been guilty of a thing."

"Yes, but the devil has found him." The burgomaster was quick to retort. "He is a halfwit, and easily taken by the hand of the devil. Promised great things, only to one day dine with Lucifer in hell."

Doctor Von Niemann was stone-faced and silent as he stared off into nowhere. He couldn't believe how well Emil's deception was working. His only thought was … he had to get back to his lab!

"Gentlemen," the doctor began, "there really isn't more I can do here. This is work for the authorities, and I will leave you to it."

Karl felt in his heart that this wasn't the work of any devil from hell. An earthly devil, perhaps. But why?

"Good day, gentlemen." Doctor Von Niemann went to exit the bedchamber when Karl shouted out, "Oh doctor!"

Von Niemann seemed a bit nervous. He placed his monocle before his right eye as he turned to answer, "Why, yes Karl."

"If you don't mind doctor, I'll be dropping by to see if you have more to enlighten us with this matter," he paused as his eyes lit up. "This murder."

"Why yes, I will be expecting you. Until then, I will retire to my study to investigate my findings."

Karl's look was troubled, as he was no doubt unsure of many things … and perhaps, even of the doctor.

Week after week, body after body, the village became crazed. Mobs now formed and stalked the hillsides carrying torches, while gunshots rang throughout the night. Wolves, wild dogs, and predators of the darkness were snuffed out, then brought back to the local tavern where bounty was paid.

In their minds, they were killing vampires and witches and would eventually kill the one responsible for these heinous acts. Their deaths first and then the life force drained.

While the simple folk drunkenly celebrated their kills, Doctor Von Niemann was far underground in a dank laboratory surrounded by the cold cut-stone walls of his chamber. He had retreated from the Gypsies who were loudly playing their wild Romani music, now focusing on his creation, the sponge-like tissue, which pulsated in its glassed box … held prisoner by his fathomless craft.

His supply of blood was dwindling fast, and he needed more.

Then, to his glee, the old wooden door was knocked upon cryptically, five times. It was the correct pattern and timing, so he crept to the chamber door.

He pressed his body against the entry before hissing with mad gaze, "Who goes there?"

"It is I, doctor. Emil." The muffled voice projected from the other side of the oaken portal.

Von Niemann undid the wrought-iron lock and lifted the latch. With all his body's strength, he slowly inched the door open. He found his servant with dark hat, long black cloak, and blood-stained hands.

"Come in, man. Do not delay!" commanded the doctor.

Emil made way to the stainless-steel table and opened his cape, where five bottles of blood were strapped inside.

The doctor's eyes went wide. "Well done! Just what I needed to continue my work." Von Niemann paused before stomping about his lab while rubbing his clasped hands together. "It will be soon now, Emil. My work is almost complete! You know, Emil, mad is what some might say." The doctor then questioned, "Is one who has solved the secret of life to be considered mad? Life created in the laboratory. No mere crystalline growth, but tissue—living, growing tissue. Life that moves, pulsates and demands food for its continued growth. I tell you, Emil … I have done it!"

Emil was stone-faced and speechless as he set the bottles upon the table. He peered deep into the doctor's wild gaze as the great man practically drooled upon his prize.

Von Niemann then glanced at Emil before saying, "You may retire now. Your work for the night is now done."

The doctor slipped him a money purse before delicately cradling one of his new bottles of blood. Emil turned and left the chamber. Soon thereafter, he heard the doctor latch the heavy door.

He slipped the purse into his pocket, his mind troubled and even more frail from the doctor's supreme control over it. He felt sickness and prestige all at once and hoped one day his name would be held high, with the greatness of the doctors who would eventually give life.

But the murders! As much as he tried, he couldn't come to terms with their control of his soul.

To forget the evils he had committed, he slipped away to the tavern where the Gypsies played their feverish Romanian music. Violins and accordions played, while women danced provocatively before them. The wives of the men hated the Gypsies, whereas the men of the wives loved them.

A dark-haired woman danced before Emil. The men began to clap as she rubbed herself against his body. She was soft and warm, pulsing with life … and with blood. Emil winced and took a long swig of his ale before setting it on the bar. He flipped a coin to the tavern keeper, and another to the Gypsy whore.

Emil could find no comfort and he never cracked a smile. He was emotionless and lifeless. His foretelling of his future had come true, from that dark night when he gazed upon the moon and whispered, *Am I a vampire?* He now truly was.

He slid from his barstool, the Gypsy woman staring deep into his eyes. She could see his tribulation, his struggles, but said not a word, as she shrugged and turned to smile at her next patron.

Curiously, she looked back at Emil as he exited the tavern. She whispered a prayer in her native language for his soul. She might have been a whore, but she was not a devil, nor a murderer, and she could see there was a demon inside him that owned his soul.

That demon's name was Von Niemann.

CHILLERS

Emil walked the dark and lonely streets for several hours before he heard the talk of several men coming from an open window. He recognized the burgomaster's voice and heard Karl Breettschneider. He eased his body beneath the window, then crouched downward out of the vast moonlight, where he eavesdropped on the rather serious conversation.

The burgomaster asked, "How else can we explain these terrible deaths? Six deaths, within as many weeks, Inspector. Our friends, neighbors that we've known for years, drained of their life's blood, found dead in bed, lifeless skeletons. Vampires are at large … this, I tell you!"

THE VAMPIRE BAT PRELUDE
THE PLAYERS
Lionel Atwill as Doctor Otto Von Niemann
Robert Frazer as Emil Borst
Dwight Frye as Herman Gleib
Lionel Belmore as Burgomaster Gustave Schoen
Melvyn Douglas as Karl Breettschneider
and
Fay Wray as Ruth Bertin

About the Author:
Brad A. Braddock is an avid fan of classic cinema and Bela Lugosi. He is the author of *Memoirs of Murder*, a prequel to the 1932 classic, *White Zombie*. He lives in an old log cabin in a remote region of Southwestern Pennsylvania, where he performs experiments in his lab.

He likes to think of himself as Tarzan the Ape Man … but, his wife says he's much more comparable to Tarzan's good friend, Cheetah the Chimpanzee.

Vincent Price as Dr. Robert Morgan, *The Last Man on Earth*

 CHILLERS

They Only Come Out at Night

by Danielle DeVor

{Author's Note: *They Only Come Out at Night* was spawned by a desire to wonder what happened after the events depicted in *The Last Man on Earth*. Morgan's plight, the Gothic state of affairs, and the changed world always fascinated me. Especially the idea that there were vampires and then there were less evolved creatures. Of course, the incomparable Vincent Price gave a wonderful sense to the role of Robert Morgan, and there is no way to top him. So, I created a whole new set of characters set in the same world. I hope you enjoy this homage to Matheson, who penned the original novella, and Price as much as I do.}

"Keep 'em coming!"

The smell of all the unwashed bodies was sour, but I ignored it. I passed the piece of wood I was handed in line onto the next person.

"Come on! We don't want to be here all night. Keep it up!" a man yelled out.

I wasn't sure what he was wanting. The line was moving pretty fast. Guess he thought he was being inspirational or something. I didn't really care. I'd been told to do my part. It didn't matter who I was anymore. It was us versus them.

"Keep 'em coming!"

Pieces of wood were added one by one. It seemed to take forever, but there wasn't a choice. We didn't have any other way to do it. No one had a backhoe or a bulldozer. They were locked up behind a metal fence. That's what I'd been told. Finally, we couldn't add any more wood to the pyre. We all lined up several feet away to watch.

Gordon, the self-proposed leader yelled out, "It is time!"

"Let me go! You don't know what you're doing!" Robert Morgan yelled, while pulling at ropes that bound him.

"We know exactly what we're doing, Mr. Morgan. The same thing you have been doing for months," Gordon stated. The tag was sticking out of the neck of Gordon's black turtleneck. Kind of killed the leadership feeling.

"Let me go!" Morgan shouted.

I didn't know what to think. It wasn't like I knew the man. You didn't get very friendly with people ever since the sickness came. It wasn't smart.

Gordon pulled out a lighter from somewhere and flicked the flint. The flame that came forth was orange and had a nice glow. Gordon tossed the lighter onto the pyre.

The wood started to crackle and smoke. Morgan began screaming. I backed away from the crowd. No one would notice a dumb boy was gone anyway.

I can still hear him at night. His cries. The way his body crackled in the fire. He had become the boogeyman. And now? He was reduced to celluloid.

It started as an experiment, or so I was told. You know how those things go. Rumors pile upon rumors until you don't know what's real or not. The plague, as they called it, was pretty simple. It was some sort of virus that progressed until it passed from species to species in some sort of accelerated replication cycle.

As the rumor went, a vampire bat had bitten Morgan during a research trip. That bat had been infected with a version of the virus that hadn't made the species jump yet. So, by the time it jumped to humans, Morgan was lucky and was immune. Well, if you want to call that lucky, I guess.

When horror legend, Vincent Price, was chosen to play him in film, I was in shock. The real man was not classy. He was more redneck than Shakespearean. But then, they hushed up the outbreak.

There's a reason most of the population is on the coasts.

Morgan had grown up the son of some farmers. Got a scholarship to the state university. He never lost the lilt of twang in his voice. Made it hard to be a scientist, I bet.

I was a teen when it all went down. Just another dumb kid going to school. I had no idea things were about to get all insane. It began with original reports of some new "flu." Of course, no one paid attention to that. Then, there were weird people showing up and knocking on doors.

It wasn't long after that when the government made new rules that all bodies had to be burned in giant pits. Of course, people skirted the rules. That's when the plague really started to spread.

Some families tried to make it to the coast. But the government had put up giant barricades and stationed military that would shoot people on site if they tried to pass through. It was how they kept most of the country's population alive.

This was before the Internet. No social media. Nothing. That's how they got away with it. Editors and newspapers only published the official word from the government. So, most of these things, no one knew about. They were told that many states were under quarantine because of the plague. That was it.

But life moves on. I got older. Things became more normal. I got work. Turned out that I was pretty good at what I did; I had some sort of innate talent for it. When the government came calling, that's when I started the first extermination business.

I had a family to support. And my working for the government helped me keep them safe. Not many of us could afford the black-market vaccine. But now, I had managed to get it for my entire family.

CHILLERS

I wasn't going to lie. I kind of enjoyed the work. It made us a lot of money killing the things. It was dangerous, sure, but if you were careful, there weren't any major problems.

The government hoped to one day make the Midwest and deep South habitable again. To do that, they needed people like me. And honestly, there weren't very many of us who could stomach it.

Kristin. My name is Kristin.

Counting. Everything. I couldn't stop it. Five packages of sugar. Three pieces of paper. One frog figurine. All were things I picked up. Souvenirs, I guess. I couldn't stop myself. I'd tried.

So, I continued counting all of my crap that meant nothing. It wasn't like I would ever use any of it. I couldn't eat any of it. I guess I should be happy I wasn't one of the mindless morons, but my gratitude level had left the building a long time ago.

I wanted a normal life. Wanted to go to school. Worry about who was going to the upcoming dance. Worrying about food all the time put a damper on things.

I couldn't even just meet a boy. No, now meeting one meant letting them know what I was. That never turned out well. Biting someone kind of put a damper on romance. Especially when you couldn't stop and ate them.

I pushed my hair out of my eyes and stared up at the sun. It was a nice day, but blinding. I needed to get away from the house. I'd kept myself locked up too long again. At least when I rode, I felt more alive. I grabbed my bike out of the garage and headed toward town. Not that there was all that much to see in town, but at least it wasn't the same walls day in and day out.

Besides, I needed supplies. Batteries. Some soap. Things weren't so easy to get now that everything was destroyed. It wasn't like I could just go to the store and buy something. *Who had money anyway?*

I got my clothes from abandoned houses. At one time, I would have been grossed out by wearing someone else's clothes. Now, I didn't even bother washing them before I wore them if I pulled them out of a closet.

The voice of the blood used to drive me crazy. It was the voice of the virus, the parasite. It made you think anything you did for blood was okay. Not many of us could keep ourselves in check. It was hardest when I met Lucy.

I was 23. I'd gotten infected a year before I started working there. Lucy wasn't more than 18. She had hair the color of spun gold and a smile that would melt the heart of the worst asshole in the world. I was still early in my extermination days, which pretty much meant I was a loner with a gun and a truck. Everything else I had to wing. She worked as the secretary for my reporting unit. Made sure we were paid. I first saw her smile at Crenshaw, my boss. Then, one day, she smiled at me. How she could smile at a sucker, I'll never know. She said later it was because I had a light in my eyes the others didn't have.

"Hi," Lucy said.

I felt the red rise to my face, "Hi?"

"Want to come to my place on Friday after work? I have some meat rations. I was going to make spaghetti," she said.

I didn't even know if I could eat human food anymore. Hadn't tried in years, "Miss, I sure would love to, but I don't eat."

She smiled softly, "You can still smell, can't you?"

I nodded.

"Well then, I'll make spaghetti, you can remember, and I'll enjoy my dinner with good company."

I later found out that before the plague, she'd been what they would call an "easy woman." Back then, it was more of a stigma. I didn't care though. What did it matter? She was pretty, and she was nice to me. That's all I needed to know.

A captain married us a few short months later.

I saw the sucker right off. She kept squinting, almost as if the sun was blinding, except it was pitch dark out. Nothing to squint at. Her hair was stringy and dirty. Might have been blonde at some point. She was obviously too far gone to know she needed to bathe.

Some evolve to where they remember. Some become stuck somewhere in between. This was one of those. Could remember how to ride a bike but couldn't remember to wash off the dirt. She was a pretty girl at one point. Now, too much dirt to see.

It was weird as he was carefully getting off the bike, making sure the kickstand was solid before leaving. Maybe she wasn't so far off from evolution. But that wasn't his problem. He was paid for bodies. She needed to bite the dust.

I looked over into the park. My son, Josh, was sitting on the bench in the center. Trying to draw more of the bastards out. Two instead of just one would be great. But one was still another down, so I couldn't complain. We just would have to see how the night went.

It helped to have fresh bait. People would think I'm a shit for using my own kid, but it wasn't like I had extra helpers. It was a family business. Plus, Josh was immune. If he got bit, I just had to worry about treating the wound. Nothing too dangerous there. The government gave us free medicine packs to kill off infections. And if we got silver cream on the wound fast enough, infection didn't even set in.

Used to be, we would have had to worry about major physical damage. When they first started, they were really strong, almost superhuman. But as food became more and more scarce, strength lessened. Now, it had gotten to the point where most of the suckers weren't strong enough to overtake a lifer. Plus, he'd trained Josh well. It would be hard for anyone to overtake him.

Sitting on a bench was boring. This was the third night in a row that I played like a nerd. I hadn't been working for dad for long. My brothers started when they were 18. I was the youngest at 16. But since they started their own businesses, Dad had to start using me.

I wasn't scared. He started training me to fight them off as soon as I was old enough to hold onto a stick as a weapon. I wasn't exactly helpless; I just kind of wished I could have been a kid like you read about in books or see in old movies.

Nothing like that was made anymore. People didn't even bother with fantasy. Reality was too vivid. There wasn't any way to forget.

I guess when we get past the plague, things will change. Right now, stuff was too fresh. The wound was still bleeding because the suckers still existed.

There was this one time, when I was about five. Mom was letting me play outside to get some sun. I was just sitting in the front yard, digging in the dirt. I used to do that a lot. Pretend my little cars were how things were before. Like I'd heard my parents talk about. Going to the grocery store. Getting stuck in traffic.

"I can't believe that man took our spot, Debbie," I spoke aloud.

I wheeled the car into an imaginary space beside the other car that had pulled in earlier when I heard a groaning noise.

"Uhh."

I looked up. It was across the street. It had once been a little girl and wore a dress with lace on it. But it was covered in brown muck. I couldn't tell if it was blood or mud or what it was. I didn't want to know.

I looked down at my cars. Toys weren't that easy to come by anymore. Not ones like these. Dad didn't run into them all that often. The blue car had belonged to my brother, Ray. The green one Dad had brought home just three weeks ago.

I needed to go inside, but I didn't want to leave my cars. But I couldn't get up with the cars in my hands.

"Uhh."

It was closer now. Almost to my side of the street. I got up and grabbed my cars, spun around, and tripped. I fell, skinning my knee.

I fought the tears and tried not to cry, but I couldn't help it. It hurt. I started wailing. The thing started moving faster.

"Josh, what's wrong?" Mom had her head poked out the window.

I looked up and pointed toward the little girl.

"Son of a bitch!" In no time, she had her gun pointed out the window and fired.

I looked at the little girl. There was a black dot in the middle of a whiter area on the dress now.

"Uhh."

She was on our yard and kept staggering forward. Her arms were reaching for me now.

"Mom!"

"Josh, duck!"

The gun fired again. This time, Mom got it point blank in the head and it fell down with its hand only a foot away from my shoe.

"Get inside this instant, Josh! No more playing outside."

I ran in and mom locked the door behind me. I forgot about the cars. I never played outside again …

I shook myself back into present reality. There was a rolling, crunching sound on the pavement. I looked up. There was one of them coming toward me riding a bicycle. Game was on. Time to pay attention.

Her being on a bicycle bothered me. It was new and showed a dexterity and physical prowess that was thought to be lost. It made me uneasy. *Was the virus mutating?* I would have to remember to bring a sample back with me.

She rolled to a stop in front of Josh. Almost perfectly handled the bike. It made me nervous. Maybe she wasn't a sucker. Maybe my senses were getting clouded. I was getting older. *Could it be that I was losing my nerve?*

"Aren't you afraid?" she asked Josh.

Josh shook his head. He'd gotten really good at faking. He wasn't a little kid anymore, even with as young as he was. They all grew up faster now. Even faster than I did. Guess it was the nature of things, but damn, sometimes you wish for a better world for your kids.

She stepped a little closer. Hesitant. Not like she was afraid of bolting, but something else. I just wasn't sure what. I sure wasn't telepathic. Josh held his ground. I had to hand it to him for that. Too many others would have flinched by now at least. He was handling this like a pro.

"This is a tough place to live now. Not like it used to be. We all have to be careful," she said.

She seemed like she was making small talk. But then, she would twitch. Still a sucker. Just had better control than most. Maybe a bit more advanced, but still not highly evolved. I started to relax. Things weren't as dire as I thought they were.

"It isn't that bad," Josh replied, "You just have to keep your eyes open and not let yourself get too nervous. I heard about a guy who accidentally broke

CHILLERS

his leg because he saw a shadow coming out from behind a building. It was his dog." Josh crossed his arms in front of his chest.

I leaned back against the truck and waited.

Josh had a knife in a holster under his arm. Smart to get near the weapon just in case he needed it. Things were going as planned now.

Josh was careful not to wrinkle his nose at the stench of the woman. You couldn't show them fear. It triggered the feed response. Dad explained it like this—if you acted normal, they may or may not know you are like them. He'd seen a group of suckers attack a weaker looking sucker. If you acted scared, they knew for sure you weren't like them, ensuring attack.

She might have been pretty if she'd been clean. Now though, she was a horror. Covered in some sort of gunk and looked like she hadn't bathed in years. Bacteria had to be crawling all over her. She didn't have any black stuff on her, which was promising. The black stuff was usually rotten blood. His father had told him about one he'd found that was bathing in the stuff. He didn't even want to imagine that stink.

She wore a flannel shirt, jeans, and an old pair of white tennis shoes. She said, "It's not like how it used to be. Now, most of the time, it's quiet. I like to take time to myself."

I breathed out of my mouth, so I wouldn't gag. Wiped my hands on my pants, trying to make my nervous look like normal nervous and not "attack" sweat, "What's your name?"

I silently cursed myself. They didn't always remember their name. Dad would yell at him about that later.

"Kristin. Yours?"

"Josh," I said and stopped it at that.

I needed to be careful. Regular small talk was tricky. I made sure not to mention the time of day to her. To suckers, night looked like day and day looked like night, so it was best to keep specifics out of it; less of a chance of giving himself away. I'd already messed up once. Best not to do it again.

Everything about this one was a little off. Suckers didn't usually stand there and talk to you. Especially not ones of her level. The smarter ones, if they were fine with being around livers, usually just did their job and spoke least as possible. That's how he'd been early on.

But this girl, she wasn't far enough evolved to work with people. And her standing there, talking to his son, made him want to just take her out with the crossbow and be done with it. But if he was somehow wrong, and she was a liver, they'd kill him. And then, who knew where his family would be.

I grabbed the crossbow from the bed of the truck and loaded an arrow, just in case. I wasn't willing to take too many chances. I'd learned that when you feel something was wrong, you paid attention. If he'd done that, his wife would still be with him.

It happened last year. Lucy started getting tired easier than usual. She would take naps during the day when she never had before. She got paler …

"Hon, are you sure you're feeling okay?" I knew enough to ask. I didn't get sick like humans did.

"I'm just getting older. I'll be all right," Lucy said.

I wasn't so sure, but the look on her face told me to drop it. I knew she hated going to doctors, but sometimes, it was worth the expense.

Two days later, I found her passed out on the floor when I came home from work. There was a small amount of blood coming out of her mouth. It took me three hours to get her to the hospital.

"I'm sorry. I didn't mean to get sick," Lucy said.

"Lucy—don't you worry about it. I'm worried about you. Nothing else."

She started to cry, and I grabbed her in my arms. When I pulled away, my shirt was wet from her tears.

We found out later that she had stage-four lung cancer. The doc said he figured it was from the leftovers of the crap they had dumped in the air to try to kill off the plague. It didn't work. The suckers still walked, thus why I had a job and was still alive.

She lived another four months.

I cursed Dad silently for making me dress like a nerd. Khaki pants and a button up shirt. Guess it helped draw them in if they thought I was weak. But I really wanted to wear something else for a change. It wasn't like I was trying to pick anyone up, but I hated being looked at as weak. It was important to be strong, but Dad's word was law.

I did all the things I was told were best. Like, before hunting, I also made sure not to take a bath for a few days, so the bacteria were the stronger smell. Made me stink a bit more like them. I couldn't go longer than that, but Dad has said it was enough. It wasn't about being perfect. Just good enough to get close.

Suddenly, she leaned in close and did that weird sniffy thing that sounded like a chatter.

I froze, and then backed away; I knew better than to sniff him. I might have just ruined it all.

Good one. Just give yourself away like an idiot. If I wanted people to talk to, I was going to have to stop giving in to my temptations.

He didn't run and stayed seated on the bench. I kept watching, but he stayed perfectly still. *Did he have a death wish?*

"I'm sorry," I said.

     CHILLERS

He was being nice to me and I was completely blowing it. He was a normal boy. Part of me hoped I could somehow manage to have my fantasy of someone to share my life with. A fantasy I thought had died.

He looked up at me with big blue eyes; I felt myself melting more and more. I wanted to have him with me.

"You aren't going to hurt me, are you?" he asked.

"I'm going to try not to," I said.

I hadn't meant to tell the truth. I wanted to keep the fantasy going longer, but I knew it wasn't going to happen. Maybe I could just bite him and let him go. Then, he'd be like me. I could control myself long enough not to drain him. Maybe. I could find food elsewhere. Let him become like me. It was even more of a fantasy than me living with him. I never had that type of control.

"What do you mean by try?" he asked.

His body was tense now. His muscles were taught underneath his shirt. He moved slightly.

Then, my nose caught his smell. I twitched.

THWACK!

"Dad, you got me in the eye, dammit."

I walked over and handed Josh a handkerchief. Her body had fallen over in a heap, with an arrow straight through the skull. My aim was spot on. "Eh, it's just a little blood," I said.

"I still don't like it in my eye."

I looked down at the body. The arm bucked and settled again, "We got a twitcher!"

Josh ran over to the truck and grabbed the flamethrower. I kept the crossbow aimed on her with another arrow loaded. Josh came back and doused the fucker in flames. Soon, the body was a crispy critter. The smell of cooked half rotten meat settled in the air. It was dead for sure now. There was no sense in wasting another arrow.

I couldn't get the look of the girl's face out of my head. Her mouth was in mid-smile when the arrow hit.

"That's just fine. You bailin' on me now, boy?"

Dad looked pissed. I didn't need that today too. It was already bad enough being upset over a kill; I didn't need yelled at. I shook my head, "Just because they are dead doesn't mean they weren't once someone's daughter."

I knew I'd stepped in it. Just said something that would earn me a lecture. *I knew they were dangerous, but wasn't there some way to show them respect for what they were? That their lives mattered somehow?*

"Josh, that's how it spread. That's exactly why. All over them, someone's mother, son, sister, brother … father. It all sucks. That's why we work. Until the plague is totally eradicated, we have to. There is no one else. No other answer. Before memorials can be made, we have to make the ones left living safe. In order to do that, we have to kill all these things."

I sat down on the tailgate of the truck and peeled off the straps for the flamethrower. I was going to have to throw away the clothes. They were dotted in blood. "Doesn't mean you can't have compassion."

Dad put his hands on the truck and squeezed. Then, he stared at me, "You think you can be all high and mighty because you're immune. Did you know the vaccine isn't 100 percent effective? I sat, sweating, waiting to see how you and your brothers would react to it. I knew a guy whose kid collapsed into convulsions as soon as the vaccine was administered. He died. Others think they are fine, but the first time they get bit, they start to turn. Life isn't a guarantee."

"Well, scientifically, you cannot have 100 percent probability. It is impossible because of too many factors."

"And the government controls what science is published. So, unless you know more than I do, I suggest you stop that attitude. You make my head hurt." He rubbed his hand over his face. "You know what keeps me awake at night, Mr. Know-it-all?"

I looked down at my feet and then back up at dad, "What?"

"Viruses mutate."

They had strung him up on a pyre. *Why?* Because Morgan had the gall to kill them instead of trying to help them.

How do you help a leech? Doesn't matter how nice it is to you. Doesn't matter where you touch it. The leech will bite you. Then, you gotta try to pry the fucker off. Get too many leeches, and you'll ex-sanguinate. And, leeches carry disease. Parasites. You get bit and it ain't over.

Morgan was a hero. Kind of like Vlad the Impaler. He tried to keep his life and home out of insanity. He failed. But, that was life. The insanity was still brewing. And, it was too late for the others to realize Morgan was right. By the time the government had figured it out, almost the entire country was gone.

The United States went from a population of about 180 million to about 500,000. That's how many non-infected there were now. We were slowly making our way through the suckers, but it was slow. A process. You had to draw them out of their hiding places. Morgan had known that. And he'd been damn good at it. They estimate he took out over 5,000 suckers by himself. If he'd had a crew, maybe so many people wouldn't have died. *If they hadn't killed him and had listened, what would things be like?* No one will ever know.

"Dad?"

I looked over at him. He seemed scared. I looked around. No other suckers, "What son?"

     CHILLERS

"Your eyes look funny."

"Like what?" I wasn't crazy about this conversation, but I'd known it was coming. Just like it had with the kids before him.

"Weird. Like a kind of milky sheen to them. You okay?"

I sighed. Just hoped he wouldn't be too upset. I loved him. He was my youngest and last kid. Probably wouldn't ever have another. Women like Lucy were rare, "They always do in the dark. You want to know why else I got you the vaccine?"

Josh hopped up into the back of the truck and started backing away from me. This is what I'd been afraid of. My own son scared to death of me.

"Right there. That's why. You know now. It's in case I lose control. Don't worry about that none. I've been like this for many years. I've never made a mistake. Never bit your mother. Your brothers know. You just finally got old enough to learn the truth."

"But, how can you? How can you kill them? They're your own kind," Josh said.

I threw open the door to the truck and hopped in. His heart was gonna get him killed someday, "You comin' or not?"

A couple minutes passed. Soon, he climbed out of the back and got in on the passenger's side. He kept his head facing forward, not looking at me.

"How many?"

I twitched, "How many what?"

"How many have you killed?" he asked.

There was this earnest look in his eyes. The same one he had every time he'd promised me when he was a kid that he would be a good boy.

I leaned back and laughed. Used to be, soldiers were the only ones really asked that question. How times have changed. "Which ones, leeches or humans?"

He bowed his head. I felt bad for laughing. He was just so innocent. I forgot what it was like. I started the truck, "Probably best you don't know. But, one thing you're forgetting kiddo."

"What's that?"

I released the emergency brake and put the truck in gear. Then, I looked over at him. His eyes were a little glassy. He needed perspective, "You're a killer. Already are. What's worse, me killing my own kind or you killing the type of thing your father is? Stew on that for a while."

I drove out of town and headed toward home. We had to get ready to do it again tomorrow. It was what my family did.

Robert Morgan. Redneck scientist who ended up killing vampires. Immortalized by a horror icon on celluloid.

He was my uncle.

About the Author:

Named one of the *Examiner's 2014 Women in Horror: 93 Horror Authors you Need to Read Right Now*, Danielle DeVor has been spinning the spider webs, or rather, the keyboard for more frights and oddities. She spent her early years fantasizing about vampires and watching *Salem's Lot* way too many times. When not writing and reading about weird things, you will find her hanging out at the nearest coffee shop, enjoying a mocha Frappuccino. Visit her at http://www.danielledevor.com

Witches and the supernatural run amok in *Haxan* (1922).

 CHILLERS

Hasten
A Prelude to Haxan
by Christine M. Soltis

{Author's note: *Haxan*, a 1922 Swedish-Danish silent horror film by Benjamin Christensen, inspired this short story. While there are many wonderful classic horror films, I wanted to do something different and focus on a different *kind* of monster. Witches.

The story of *Haxan* itself was a controversial piece and was banned due to its graphic nature, even though it was meant to be a documentary. It is known for having special effects that were ahead of its time, which is evident when you see witches flying on the silver screen.

For me, I have always had a fascination with witches, and having recently visited Salem, Massachusetts again, I was ready to write another witch story. While there were time constraints for me during the creation of this story, I wanted to focus on the medieval witch ointment that was sought after and was allegedly powerful enough to make regular women fly. I also recently ordered and received a translated copy of the *Malleus Maleficarum*, or the *Hammer of Witches (1486)*, which I am highly excited to read.

In the Middle Ages, witchcraft was considered to be a result of a pact with the devil. In my story rendition, I wanted to show that a witch would actually commit an evil act if aligned with the devil and could actually *get away* with it. So many of those in our history who were wrongly accused and considered to be witches did not actually commit an evil act when they were prosecuted, hanged, stoned or even burned for being "witches." It has always been in my opinion that an actual witch with a devilish pact to be evil would never be caught, and I have expressed this in my story.}

Levyla.
Levyla, the only real, known witch that had a pact with the devil.
Inside of her small stone cottage, the witch's thick arms swayed left to right, back and forth and then in a circular pattern, as she stirred the black cauldron brew. The witch used her broom upside down to stir the contents, for medieval times were tough, tools were scarce, and even her clothing told of her poverty level. Her brown dress was like deteriorated rags, covering her thick form all the way to her toes.

The witch's body was akin to two pumpkins plopped together as she swayed back and forth. Her round, elderly face comprised a smaller pumpkin that was lumped on top of a larger pumpkin shape to compose her body. A brown piece of cloth hid her hair from her face and she squinted as she smiled and stirred. Dark brown eyes widened with delight as her pointed nose twitched back and forth, up and down, with each silent facial movement. The crinkles around the witch's lips deepened as words then sang from her dry, cracked lips.

"Witches ointment! Hasten! The finest in the land," she chanted with a toothless grin, "Come to me, all, where we shall be, and where the devil holds your hand. Hasten!"

Levyla closed her eyes and from her mind, she summoned all of her powers into her brew. She felt energy coursing through her wide chest, coming together like electricity down her arms and connecting with the broom as she swayed and stirred, swayed and stirred. Her fingertips tingled as her mind made the contents of the cauldron bubble slightly, while singing her magical incantations. The fire below the cauldron sparked and sizzled in reaction to her magic.

From an open window far behind the witch, the devil appeared; his face existed as a large, white, pointed mask in the light as he bounced into view. The devil could feel the evil energies of the witch as she created the witch's ointment. He roared with delight as he thought of the upcoming Witches Sabbath and the creation of even more witch pacts with the devil himself.

The witch was too deep into her spells to be disturbed by the devil's joy.

The devil's face stiffened and then turned to an orangish glow; he sensed an opportunity for evil in the neighboring streets. The devil disappeared outside to take a peek at what roamed in the night.

Less than an hour later, the witch's ointment was complete.

With one swift, gray breath, Levyla blew out the flames underneath the cauldron. She removed her broom from the cauldron and rested it against the wall as she allowed the ointment to cool.

The witch waddled to a nearby oval shaped stone table and looked over her remaining ingredients; there were some fat children left that had been dug up from the graves, some *conium maculatum*, also known as poisonous hemlock; *datura stramonium* also known as the devil's snare or jimsonweed and her favorite, atropine. There were plenty of ingredients left if the devil preferred another batch of the witch's ointment for the upcoming ceremony.

Levyla smiled and sat on a wicker chair. She laid her head on the wall, preparing to take a brief nap as the ointment cooled. Just as she began to fall asleep, there was a rapping sound at the front door that echoed through the halls.

Tap, tap.

The witch jumped up in alert and went to grab her broom.

Tap! Tap! Tap!

There was a sense of urgency as someone rapped against the front door and window.

Levyla left her broom and went alone to the arch shaped, wooden front door. She looked out the window just to see a middle-aged woman standing there with a small brown pouch in her hand. The woman had shoulder length brown hair that was mostly obscured under a beige hood.

The witch looked the woman over through the window with distrust. The woman looked up, as if sensing Levyla's presence, and held the brown pouch up to the window. Levyla knew there were coins inside the pouch and, reluctantly, the witch opened the door. Through scarce light, Levyla could see desperation in the woman's brown eyes.

"Please, let me in," the woman pleaded, "My name is Marion Gray and I need to purchase a love potion. I am sick, I am lovesick and my love does not even see me. Please, witch, I know you can help me. I need him to love me too."

Levyla did not say a word. Her eyes glanced at the pouch. Levyla put her hand out and the woman, Marion, placed the pouch into the witch's hand.

"It is all that I have," Marion said, "But it is worth it to me to have love."

The witch looked into the pouch, which contained five gold coins. Levyla's eyes widened and she stepped back to let Marion inside.

"Thank you, thank you," Marion said.

Marion stepped inside of the cottage and looked around, observing that the witch's chambers looked much like the inside of a sandstone cave. A strange, orange light seemed to illuminate every corner but there was no visible torchlight or source.

Once inside, Marion followed the witch down the sandstone corridor to a large, open room. An oval shaped stone table held several questionable herbs and ingredients, but what caught Marion's eyes was the large black cauldron of thick, gray-white looking blubber.

"Is that the love potion?" Marion asked.

Her eyes grew wide with wonder as she stared at the cauldron while considering just how much her love interest, Michal Roman, would want her once he tasted that much potion.

The witch began to shake her head "no" but then stopped. She looked up and to her left, where she saw the devil peeking through the back window, with a quiet grin and smirk upon his face.

"Yes, yes, that is the love potion," Levyla said to Marion, while winking her left eye at the devil.

The witch turned to Marion then, "I have just cooked up a fresh pot of it. You are in luck."

Marion smiled, laughed, giggled and cried all at once.

"I am so happy," Marion cried, "He is such a pious man and I love him. I cannot wait for him to see how much he loves me too," she said.

Levyla found a flask and began to scoop up the witch's ointment with her broom end into the flask opening. The witch continued until the flask was full and then placed the cap on tight. The witch wiped some of the overspill onto her ragged clothes and then handed the flask to Marion.

The witch stuck out her pointed finger as she provided instructions, "Make sure to put this potion into your love interest's food or drink and make sure that they take all of it. At the same time, pour some for yourself too and take a hearty swig. This will ensure that you are both taking in the potion. Otherwise, the potion will not work. You both must take it."

Marion smiled as she grasped the flask, "I can never thank you enough for finally ending my days of loneliness," she wept.

"The pleasure is mine," Levyla slyly shrieked, as she turned to show Marion to the door.

Levyla waddled forward, holding a toothless grin the entire time. Marion exited the witch's cottage and skipped all the way home. The witch watched her leave and then went back inside.

The devil was still peering through the back window and busted into roaring laughter as Levyla waddled back into the room. The witch matched his laughter with a high pitched, shrieking intensity.

Witch's ointment could make you fly, if externally applied, but consumption of the toxic ointment had one result … Death.

The next day, Marion Gray giggled as she cooked breakfast for her master, a pious monk by the name of Michal Roman. Marion doused her love interest's cup with love potion while setting her own matching cup right beside it.

As she served her master, she watched him eat and drink heartily as she chugged her own mug of milk and potion. Both of them simultaneously spit out the ingredients after the first sip. But it was too late. Some of the toxic potion had been ingested.

Marion and Michal writhed pathetically; their bodies convulsing from their heads to their limbs, all the way to their toes.

The devil's freakish white face and body appeared in the room, cloaked in a smile as he waited for their souls to pass. The devil grabbed Marion's writhing body and began to dance with her, pulling out her arms as she twitched like a puppet doll. The devil spun her around then threw her to her love, Michal, who was now dead, face-first onto the table. Marion fell onto the back of his chair as she died, with her head striking the floor and her body looping over the chair so that her feet touched the ground.

The devil stopped and laughed. He took the remaining flask of witch's ointment and rubbed his finger inside to pull out a small amount. The devil rubbed the ointment across his back to test it out. He stepped to the window and jumped, just to fly into the air without using his own powers.

The witch's ointment worked!

The pacts would be secured.

Tonight, was the Witches Sabbath. Beautiful women would come in hoards for a chance to fly with the witch's ointment.

The feast, the dance, the sex!

The devil could not wait.

Hasten!

About the Author:

Christine M. Soltis wrote her first novel circa 2002-2003. She has crafted 22 books at this time, most of which are available on Amazon.com.

Recent releases include, *The Keeper of the Blackland* (2018); *Final Moon* Re-Release (2018); *Estranged Decisions* Re-Release (2018) and *Transference* (2016), among others.

Christine runs an arts business, SolsticeNightSky Productions & Radio, which can be found on Facebook. She is also a Private Investigator. Her days consist of constant travel, investigating, writing, editing, reading, events, networking and otherwise trying to create more time out of time.

Dr. Waldman (Edward Van Sloan) demonstrates the "normal brain" and the "dysfunctio cerebri" or dysfunctional brain from *Frankenstein* (1931).

Dysfunctio Cerebri
by Dwight Kemper

{Author's note: For years I would watch *Frankenstein* and wonder about those naked feet sticking out from under the torn sheet. Dr. Waldman would indicate the dead man before us, whose life was one of brutality, of violence, and murder. I always wondered who that subject was. Who donated the Monster's brain? This story is my answer to that question.}

A den of thieves is just what the nondescript bar in the most notorious part of Goldstadt was. Not that this discouraged the medical students of the nearby university from experiencing the seedier side of life first hand. But Herr Frankenstein was not here to get a sample of the local color. He cared not at all for the garishly painted ladies of the night, nor the buxom barmaids, nor the smoke-filled atmosphere. No, he and his hunchbacked assistant Fritz were here for a different kind of assignation. At one of the darkly lit booths was the objective of this little get-together. He was a tall, gaunt man with gray hair, a twisted smile, and an oily demeanor. Frankenstein sat opposite him in the booth. "Grimm?" he asked the gaunt gentleman, who flashed Frankenstein a twisted smile, "Grimm's the name," he lisped. "Grimm by name, and Grimm by reputation."

Fritz hovered at Frankenstein's side, cowering at the piercing gaze those heavy-lidded eyes of Grimm flashed him. "And who is this charming gent?" Grimm asked.

"This is my laboratory assistant, Fritz." Frankenstein grew impatient. He ran his fingers through oily coal-black hair and stared with equal intensity at the man. "Is it true that you ... procure specimens for Goldstadt Medical University?"

"You mean, am I a grave robber? That is my occupation, kind sir." Grimm took a sip of his whiskey. "And is it true that you ... left the University to experiment on you own?"

Frankenstein eyed Grimm narrowly. "How do you know about that?"

"In my line of work, it pays to keep one's ear to the door, particularly if there's extra work to be had. That is why you arranged this little *tete-a-tete*, is it not?"

"What I need are bodies. The fresher the better," replied Frankenstein.

"Male or, uh, female?" asked Grimm.

"Male. For now."

"And how fresh?"

"Preferably no more than three days old."

Grimm paused to consider this, scratching his lantern jaw. "Now that's a tall order, Herr Frankenstein, a very tall order. People 'round here have been unusually healthy of late. Although *accidents* do occur. Which leaves me the question of the condition of the bodies."

"Any damage will prove to be of no importance. I plan to ... use the best parts."

"I see. So, what you're interested in is dissection and all that?"

"Something like that, yes." Frankenstein leaned in. "Can you do it?"

"Can you pay?"

"Of course, I can. The fresher the subjects, the greater the reward."

Grimm nodded in the direction of Fritz. "Do you suppose your assistant would be interested in acting as a lookout? I can always use a second pair of eyes."

Frankenstein repressed a smile. He could use a second pair of eyes as well, but not as a lookout. "Well, Fritz?"

Fritz shivered with apprehension. "You mean sneak around in graveyards in the dead of night?"

Grimm smiled reassuringly. "You needn't be frightened. The dead make good, if not terribly garrulous, company." Adding with a chuckle, "And after all, every Burke needs a Hare."

Frankenstein glared at his assistant. "Go on. There's nothing to be afraid of."

Fritz reluctantly nodded his head. "When do we do it?" he asked Grimm in a hissing whisper.

"No time like the present." Grimm finished his drink. "I know of a body of a freshly hanged lad not a mile from here." He asked Frankenstein, "And where are the items to be delivered, Herr Frankenstein?"

"Do you know the abandoned old watchtower on the hill overlooking the town?"

"I do indeed."

"You will meet me there. Tonight. Payment on delivery."

"Excellent!" Grimm motioned to Fritz. "Let's go, lad. I hope you're a good climber."

It wasn't long before Fritz found himself a passenger of Grimm's horse drawn cart. In the bed were old blankets and ropes, along with other tools of the trade, shovels and picks, etc. A lantern hung from a pole by the buckboard.

"Considering your master's interests, you certainly are a nervous sort." Grimm observed.

"I can smell the ghosts already!" Fritz said with a shudder.

"There it is," Grimm said, pointing ahead at the silhouette of a gallows and hanged man in bold relief against the gray evening sky.

     CHILLERS

Pulling back on the reins, Grimm maneuvered the cart, so its bed was directly beneath the hanging corpse. Handing Fritz the knife, Grimm pointed at the gruesome prize. "Climb up and cut the rope."

Reluctantly, Fritz did as he was told. The body landed in the bed of the cart with a dull thud. Grimm hurried around to cover the body with the blankets. Mounting the buckboard, he smiled at the nervous dwarf. "Now wasn't that easy? Like taking candy from a baby. Easier than unearthing a coffin, let me tell you."

"I wish you wouldn't."

It was on their way up the winding path that led to the watchtower that Grimm and Fritz happened upon a tramp walking along the side of the road in the opposite direction. Pulling up to him, Grimm asked pleasantly, "Where are you bound, my good man?"

"Goldstadt," the Tramp replied.

"As it happens, that's just where we're going after I make a delivery. Would you care for a lift?" Fritz was about to protest, when Grimm shushed him curtly.

Smiling, the tramp hurried around to the back of the cart and climbed into the bed. "Many thanks, brother!" he said. It was then that he felt the outstretched lump beneath the blankets. No sooner had he uncovered the corpse's pale face that a lead gat connected with the tramp's skull, killing him instantly. "He said he wanted 'em fresh," Grimm explained to Fritz, adding with quiet menace as he covered his latest prize, "I'm sure I can rely on you to remain discreet."

Fritz nodded nervously.

Herr Frankenstein was the perfect customer, as it turned out. Although a freshly bleeding corpse would have raised suspicions, he seemed inclined to ignore such paltry details in favor of worthwhile materials.

In the coming weeks, Fritz and Grimm would visit morgues, charnel houses, and dig up the occasional freshly made grave. And as they made their deliveries, Fritz would nervously describe just what Herr Frankenstein was doing with those bodies. This piqued Grimm's interest no end. He was not a scientifically minded man, but he had been around enough of them to piece together the nature of Frankenstein's experiments. And piece together was the right expression, because it seemed Herr Frankenstein was building a whole body from the bits and pieces Grimm had supplied. Given time, there might be blackmail money to be had. But for now, he was content to ply his trade.

"CHILD MURDERER AT LARGE" read the fliers posted to every vacant lamppost and fence in town. The victims were all little girls. At first the police thought they were accidental drownings. The Goldstadt coroner never found a trace of sexual assault. But the death of six little girls over a period of three months, could all of them be from accidental drowning? That was too much of a coincidence in a town with such a small population. What the coroner didn't know was that not *all* the victims were found washed up on the shore of the lake. Nearly a quarter of them found their way onto the dissecting slabs of Goldstadt Medical College. All of them supplied by Grimm, who fancied himself something of a pied piper when it came to charming little girls into his murderous web. He would use his horse to gain their trust, then suggest a game that took them well out of sight of their parents or guardians, and then spring his trap. It gave him a thrill to lead the little ones to their deaths, all under the pretext of a harmless game. But he never raped them. Oh, he wanted to, surely, but there was a part of him, possible a glimmer of a conscience, that made him feel that was going a bit far. He derived more than enough release through the simple act of drowning them. And what little girls he didn't let the river claim only added to his coffers, thanks to Dr. Waldman and the other professors at the university who were grateful to have child corpses for the medical students to examine. Grimm was amused by the idea that if there were a rape committed on these young innocents, they were committed by none other than the learned men of science. My, how that tickled him!

But now things were heating up, and Grimm decided that his favorite pastime would have to wait. Then it occurred to him that if the good people of Goldstadt got too itchy to find a poor soul to pin the deeds upon, perhaps Fritz was as worthy a scapegoat as any. It was during one of their frequent nights out looking for bodies that this notion first presented itself. Grimm gave Fritz a quick glance, sizing him up as a possible child murderer.

"Why are you looking at me like that?" Fritz asked nervously.

"No reason, friend Fritz," Grimm said reassuringly. "No reason at all."

Grimm snapped the reins and the horse quickened his pace.

It was during a night at the dank tavern that Grimm got careless. He had had too much cognac and his mouth began boasting of his prowess providing cadavers for a young scientist. Two gendarmes were at the bar hoisting a few when they overheard Grimm's boasting.

"May we have a word?" one said, as they surrounded the body snatcher.

"Why, certainly, officer," Grimm smiled. Catching one of the Gendarmes off guard, he gave him a swift kick to the solar plexus and made a run for the exit. The denizens of the tavern knew what to expect and ducked for cover as shots rang out and Grimm's body hit the filthy floor with a thud. The Goldstadt coroner collected the body and soon Grimm found himself on a marble slab with gold water running from an overhead pipe on his face, to keep him from decomposing. It was then that Dr. Waldman came by.

"I beg your pardon," Waldman asked the night attendant. "I am from the Medical University and I'm in need of, well, for want of a better term, a criminal brain."

"For what purpose, Sir?" asked the attendant.

"Instructional. In a few days I'll be giving a lecture on the differences between a normal and an abnormal brain of a typical criminal. I was hoping you might have such a specimen."

"I don't know, Sir," the attendant hesitated. "Any criminal type would need to be examined by the coroner." He held out his hand and cleared his throat.

Waldman smiled as he reached into his pocket. "Of course." He produced 50 crowns and placed them in the attendants waiting hand.

The attendant smiled. "As it happens, Sir, I know just the chap for your lecture." He led Waldman into the morgue proper and to the naked, stretched out body of Grimm. "This one's a thoroughly bad sort, Sir. Body snatcher, murderer, maybe even the child killer, I shouldn't wonder.

Waldman tried not to let on that he recognized Grimm as the chief supplier of cadavers. It probably would be for the best if the body were ... disposed of. "He will do nicely," Waldman said. He quickly got his student helpers to wrap the body in a burlap sheet and quickly hustled into the back of a waiting van.

"What's become of Grimm?" Herr Frankenstein asked Fritz testily. He paced the floor of the watch tower, pausing to look out the grate covered peep hole in the heavy wooden door. "He's usually here by now! I only need a few minor pieces to complete my work." He glared at his assistant. "Did he say anything to you?"

"No," Fritz answered, flinching and shaking his head adamantly. "He never even came to see me to go with him."

"Well, we can't wait any longer!" Frankenstein insisted. "There's a body being buried in the cemetery tonight. And there's a hanged man that will do well enough for a donor brain. If Grimm won' supply them, we'll have to go ourselves!"

And so, Frankenstein and Fritz became their own grave robbers. First digging up a freshly interred body. "He's just resting," Frankenstein said, patting the coffin. "Waiting for a new life to come!" Fritz again climbed the gallows and cut down a hanged man. Only, for Frankenstein to discover, "The neck's broken. The brain is useless. We must find another brain!"

It was then that Fritz was sent to the university to obtain a perfect cerebral specimen. Frankenstein had heard of Waldman's upcoming lecture concerning the normal versus the criminal brains. Fritz climbed up to the window of the operating theater and watched as Waldman presided over a sheet-covered corpse.

"Here we have the finest specimen I've ever had the good fortune to come across," he said, using a pencil to indicate the jar with the normal brain.

He then directed his student's attention to the jar marked, "DYSFUNC-TIO CEREBRI."

"And here we have the abnormal brain of the typical criminal. Note the degeneration of the frontal lobe, and the distinct degeneration of the middle frontal lobe. This matches the case history of the subject before us, whose life was one of brutality, of violence and murder! Both these jars will remain for your further inspection."

The torn sheet covered Grimm's naked feet as the attendants wheeled out the stretcher carrying the grave robber's body to the furnaces, where it would be cremated. Grimm's life had come to an end.

At least, his former life as a human being was done.

Henry Frankenstein (Colin Clive) and Fritz (Dwight Frye) dig up another grave to retrieve body parts for Henry's experiments from *Frankenstein*.

Anton Phibes without the "Vincent Price" makeup and wig

CHILLERS

Dr. Phibes' Overture
by Brad A. Braddock

{Author's note: Vincent Price as "the abominable" Dr. Phibes, and the beautiful Virginia North as Vulnavia, his lovely assistant who doesn't mind the sight of blood, make a wonderfully macabre on-screen duo. After Dr. Phibes' wife doesn't survive the operating table, Dr. Phibes blames the surgeons that failed her, and in poetic fashion, visits death upon those that he holds responsible for her demise. The film is notorious for its dark humor and wit, and it does not fail to be horrific at times. It's one of my favorite Vincent Price films. My favorite death scene is when Dr. Phibes helps one of the poor doctors at a masquerade party by tightening his frog mask … unfortunately for the doctor, the mask becomes a little too tight around his neck.

My short story gives a backdrop to when the doctor first encounters the beautiful Vulnavia. I certainly do hope you like it. Enjoy.}

1921 Switzerland. Anton Phibes rushed down the mountainous, winding roads of the Swiss Alps. He was on holiday with several of his friends, composers of works of genius—as Anton would call them—when he had to leave immediately.

He was reached by family that his wife had fallen terribly ill and was to be operated on promptly. The wheels of his Mercedes Benz squealed as Phibes hugged the bends. He was breathing heavily as he headed for the airport. One last plane was flying from Switzerland back to England that night, and he had to make it.

It was possible that this was the last time he may ever see his darling wife.

Dr. Phibes was almost to the bottom of the steep mountain when his tire blew, causing him to go over an embankment before striking a large tree. He was thrown through the windshield, his face catching on the glass before being torn completely off. With no face left, he crawled from the wrecked automobile as it caught fire. Shortly after, the car exploded and remnants of it rained upon him, one piece of metal striking his head, causing him to pass out.

When he awoke, he was bandaged and in the bed of an unknown home. A beautiful young woman sat by his side, as if to comfort him. She was silent and never spoke a word. In turn, Dr. Phibes' vocal cords had been torn out, causing him to be her silent partner.

She pointed to his driver's license and smiled at him. She pretended that she was playing an organ, indicating that she knew very well who he was. She lipped the words … *I love you.*

Dr. Phibes could make out what she was trying to say, but at the moment he was rather unimpressed. He was frantic of his wife's condition, if she was alive or dead. His heart raced from the pain he was in. He reached to his bandages and began to tear them off.

Vulnavia stopped him. She grabbed hold of his hands and shook her head no. Dr. Phibes stopped and she administered a needle with a clear liquid. Morphine, and within a few minutes, Dr. Phibes passed out.

When Dr. Phibes awoke, he found a chalkboard setting next to his bed, along with a glass of water and two small white pills. Out of the corner of his eye he caught Vulnavia in the doorway, gazing at him. She motioned with her hand for him to take the medication.

He wrote on the chalkboard: *my wife?*

Vulnavia walked to the board and wrote underneath it: *No more.*

Phibes threw the chalk against the wall and hung his head in his hands. She picked up the chalk and wrote: *I'm sorry for your loss, but I'm here to help and take care of you.*

Phibes cried as he looked into her eyes. She hugged him. Even without a face, she loved him.

Weeks turned into months; before long, several years had passed. Dr. Phibes used his intelligence to reconstruct his face using prosthetics that Vulnavia had brought him. Through his knowledge of acoustics, he had a microphone system that allowed him to communicate with Vulnavia with his voice. He had gained it back, and it was one of the few things that still made him happy.

He and Vulnavia sat by the crackling fire of her little stone cottage one night. They shared brandy and he talked to her. She loved to hear his stories when he was a famous concert organist.

He held the microphone to his neck. "I played the greatest halls in all of England." He sipped his brandy. He became a bit poetic when he thought back to the death of his wife. Vulnavia was not jealous when he went into his fits about the surgeon's incompetence. The doctors that he felt killed his lovely wife.

Vulnavia went to her chalkboard and wrote the word: *Vengeance.*

He squinted at her through his prosthetic face. "Nine shall die. The plagues visited upon Egypt shall be my inspiration."

Phibes had taught Vulnavia how to play the violin, and she took it and sat by the fire. She began to play a melancholy tune as he went on with his madness.

"Nine shall die by the hands of vengeance. Those that claimed my wife will rot. The plagues that visited Egypt will find these heathens that claimed my wife's soul."

Vulnavia took the brandy from him and looked deep into his eyes. She then led him to her bedchamber to comfort him. She loved the doctor.

When Phibes awoke the next morning, he had a slight headache from the amount of brandy he drank. His prosthetic face had fallen off, and he was frantic to put it back on before Vulnavia returned to bed. As he was starting to put himself back together, she stepped in the doorway, and froze still. The doctor was frantic and motioned for her to get away. Instead, she walked to his side and took the false face from his hands. He fought her at first, before he released it, and she kissed him upon his teeth that bared no lips.

He took his microphone and placed it to his neck. "Why do you love me?"

She kissed him once more before leaving the bedroom to retrieve his breakfast. She set it in front of him and kissed him once more. She wrote on the chalkboard: *You need not worry about your face. I am in love with your heart, not your exterior. Love means never having to say you're ugly.*

Dr. Phibes wept.

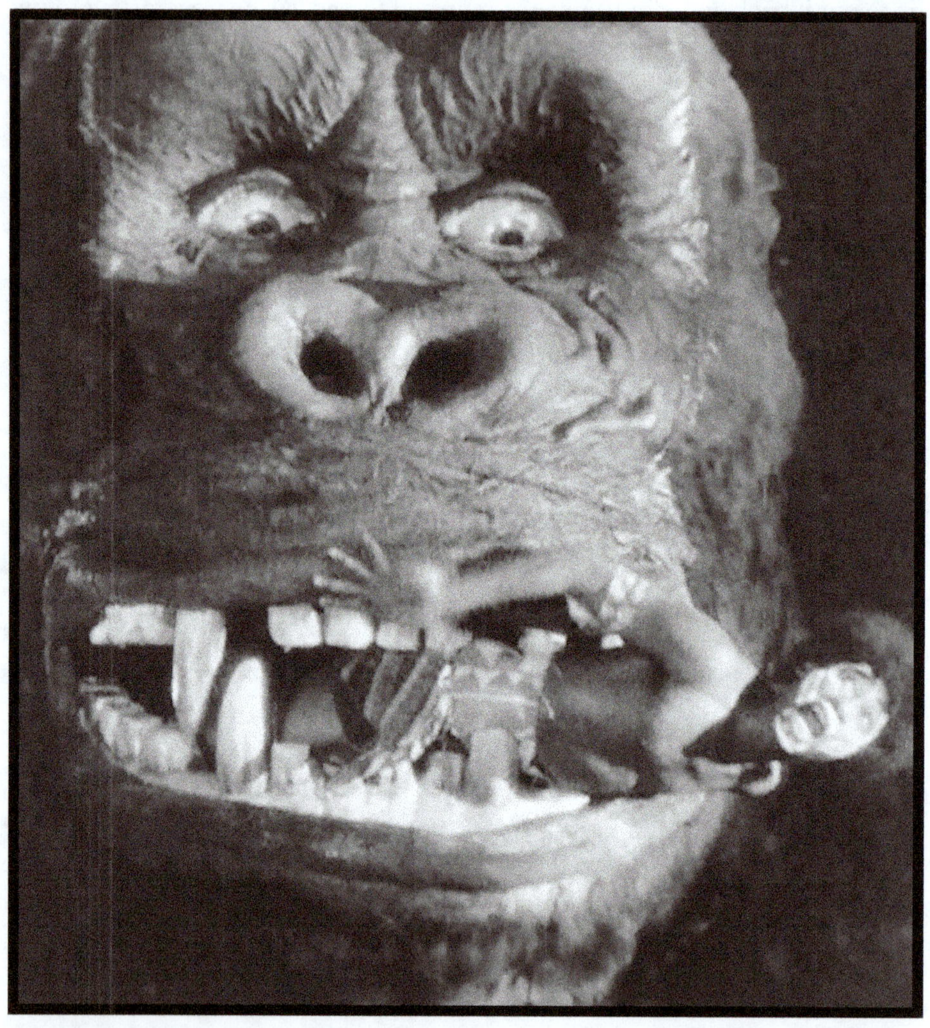

One of the "censored" sequences from *King Kong* 1933, discovered by the late film historian Wes Shank

Emmy Knows Monsters

by Frank J. Dello Stritto

{Author's note: I have loved classic horror movies for most of my life, but never more than when I first saw them as a boy. The films conveyed a sense of wonder then. I can recall those early emotions now, but no longer genuinely feel them when I watch the movies again. Oh, to recapture that first sense of awe, that feeling that I was not just watching a movie, but peering into dark history, into dark truths. Perhaps my life-long study of the classics, and the people who made them, has been an unconscious attempt to relive those first wonders. But the only real way to do so is through the eyes of a child.}

The afternoon of the third Sunday in June is one of Jim Matteo's favorite times of the year. During those usually sunny three hours, he drove home from the annual Monster Bash. The Monster Bash is a conference for fans of monster movies, focusing mostly on classic monster movies from the 1930s and 1940s. Actors and filmmakers, authors and historians, artists and modelers are the usual guests. They give talks and interviews and show their latest works. Films are screened, and the "dealers' ballroom" sells DVDs, books, magazines and countless collector's items.

Jim was a second-generation monster kid. His father, Jim, Sr., attended the Bash with him. Jim acquired a love of the classic monsters from his father, who many years ago sat with his then-young son, as they watched Frankenstein and his Monster, Dracula, The Wolf Man and the others on television. Among Jim's earliest memories was his father's explanation of the monsters. How Frankenstein's Monster came to life, why Dracula casts no mirror reflection, how a vampire's or a werewolf's bite is infectious. Jim, Sr., had given much thought to such questions, and passed his curiosity on to his son.

At the Bash, father and son shared a hotel room, and they attended the films and talks together. Both bought what Jim's wife called "monster junk" to add to their important collections of unimportant items. As Jim headed home, he thought back on his weekend of being with Dad, seeing old friends and making new ones. Mostly, he felt a sense of renewal in seeing old monster movies again.

The Monster Bash was Jim's "getaway weekend of the year." His wife, Alice, and six-year-old daughter, Emmy, stayed home. Alice had no taste for horror films, old or new. Jim hoped someday to bring Emmy to the Bash.

Fifty miles from home, Jim tuned his car radio to his Public Radio station, which re-broadcast *Science Friday* on Sunday afternoons. That day, the program aired a 1996 interview with astronomer Carl Sagan, made shortly before Sagan's death. Jim's mind wandered as he drove.

All children have an intact sense of wonder. When I teach kindergarten or first grade, I have a room full of scientists, at least as far as wonder is concerned. They are not up on the skepticism quotient yet, but that's fine. That's something that can be taught to them. But by the time they get to high school, when I talk to seniors, 12th graders, it's all gone. There are no follow-up questions. They're not listening to what their colleagues are saying. They're worried about how their questions will be received by their peers. Their minds have been turned off. The sense of wonder is almost gone. Something dreadful happens to students between first and twelfth grades, and it's not puberty.

Alice greeted Jim in their driveway. "Well, your daughter is a chip off the old block."

"How?"

"Emmy figured out how to use the DVD, and she popped in one of your monster movies and watched it. She's still watching it. I'm surprised."

Jim laughed. "And she wasn't scared? Not a scaredy-cat like her mother?"

"No child watches what scares them. No, she's fine. Like I said, a chip off the old block."

Inside the house, Emmy jumped into her daddy's arms and hugged him. He carried her into the dining room, where supper waited. Jim was starving and was glad to see lasagna steaming on the center of the table. He served up three plates, sneaked a mouthful and declared it delicious. Then everybody sat down to eat.

"So, what did you do today?"

"I watched *King Kong*!" Emmy said pride.

"Which one?'

"There's more than one?"

"Yes. There's the first one, made when Grandpa was a little boy, and then one made when I was a little boy, and one made when you were a baby. Then there's other ones, like *King Kong versus Godzilla*."

Jim made a scary face as he said Godzilla, and Emmy laughed.

"Was the one you watched black and white or color?'

"Oh, there was no color. It was like the old movies you always watch."

"Did it scare you?"

"No. Maybe a little. I didn't like it when the spiders ate the men."

Alice swallowed a bite of lasagna and spoke. "I don't remember spiders in *King Kong*."

Jim studied Emmy. Her face, as it always was, was disengaged innocence. She ate her lasagna, and only looked up when spoken to.

"There aren't any spiders in *King Kong*. At least not in the finished movie."

"Oh yes there are," answered Emmy. "King Kong shook the men off the log, and the spiders got them when they fell."

Jim left the table and returned with the DVD case for the *King Kong Collection*, a deluxe multiple-movie set issued in conjunction with the release of the 2005 *King Kong* remake.

"Is this what you watched today?'

Emmy nodded. She did not understand her father's new tone, but she sensed something amiss.

The *King Kong Collection* contained the three giant ape movies produced by Merian C. Cooper: the original *King Kong*, its sequel *Son of Kong*, both released in 1933, and the 1949 film *Mighty Joe Young*. Jim scanned the case for *King Kong*.

"There's an extra here called *The Mystery of the Spider Pit Sequence*. The original plan was that after Kong shook the men off the log and into the pit, giant spiders devoured them. That's the spider pit sequence."

"Sounds charming. Perfect for a six-year-old to watch."

"But it was cut from the final film, and as far as I know the footage no longer exists. The men who made the 2005 movie recreated it using the 1933 technology, stop-motion animation instead of CGI. They did it almost as a lark."

"Well," said Alice, "she must have hit some buttons and watched it."

"But it's on a different disk. She would have had to switch disks to see the movie and the extra. Did you watch two disks today, Emmy?"

Emmy shook her head. "No, just one. It was in the movie. After the spiders, Kong had to fight a dinosaur."

Soon after the Monster Bash in late June came the July 4th holiday, and then Jim's busy season, with his job's Budget and Planning cycle. Jim was the company numbers man and cranked out economics based on production and cost estimates. Lots of late nights at work through July and August. August 16 was one such day, and Jim got home after 8:00 p.m. An angry Alice greeted him at the door.

"You have to go upstairs and console your daughter. She's been crying ever since she watched this." Alice pushed a DVD case into Jim's hand. *Freaks*, Tod Browning's 1932 classic set in a circus sideshow. The title characters were actual circus attractions, whom Browning recruited from across America. Jim had purchased the DVD at the Monster Bash five years before but had only watched it once.

"This was way in the back of the DVD cabinet. Emmy must have really dug to find it."

"Well, she did, and now she's paying for it. Go up and talk to her, and I'm putting a lock on that cabinet tomorrow."

As Jim walked to Emmy's room, he ran the movie through his mind, and was surprised how much he remembered of *Freaks*. Cleopatra, a trapeze artist, conspires with Hercules, the circus strongman, to get the large inheritance of Hans, a sideshow midget. Cleopatra marries Hans, and with her lover, slowly poisons her husband. The clan of sideshow freaks—including Siamese twins, pinheads, armless women, a human torso, and others—learn of the plot and extract furious revenge. Hercules is killed, and Cleopatra is mutilated. The movie ends with her quacking in a pit, the duck lady, a star attraction of a sideshow. Jim could well understand Emmy's reaction. He remembered his own when he first saw *Freaks* at a revival theater in New York at age 19. Even then he knew the plot well, but seeing the actual human oddities on the screen unsettled even dedicated horror movie fans

The worst was over when Jim entered the room. Emmy sat on her bed, wiping away the last of her tears. Jim sat with her and said that he wished that she hadn't watched the movie, and that he never meant her to. He explained that "God made some people different," and long ago such people were treated very badly, but their lives were much better now. Emmy listened in silence, her big eyes locked on his.

"But what did they do to Hercules? What happened to him?"

"Hercules was a very bad man, and Hans' friends killed him in revenge. They should have called the police, but they were just so angry."

"No, they didn't. They did something terrible to Hercules. At the end of the movie, he's singing with the voice of a little girl. He looked so different. He looked so sad. What did they do to him?" Emmy's big eyes searched her father's face.

Jim remembered what he had read in the monster magazines about *Freaks*. The movie was originally 90 minutes long, but first the studio and then the censors cut it to a little over an hour. Still, it was banned in Britain, other countries, and some parts of the USA. One of the scenes removed involved Hercules. Originally, he was not killed by the freaks, but mutilated along with Cleopatra. The movie ended with his singing as a castrato.

No one outside the studios or the censorship boards had ever seen the full film. The footage of Hercules' fate no longer existed, nor did any photographs of the scenes.

Jim and Emmy talked a bit more before she fell asleep. Whatever trauma *Freaks* had caused passed. Jim went downstairs to Alice.

"How long was she watching the movie?"

"Let's see. After you called saying you'd be late, we ate dinner. We finished at 6:30. I remember, because I put the radio on, and *Market Report* was just starting. I could hear a movie on the TV right after that. It finished a few minutes before you got home, and Emmy ran in here crying. So, I don't know—an hour and a half maybe."

Jim looked at the case. The blurb on its back mentioned among the extras "Three Alternative Endings." Jim had never looked at the extras. The DVD

CHILLERS

was still in the player, and he watched them all. Film historian David Skal, whom Jim and his father had met a few times, did mention Hercules's original fate, but only in passing.

Had Emmy hit a button on the remote control, and played Skal's documentary? Even if she had, would a six-year-old sit through the long spells of talking heads, and pick out the one mention of the original ending?

When Jim returned home from work the next day, a lock hung on the DVD cabinet.

After school every day, Emmy watched television. Playing outside with her friends bored her. Television was all that interested her. Her television revealed a world so much more interesting and exciting than the world outside her window. "You watch too much television," her mother said almost every day, "like your father." Emmy sometimes went outdoors, but only to please her mother. Sometimes she played on her computer, but only to keep up with her friends. When she made these concessions, she always looked forward to when she would be back in her room, watching her television.

Her television set was in her room. It was a small set, and parental controls reduced the cable channels that she could watch, but it was her set and hers alone. It was the only pink television Emmy had ever seen, with a pink remote control that, despite her years, she had mastered fully. She received the set on her last birthday.

In the family room of Emmy's home stood the chest holding her father's DVDs. Hundreds of them, but she had watched only a few before her mother put a lock on it. It was an old chest that her mother had bought in an antique shop. Emmy had been with her that day, but recalled very little, for she had been so young. She did remember two big men carrying it into the house the next day. The chest was a birthday present for her daddy. "Imagine," her mother had said, "over 100 years old and just the right size for storing Daddy's DVDs." Emmy did remember her mother saying that.

Alice Matteo returned to the antiques shop to buy an old hasp and lock that matched the chest design as best as she could. Emmy watched as her mother screwed the hasp into the old wood of the chest and locked it. The key was big and funny looking, like the ones Emmy sometimes saw in cartoons or in Daddy's old movies.

Now, the locked chest, taller than Emmy, almost as tall as Alice, stood undisturbed. Emmy imagined the treasures inside. Treasures that Emmy thought she would never see, for Alice was adamant that the DVDs were off limits to her daughter.

October came and brought the first Halloween season of Emmy's young life that she would remember. On her television came the advertisement:

Tomorrow at 4:00!
The Wolf Man, 1941, starring Lon Chaney!
Classic Horror All Month Every Friday at 4:00!

Emmy never thought to record the movie (though she had just figured out how to). She would be in front of her television the next day.

Lawrence Talbot reminded Emmy of her father. Both were big and strong, and always ready to laugh. He was so sad after he killed a wolf with his cane, and no one believed him. Everyone—his father, the doctor, the police—kept telling him that he had killed a man. It made no sense to Emmy that they wouldn't believe him. Her father always insisted that she had not seen things that she knew that she had. Couldn't they see that claws and teeth had ripped Lawrence's suit? Couldn't they find out whose blood was all over Lawrence's suit?

Lawrence was so sad that he went to the church and opened a coffin. The Gypsy opened his eyes and stared at Lawrence. Lawrence had never seen such eyes, neither had Emmy. He pulled away from the coffin, but the Gypsy reached after him. Emmy was terrified, but she kept watching.

Jim was always home early on Fridays, and he popped his head into Emmy's room. "Oh, you're watching *The Wolf Man!*" Jim looked down the stairs to make sure Alice was not nearby. Then he whispered, "That's one of my favorites."

On the television, Lawrence Talbot showed his father the scar left by the wolf bite, and told him it was the pentagram, the mark of the beast. Sir John dismissed him. "That wound could have been made by any animal."

"I like it, too, Daddy, but I was a little scared when the Gypsy reached out of his coffin."

Jim sat down and took Emmy in his lap. "You couldn't have seen that Emmy. It's not in the movie. It might have been filmed, but it's not in the movie."

Jim picked up the pink remote, pressed the "reverse" button until the film reached the scene of Lawrence Talbot in the church. He watched it and saw nothing that he had not seen dozens of times before. Lawrence Talbot enters the crypt, approaches the coffin, but hides in the shadows when the priest and the Gypsy's mother arrive.

"Emmy, you didn't see the Gypsy reach out of the coffin. It's all in your imagination."

"But I did see it, Daddy."

Jim pressed "forward" on the remote until the film returned to Lawrence and Sir John and left.

    CHILLERS

Emmy watched the rest of the movie alone. At the end came another announcement:

Next Week at 4:00!
The Mummy, 1932, starring Boris Karloff!
Classic Horror All Month Every Friday at 4:00!

Emmy's school scheduled parent-teacher conferences in October, to identify any problems or issues early in the school year. Jim usually left that duty to Alice, but now both met with Emmy's teacher, Ms. Callahan.

Ms. Callahan resented a new policy that required the school psychologist, Jeffrey Garth, to attend all parent conferences. She thought his presence detracted from the intimacy of the meeting, and burdened it with an unnecessary air of formality. She also knew the school was mainly interested in protecting itself: an added witness in case of later disagreements over what had been said and promised. Garth, she thought, tended to dominate the meetings. He was more interested in being listened to than in listening.

Most conferences with parents fell into a few types. Some parents only wanted to hear praise for their child, while others wanted to hear only the opposite. Some came prepared to spend all day, while others hurried the meeting. In many conferences, one parent did all the talking, and one sat listening. It was the listeners that made the meetings interesting. Out of nowhere they might spring like cats, with questions that cut to the heart of whatever concerned them.

Such was the meeting with the Matteos about their daughter Emmy. After a run through of test scores and behavioral summaries, the father spoke up.

"What kind of person is my daughter?"

"Surely, you have opinions of that," Garth answered. Callahan winced. She wasn't sure that Garth had even met Emmy. He tended to stay in his office, studying data, and only spent time with "problem" students, which Emmy was not.

"I know what kind of person she is around me, but children are often different around their parents."

Callahan answered. "Emmy seems to be a happy child. She is a bit of a loner. No, maybe more than a bit. She plays well with the others, but I always get a sense that she would much rather be alone. She never talks in class. She sits at her desk listening or working on her activities."

"Aloof?" asked Garth. Callahan turned towards the psychologist but kept speaking to the parents.

"Not so much aloof as preoccupied. There's a lot going on in her mind."

"Just like her father," laughed Alice. Jim took Alice's hand, and squeezed it.

"There's something I want your opinions on. Something at home that I cannot explain."

Jim told in some detail about Emmy's claiming to see scenes in movies that were not in the films. He took pains to distinguish the old classics from the explicit gore fests of modern horror.

Callahan spoke. "Imaginative children often fill in gaps on their own. Emmy has quite an imagination. Perhaps she is seeing what she expected to see, and doesn't realize that she's making something up."

"The scenes she remembers were actually filmed. They were deleted from the release versions, and the footage no longer exists. They are part of the movies' histories, but they simply don't exist. Yet she describes them in detail."

Jim told as much as he knew about the history of the deleted scenes. Whenever Emmy told of seeing a missing scene, Jim read what he could find about it. Her accounts squared exactly with what was known. He explained the possibility that Emmy might also have read about the lost scenes, but he thought it very unlikely. Jim himself had not looked at the books that he needed to consult for some years. He could tell that they had not been disturbed recently, and he doubted that a six-year-old could have waded through the information even if she tried.

As Jim spoke, Alice became uncomfortable, as she always did when Jim spoke of his passion for old horror films in front of others, especially at a parent-teacher conference. She had visions of a call from Child Services. Garth had dropped his detached air, and listened intently.

"But you knew about these so-called 'lost scenes' before Emmy watched the movies?"

"Yes, but I know more now than I knew a while ago," Jim said.

"Perhaps Emmy is mediumistic. Such things are not unheard of between a parent and child. She is a conduit for all the intangible forces around her."

"Sounds like a lot of supernatural baloney," mumbled Alice.

"Supernatural perhaps. Baloney perhaps not."

Alice spoke louder now. "I'm worried about Emmy's liking these strange movies. Her father was —is —a 'monster kid.' So is her grandfather. They are almost proud of it. I guess I don't mind Emmy becoming one of the club, so to speak, but it seems strange for a six-year-old. I don't care as much about her seeing what's not there as seeing what is there. She might be home with the babysitter now, watching one of those movies."

Jim seethed as Alice spoke. Callahan saw many arguments between parents in her meetings, and braced to manage it. Garth, delighted that the conference was no longer the mundane exercise he expected, took over.

"I know something about these movies, but frankly I don't care for them. My father was into such films. Voodoo and vampires and such. But he never swayed me. I don't like them."

"Maybe I should speak to your father," Jim said. "You seem to have made up your mind about them."

"My mind is just as open as ever it was, but it's a scientific mind, and there's no place in it for superstitions. You're up against stern reality. If your daughter were an adult, I would say that she is delusional. For now, we just call her an 'imaginative child.'"

The parents leveled hard looks at the psychologist. The teacher tried to enter the conversation, but Garth was not to be stayed.

"Emmy's strength lies within herself—that is, if she has the will to see reality. Put it to a test. The next time one of these movies is on television, don't avoid it. Let her watch it, let her know that you want her to see it, watch it with her. Score the first victory. That's the secret."

The Matteos' drive home might have been more heated if not for Dr. Garth. Neither was happy with what the other had said at the meeting, but both agreed that the doctor was a jerk. As tempers cooled, Jim reflected on Garth's advice.

"Maybe he has a point. Maybe the movies are forbidden fruit to Emmy, and that's why she watches them. She's never been rebellious, and maybe this is it. Maybe if she saw more of them, and knew that we didn't care, all this would stop."

"What about these mysterious lost scenes?" Alice had known nothing about them a few months ago. Now, she knew more than many horror film fans.

"I can't explain that. But we must do something. How about this: the October Monster Bash is next week. Pop always goes, and he's always wanted me to go, but I never wanted to take the vacation days. I could go and take Emmy."

"What about me?"

Jim's laugh was the first one in the car that afternoon. "You've always been welcome to go, and you've never wanted to."

"I still don't. Three days of that stuff. I couldn't take it." Both sat silent for a few minutes as the car turned onto their street. "If you and Emmy went, and if your father helped you look after her, it would solve one problem."

"Aunt Julia's estate?"

"Yes, I could go through that stuff in three days. Let me think about it. We'd have to take Emmy out of school."

"After today's meeting, I don't think Ms. Callahan would object. If she did, I'd call in Dr. Garth."

Jim and Alice laughed as the car entered their driveway.

At the dinner table, Alice asked Emmy, as she often did, "What did you learn about today?"

"Reincarnation."

Jim and Alice looked at each and then their daughter. Jim was chewing a ravioli and didn't wait to swallow.

"They're teaching reincarnation at school! I'd better talk to Ms. Callahan about that!"

"Not school. On TV. It was in the movie. *The Mummy*. I watched it this afternoon."

The Mummy was one of Jim favorite films. Boris Karloff plays a mummy brought to life by an incantation from the Scroll of Troth. In modern Cairo he finds the reincarnation of his lost princess. Jim explained the plot to Alice. As he spoke, he was surprised that Emmy picked up on reincarnation, which is mentioned, but not emphasized.

"Daddy, you left out all of Helen's lives. You see her again and again in different costumes, living different lives. The Mummy looks in his magic pool and sees all her lives."

Jim retrieved from his office a book, *Universal Horrors*, and perused its chapter on *The Mummy*. Alice and Emmy kept eating their dinners. Jim read of scenes of Helen Grosvenor—the modern half-British, half-Egyptian woman—reliving her past lives. Imperial Rome, Viking conquest, Medieval Saxony, 18th Century France. The lengthy sequence was deleted from the final film. Only a few photos of those scenes remain.

"I had forgotten all this,' he said. "I had read this long ago and haven't thought about it since." He looked at his daughter. "If you're reading into my mind, you must be reaching deep."

Alice rose and brought Jim his telephone. "Call your father. You and Emmy are off to the Bash next week. I'll handle Ms. Callahan. I want this all behind us when you come back."

Jim had never been to the October Monster Bash. His father had been going since retiring and had already reserved a room at the hotel hosting the conference. Two double beds. Plenty of room, Jim Sr., said, for his son and granddaughter. Father and son would share one bed, and Emmy could have the other. Jim Sr., was delighted to get Jim's call that he would be coming and launched into one of his frequent reminiscences on sharing a bed with his brother, Jim's uncle, until he left for college.

Jim found the October Bash more sedate than its June version, mainly because there were fewer children. But the same collection of unusual, lovable people assembled. Before Jim and Emmy registered at the hotel, Jim said hellos to the Catholic priest who conducted the Bash's Sunday morning mass, the eccentric producer of very low budget direct-to-DVD monster movies, the kid from the West Coast who interviewed everyone for his blog, and the retired production manager who had worked on some top movies and always had stories about working with famous and fabled.

The stars and prime movers of the classic horror films were long dead, but the Bash somehow always found people who had worked on the productions or knew the stars. Hardly a child-actor who had appeared in an old movie had not received a call 60 years later, inviting them to be a guest at the Bash. And there were the historians who tirelessly dig through libraries and archives unearthing new facts on old movies. Some had been doing so for 50 years. They had met and interviewed anyone connected with the old films and were the last living link to their memories. These serious students of movie horror brimmed with facts and anecdotes that movie fans loved to hear.

Fellow travelers of the historians were the owners of cherished movie props who proudly displayed them for the sheer love of doing so and told one and all the stories behind the prized relics.

For some attendees, especially young ones like Emmy, the marvel of the Bash was the dealers' ballroom, where countless treasures could be purchased. Among the offerings were magazines, books and photographs—old and new— collectibles of all sorts, life-size and scale model reproductions of movie mon- sters. The monster craze of the 1960s had produced countless monster-themed toys and ephemera, which could once be purchased for pocket change. Now, they fetched high prices. Of all the items for sale, the most valuable were vin- tage movie posters. Autographs once rivaled the posters in cost, but forgeries became so common, and so realistic that few aficionados dared take a chance on them.

Mixed among the dealers were the artists, who painted or sculpted or oth- erwise reproduced scenes from their favorite movies. Some were kitschy, but just as many were superb. An artist needs not only talent and training, but also inspiration. A surprising number found it in old movies.

Wandering throughout were people—attendees, artists, dealer, authors— who came in costume. Maybe, some feared or hoped, they were the real thing. Some Bash-goers believed in the supernatural, and what better place for a hideous monster to hide than at a monster convention. Real or not, the living monsters thrilled Emmy most of all the wild things to see.

Jim sat on the edge of the bed in his hotel room and studied the Bash schedule. The theme was the Universal Frankenstein films. The first three of the eight films would be screened on Friday, the next three on Saturday, and the last two on Sunday. Before each film came a talk by a historian. Jim marked the two or three that he wanted to hear. He knew these would bore Emmy. He arranged with Jim Sr., that he would look after Emmy while Jim was at the talks, and the family would watch the movies together.

Friday fulfilled all Jim's hopes, and Emmy had a wonderful time. She and the two Jims sat through *Frankenstein*, *Bride of Frankenstein*, and *Son of Frankenstein*. Emmy loved them all, and asked lots of questions. Jim had to shush her once or twice, but the audience didn't mind. They were mostly older fans, quite pleased that a young recruit had joined their ranks. None of the talks that day interested Jim. Between movies, the three Matteos roamed the dealer ballroom, and the hall of guests and authors. Emmy proudly showed her attendance badge whenever she passed a checkpoint. She asked many questions, and Jim had great conversations with a few of the guests.

Emmy slept very well that night. After they put her to bed, the men ordered hamburgers from room service. Their room overlooked the hotel atrium, and they could watch the Bash evening festivities as they ate.

Burgers finished, and nibbling on French fries, Jim told Senior of Emmy's strange claims. He went through the full story: the giant spiders of *King Kong*, the castration of the strongman in *Freaks*, the Gypsy rising from his coffin in *The Wolf Man*, and reincarnation in *The Mummy*. Jim need provide no explanation of the scenes, for his father knew at least as much about the movies' history as Jim did.

Then Jim told of his meeting with Dr. Garth and got a response from his father that he had often heard before. "Anyone who listens to a psychiatrist should have his head examined."

Senior dabbed a fry in ketchup, placed it in his mouth, and looked at his son a long time. "She's just like you were, you know."

"Yeah, we both like old horror movies."

"Not that. You both see things that aren't there but used to be."

Jim said nothing.

"You were her age when you first saw *Frankenstein*. You claimed you saw The Monster throw little Maria into the water."

"But that's in the movie."

"Not when you saw it. The censors removed that scene, and it was not put back until later. I thought that was a mistake by the censors, by the way, because instead of seeing her death as an innocent accident, it was left to the imagination what The Monster did to her. The station played the movie again the next night. I watched, and knew the scene wasn't there. But you saw it, or at least you said you did. The same thing happened with *King Kong*."

"The spider scene—I've never seen that. It doesn't exist."

"Not the spider scene. The scene where Kong rips off Ann Darrow's dress, same as in *Frankenstein*. The censors removed the scene, and it wasn't returned until later. I watched that movie with you. I know the scene wasn't in what we saw, but you somehow saw it. You described it. You saw it. The same with *Murders in the Rue Morgue*. The censors trimmed Dr. Mirakle's speech on evolution. It was put back later. You can tell when you see the movie now—the restored footage is in a different state of preservation. You said you saw it, even though it wasn't there."

"What did you do about it?"

Senior shrugged his shoulders and put more fries in his mouth. He spoke through them.

"Do anything? Why do anything? You saw what you saw when you saw it!"

The two Jims laughed. "I Saw What I Saw When I Saw It" is an oft-repeated line in their favorite film, *Abbott & Costello Meet Frankenstein*. It would play at the Bash on Sunday.

Senior became more serious.

"It was a simpler time. We didn't go looking for things wrong with our kids. Besides, what was the harm? You grew out of it soon enough. There were a lot of things you had to outgrow. That was the least of my worries. It was no worry at all. I thought it was neat. But you outgrew it. It never happened again. I forgot about it until now."

"Are you telling me the truth?"

"Always." Both men laughed. Emmy turned over in her sleep.

Friday had been a full day for everyone, and all slept a little later than usual. Senior took Emmy to McDonald's for breakfast, and Jim attended the morning talk on *Ghost on Frankenstein*, a 1942 film, the fourth in Universal Pictures' *Frankenstein* saga. The focus of both it and its immediate predecessor, *Son of Frankenstein*, is how Henry Frankenstein's sons, Wolf and Ludwig, deal with the legacy of their father and his creation. "There's another classic story," said the speaker, "of a son seeking redemption and justice for a dead father. Next slide, please."

Some of the audience gasped, some laughed as a slide of Laurence Olivier, flashed on the large screen. "*Hamlet*, of course. I'm not saying that *Son of Frankenstein* and *Ghost of Frankenstein* are adaptations of *Hamlet*, but both movies borrow from it." The presenter spoke in a manner equal parts folksy and scholarly, spiced with a distinct New York accent. Jim wasn't sure that he bought the parallels between Hamlet and Henry's sons until slides appeared showing similar scenes and dialogue from the movies and the play. During the questions that followed the talk, an attendee conceded similarities to *Hamlet*, but asked if they were intentional. Could 1940s monster movies be borrowing from Shakespeare?

"The screenwriters were educated men," was the answer. "If Shakespeare were plucked out of England, and plopped into Hollywood, there's a chance that the only job he could get would be writing horror films."

The film started a few minutes later. Emmy sat between the two Jims, and all watched the movie. In *Ghost of Frankenstein*, Ludwig has his father's monster strapped on an operating table, and prepares to destroy it by dissection. The ghost of Henry appears and instructs Ludwig to give The Monster a new brain, just as in *Hamlet* the father's ghost tells his son to avenge "his foul and most unnatural murder." With the new brain, The Monster can speak, but goes blind due to a mismatch of blood types.

Some minutes before the next talk, and the Matteo men walked among the guest tables, each holding Emmy by the hand. She held tight, lifted her feet, and swung between them.

Jim wanted a word with the *Ghost of Frankenstein* speaker, but when Jim reached his table a spirited discussion was underway which had nothing to do with Frankenstein or his sons.

"Vanity press! A vanity publication! Why do writers always get that label? If a painter takes lessons, rents a studio, and never turns a profit, his stuff isn't vanity art. If a singer or actor rents a hall and never turns a profit, that's not a vanity performance. They're all starving artists. But writers who want to see their works in print are oh-so vain!"

Language might have gotten stronger, but the men noticed Emmy watching them. As Jim and Senior walked on, Jim said, "That New York accent certainly punctuates his argument."

"That's a New Jersey accent. You can only tell the difference when they get upset."

Senior and Emmy went into the dealer ballroom, and Jim went into the talk on *Frankenstein Meets the Wolf Man*.

That talk—a detailed history of the pre-production and filming of *Frankenstein Meets the Wolf Man*—was more to Jim's taste. Jim had read much about the movie long ago, but the speaker, Greg Mank, was noted for the in-depth histories he compiled by poring through studio archives and interviewing every survivor involved with the film.

Original plans called for Lon Chaney to play both The Monster and The Wolf Man. Daily application and removal of makeup for any of the monsters was grueling enough. Doubling that agony was asking too much. The Wolf Man was, in Chaney's own words, "my baby," and someone else would have to the play The Monster. That would be Bela Lugosi.

At the end of *Ghost of Frankenstein*, Ygor's brain goes into The Monster, who then speaks in Ygor's voice. Lugosi, the famed portrayer of Count Dracula, had played Ygor, and The Monster thus spoke in Lugosi's distinctive accent. In most Frankenstein films, The Monster does not speak at all. Lugosi's 110 words of dialogue at the close of *Ghost of Frankenstein* beat Boris Karloff's 90 words in *Bride of Frankenstein*. Thus, Lugosi has claimed to be the voice of The Monster as well as the voice of Dracula.

The audience laughed.

In *Frankenstein Meets the Wolf Man*'s shooting script, Lugosi's lead over Karloff was to be greatly extended. The Monster escapes from a tomb of ice with

 CHILLERS

Ygor's brain and voice intact, but he is blind. He speaks another 450 words before regaining his sight for his death-duel with The Wolf Man.

When studio executives previewed the film, they thought Frankenstein's Monster speaking in Dracula's voice ridiculous. They were not enthused with a blind monster. They ordered all The Monster's dialogue be removed from the release print, and all references to his blindness cut. Where practical, scenes were removed from the print, otherwise Lugosi's voice was removed from the sound track. The speaker pointed out scenes where The Monster's lips are moving, but no voice is heard. He stumbles into obstacles as he walks with his arms outreached. To a viewer unaware of the post-production editing, The Monster's behavior makes no sense.

The talk ended, and the houselights came on. Those that had seen *Frankenstein Meets the Wolf Man* often enough left the auditorium. Those who never missed a chance to see it on the big screen filled their seats. Senior brought in Emmy. He wanted a nap, he said, and left her with her father.

The room filled until not a seat was left. Jim put Emmy on his lap so that a forlorn-looking woman could sit. Jim glanced at her. A Chaney fan or a Lugosi fan? He could not decide until he saw her tee-shirt.

Jim wanted to tell Emmy a little about the history that he had just learned, but the houselights dimmed. The opening credits flashed on the screen.

The only truly frightening part of the movie—Jim thought—was the opening. Grave robbers break into the Talbot crypt to take the money, gold ring, and watch that were buried with Lawrence Talbot when he "died" four years before. Under the full moon, Talbot transforms into The Wolf Man, and slaughters one of the desecrators.

Emmy sat enthralled by the scene and showed no hint of fear or worry. As the story unfolded, she whispered a few questions to her father, which he quietly answered.

In the movie, Lawrence Talbot realizes to his horror that he is cursed to an eternity of killing and waiting, killing and waiting. He becomes obsessed with his own death. Talbot learns of Dr. Frankenstein's work, and travels to Vasaria. He is too late: the doctor is dead, and the monster that he created destroyed. Under the full moon, The Wolf Man kills a girl, and hides from the avenging villagers in the ruins of Frankenstein's castle. He falls into a forgotten cellar and awakes in the morning as Lawrence Talbot.

Emmy's interest never waned. She remembered Lawrence Talbot from *The Wolf Man*, and—like so many children before her—rooted for the monster. Talbot's lonely, unhappy life touched her, and she obviously wanted Talbot to somehow find peace.

In the cellars, Talbot stumbles on The Monster trapped in ice, and frees him.

"Oh, Daddy. Do you hear him? The Monster talks just like Dracula." Emmy's whisper was a bit loud and earned a "shush" from the Chaney fan sitting next to her.

"No, Emmy. The Monster's lips are moving, but nothing is coming out."

"Yes, Daddy, yes. Listen!"

Jim hugged Emmy, squeezed her tightly, and looked at the screen. He stared in wonder at a setting that he had never seen in the movie. The Monster and Lawrence Talbot sat huddled at a campfire. As The Monster warmed his hands, Jim heard a distinctive voice that he knew well.

If Dr. Frankenstein were still alive, he would restore my sight. He would give me back the strength I once possessed—the strength of a hundred men—so that I could live forever. Die? Never! Dr. Frankenstein created this body to be immortal.

"Daddy, can you hear The Monster?"

"Yes, Emmy! Oh God, yes! I can hear him! I can hear him!"

His son gave me a new brain, a clever brain. I shall use it for the benefit of the miserable people who inhabit the world, cheating each other, killing each other, without a thought but their own petty gains. I will rule the world! I will live to witness the fruits of my wisdom for all eternity!

Father and daughter watched a movie which no one else in the room could see, and which they themselves would never see again. Memories of The Monster's rant, the spiders of *King Kong* and the other scenes of lost horrors soon faded from Emmy's mind. They would remain only indistinct, distant images. Unless, in her later life, Emmy would be as lucky as her father.

The story of my creation is written in Dr. Frankenstein's diary. He knew the secret of immortality—and he knew the secret of death!

About the Author:

Frank Dello Stritto is best known to movie film fans and scholars through his books *Vampire Over London—Bela Lugosi in Britain* (first edition 2001, second edition 2015), which he co-authored with Andi Brooks; *A Quaint & Curious Volume of Forgotten Lore—The Mythology & History of Classic Horror Films* (2003); *I Saw What I Saw When I Saw It—Growing Up in the 1950s & 1960s with Television Reruns & Old Movies* (2014); *A Werewolf Remembers—The Testament of Lawrence Stewart Talbot* (2017); and *Carl Denham's Giant Monsters* (2019). His books are available on www.cultmoviespress.com.

He was a regular contributor to *Cult Movies Magazine* until it ceased publication and is now a frequent contributor to *Monster Bash Magazine*, and an occasional contributor to *Scary Monsters*. Frank was born in Hoboken, New Jersey, and is a retired oil company engineer. He and his wife Linda live in Houston, Texas.

JEEPERS! THE CREEPERS ARE AFTER BUD & LOU!
BUD ABBOTT
LOU COSTELLO
THE WOLFMAN LON CHANEY JR.
DRACULA BELA LUGOSI
THE MONSTER GLENN STRANGE
STARRING IN
ABBOTT AND COSTELLO MEET FRANKENSTEIN
UNIVERSAL-INTERNATIONAL PRESENTS
BUD ABBOTT LOU COSTELLO LON CHANEY JR. BELA LUGOSI GLENN STRANGE LENORE AUBERT JANE RANDOLPH
IN A FILM BY CHARLES T. BURTON "ABBOTT AND COSTELLO MEET FRANKENSTEIN" PRODUCED BY ROBERT ARTHUR
SCREENPLAY BY ROBERT LEES FREDRICK I. RINALDO JOHN GRANT DIRECTED BY CHARLES T. BURTON

CHILLERS

Afterword

We lost most of our cinema heroes years ago ... horror icons like Bela Lugosi and Boris Karloff. When we view one of their films on a dark and stormy night, it feels like we are visiting old friends. They transport us to lands long forgotten, dark worlds of a macabre age. Vampires and men brought back from the dead. Films like *Frankenstein* (1931) and *Dracula* (1931) have continued to frighten and stir our imaginations for nearly a century now ... the films we love have inspired and brought us so much joy.

I can remember seeing *Edward Scissorhands* for the first time. Watching an elderly Vincent Price work his magic in Tim Burton's universe. Witnessing Burton's vision come to life. Not only was the director creating his dream come true on the silver screen, but Burton was also fulfilling another dream, working with one of his heroes, Vincent Price.

I not only admire Burton, but also secretly envy him. To work with great actors like Vincent Price and Christopher Lee would have been a lifetime dream come true. Unfortunately, we'll never have the opportunity to see new films created by those we love, but there is nothing stopping us from creating new literary works based upon our heroes and the incredible films that they have left behind for us to cherish.

This book churns new fiction from the cauldron of creative fire, works inspired by some of our most beloved films and characters. I can only hope that those icons that have inspired us would look upon these new works of fiction with a gleam in their eye. Happy to see that all those many years later they are loved now perhaps more than ever. New works of fiction that I truly hope they would find fitting to represent them on the silver screen.

So, we raise a toast to all those of the golden era that we cherish and love. May a loving warmth forever glow with you.

And remember there is more of the same forthcoming if this first volume warrants (sales-wise) a sequel or two.

Brad A. Braddock
September 2019

You can
find
*Midnight
Marquee*
books
at

www.midmar.com

